GW01607419

illustrations by
shirley r. hussey

WiDDERSHiNS

a novel by

judith w. monroe

Acknowledgements

My gratitude and affection to Armane, Patty and Sandy M., who shared their rituals with laughter and love, and to Sally, Shirley, Mary, Belinda, and Dorothy who labored as creative and conscientious editors, and most particularly to Elizabeth who wanted to see *Widdershins* in print and made the dream reality. Each of you, in your own way, served as a midwife in the delivery of this book.

Library of Congress Cataloging-in-Publication Data

Monroe, Judith W., 1932-
Widdershins: a novel / by Judith W. Monroe.
p. cm.
ISBN 0-9615216-5-1: $9.95
I. Title.
PS3563.05275W5 1989
813'.54–dc20 89-15786
CIP

Paper edition
Printed in the United States of America

COVER DESIGN BY SHIRLEY R. HUSSEY

Crone's Own Press
310 Driver Street
Durham, N.C. 27703

"To have a life of one's own," cries Laura, "not an existence doled out to you by others." *Lolly Willowes.* Silvia Townsend Warner.

This book is dedicated to Sandy
whose poem appears
in these pages

Seven women were moving in single file, marching quietly and slowly, each making her way, torch in hand, along the narrow rocky beach. The calm waters of the tide rose imperceptibly but steadily only a few feet away. The meeting place in a sheltered and private cove was close at hand, and the full moon was just now lifting above the hill of the island where they had come to celebrate the summer solstice.

Another woman stood waiting for them at their destination. She watched as their torches intensified the pink of the granite rocks edging the shore. As they arrived, she moved off into the darkness and, with a touch of a match, set fire to a huge triangular structure built of drift wood, twigs and branches. The red-yellow flames shot upward, a narrow funnel of heat directed straight to the star-filled sky. The watchers exclaimed, then fell silent.

Carefully the women placed their torches along the beach to the north, south, east, and west. All but one moved inside the torches to form a circle where their leader joined with them to invoke the spirits of Fire, Water, Earth and Sky. The lone woman stood watching as the others moved in the direction of the moon's path and began their ritual.

Rachel remembered the scene with a rush of love. There had been many ceremonies since, but the first had been the most daring, even iconoclastic, and certainly the most beautiful. More important, however, were the people she had met on that occasion five years ago. All had helped to change her life.

She thought of the series of events leading to that first solstice, beginning with the morning she woke (only a week before her 73rd birthday) and boldly began to orchestrate her future. The work at the insurance office bored her, and furthermore, even if after fifty-five years of faithful service they couldn't in good conscience fire her, they certainly didn't want her there anymore. The chief underwriter had literally stripped her of interesting tasks when he decided to have computers installed. Her blasted terminal did all the good work. Any damn fool could sit there and feed it data.

Rachel read constantly, sometimes a book a week. The book that intrigued her then was about Lolly Willowes, a woman of the Victorian era, who had been sheltered by her family until she finally broke away from their possessive love.

Rachel had been brought up in Maine as the only child of parents with equally Victorian attitudes. Like Lolly, she had been expected to stay under the protective wing of family until she married. And like Lolly, she did not marry at first as a kind of protest, later as habit. When she was eighteen, she had one wrenching and poignant romance. Pregnant by her handsome lover, a man from "away," her parents had taken her on a tour of Europe so no one would know about the baby. Actually, she had spent six months in seclusion and then, following the birth, two months touring Europe.

She had never seen the baby's father again. There was no question of marriage. He was not a Yankee. He was a budding genius with great musical gifts, who had taught during her Sophomore year at Bates College. She attended his recital at the chapel and fell in love with his wonderful hands and with his deep-set eyes and mane of dark curly hair. Her parents admitted later that it was a mistake to have allowed her private lessons. He might well be pleasing from a distance appropriate to an audience, her mother said afterwards in her cool, clipped voice. He would never be acceptable as a family member, no matter how gifted.

The baby girl had been taken from her at birth and given up for adoption. She decided then and there never to marry, and furthermore, never to go home. She had lost her lover to social convention and her baby to strangers. How could she forgive her parents for what they had done? In spite of her anguish, she was not the kind to think of suicide. She thought, instead, of independence.

She moved out of the family homestead as soon as she was strong enough, found work as a typist in the insurance agency where she stayed on and slowly made a career for herself. She refused to see her parents again.

From the beginning she worked hard at her job, receiving enough pay to assure that she never went hungry and could rent a room. In later years she was promoted several times and found she could afford not only to rent a decent apartment in Portland but also to buy a wonderful old farmhouse on a Maine island.

She was amazed, when she thought of it today, that she had survived and toughened up, had actually made the move to her own freedom. In the early years she felt an occasional longing to have a loving relationship again with her parents, especially during the Christmas season when everyone else in the office talked about their holiday plans, but her pride held fast, making it impossible for her to go home again. Then, when she was in her thirties, her parents died unexpectedly in an automobile accident. With their death her feelings of loneliness had disappeared.

Now she thought of Lolly Willowes who slowly cut her ties with society and felt herself moving closer to nature in a kind of mystical experience. Lolly became a witch. Rachel decided to follow her example. It was a most intriguing answer to a life that had become too narrowly circumscribed. She was quite different in some ways from Lolly. She did not, for instance, want to separate from people entirely, and she certainly had no aspirations to make the connections with the devil that Lolly had made. For Rachel, witchcraft was simply a re-declaration of spiritual independence, as well as a way to make new contacts and to learn about magic. It was a way out–of work, of the city, of sameness, of predictability. If there was one thing she hated, it was predictability.

Looking in her mirror she saw that her long thin face was still an interesting one. She had her height although that little widow's hump was gaining. (She imagined witches needed to be tall and commanding.) Even the small bald spot beneath the tangle of gray strands could be hidden through careful combing. She studied herself carefully. She'd always worn bright colors. Perhaps she'd add a dramatic shawl to her usual outfits and lengthen her skirts a bit. Or would that be too gypsy-like? The twenty bangle bracelets she had collected over the years and which she felt distracted from her skinny arms would remain. They were appropriate.

She was trying now to explain her decision to her friend and neighbor, Clarissa. Clarissa was an odd person. It was not easy at times to reach her. No two people, Rachel thought, could be so different from each other. Rachel was tall and thin, Clarissa was short and round. Rachel looked her age. Clarissa looked ageless, her skin clear and unwrinkled, her hair the same as it had been since Rachel knew her, a nice soft curly brown.

Rachel was certain that Clarissa would assume she was "failing" if she mentioned the subject of retirement. She had no idea how she would respond to the idea of Rachel's becoming a witch. Clarissa was obsessed with health issues.

When Clarissa heard about Rachel's scheme to get involved with witchcraft, she did not lecture her about health. She spoke of sex. Rachel automatically took umbrage. "No, that's not what it means," she snapped at Clarissa who perched daintily on the end of the day bed in Rachel's little living room, gazing at her with great concern. Daily, she stopped by after work to check on Rachel's welfare. Sometimes Rachel wondered if she expected to find her dead. The thought was irksome. She was convinced that Clarissa's excessive concentration on health was itself unhealthy.

"Witches are not sex crazed," Rachel continued, now incredulous that Clarissa was so naive, "and the broomstick," she continued didactically, "is not a phallic symbol. Witches don't have to have a broomstick at all." She got up from her chair and walked to the other side of the room, turning her back on Clarissa to get her thoughts together. This was one of those times when Clarissa got on her nerves. She was an odd thinker and an odd dresser, Rachel thought. Look at those damn cloddish shoes, Birken-something-or-others, that made her feet look like pita bread, another thing that Clarissa was fond of. Flat, tough, tasteless stuff she filled with grass and seeds for her lunch.

"Now, Rach," Clarissa soothed, "don't get defensive. I just mentioned what I've heard on the subject," she ended lamely, flapping her hands in little circles and feeling sorry she'd said a thing. There were days when Rachel could not be pleasant.

From her work at Cornucopia, the alternative market, Clarissa had become totally convinced that mental health was greatly affected by diet. As far as she was concerned Rachel's cluttered kitchen revealed all. It was stuffed with canned goods and convenience foods, all full of additives, for heaven's sake, and not a smidgen of oat bran in sight. "You might consider a multiple vitamin," she suggested mildly, recognizing immediately that the comment would seem a non-sequitur to Rachel. "It's a good remedy for memory," she added hoping to explain herself.

"Whose memory are you worried about anyway?" Rachel shot back. "I've got no problem remembering anything. I'm just beginning to realize who I am. If I were you, I'd do a little self-exploration just to keep up." A good argument felt so invigorating. Who was the fuzzy thinker, anyway?

Clarissa, rounding off her sixty-first year, was happily content to find herself "a senior." She needed no new definitions of herself, least of all "witch." She had two discounts now, one at the Cornucopia and the other at the drugstore, the first intended for employees and the second for older citizens. Rachel, she decided, might be having some kind of delusion, in which case niacin, or a combination of B12 and B6 might help. That would be a good gift to bring Rachel for her birthday. "You are what you eat" was her accepted maxim, and she governed her appetite accordingly.

Returning to the subject at hand somewhat reluctantly, she said, "Then what are witches–what do they do? Isn't it late in life for such a radical change?" she added, the warning in her voice all too distinct. Clarissa knew all about Rachel's knee problems and could hardly picture her dancing around a bubbling cauldron. And what about sacrifices and black masses? She could not bring herself to ask Rachel about those things.

"Witches are people who look for wisdom through the non-rational. I've had the rational up to my ears," Rachel was saying sharply, reminded of her work at the office. "Witches heal through magic. They have a great concern and respect for the earth and the environment." That last bit ought to please Clarissa who was, if not interested in magic, certainly concerned with the environment. "And no, it is not too late for me," she concluded somewhat breathlessly.

Clarissa and Rachel had lived in the same apartment building for over ten years in Portland, Maine. As often happens when people have been admitted to each other's inner lives, they had developed a relationship which vacillated between affection and annoyance. Neither had married and neither had any close relatives, and so they had, by default, become family.

Rachel ignored Clarissa for the moment. She took up the city paper, and began to scan the personals, then decided the subject was too interesting to exclude Clarissa after all. "I'm looking," she said, running her finger down the paper, "for a coven."

Clarissa suppressed a laugh. She was sure those advertisements specialized in sexual come-ons. She'd naively composed a letter a few years back in a last-ditch effort to find a male companion. She understood that it would be difficult to find someone who'd share her favorite greens, Bazmati rice, olive oil and unsweetened carob. Perhaps it was more honest to admit that she herself was reluctant to share another person's fried food or dairy products. Startled by some of the graphic language in the ads, she conceded that the real issue was that of sharing someone's bed and she was not ready for the terms the ads proposed. "Knock your socks off," indeed. Well, she did not know a man her age who ate health food anyway, so it was an academic question. Perhaps a youngish man . . . . Ah, but Rachel was not looking for a man . . . .

"What do you need a coven for?" Clarissa asked in her mildest voice of inquiry. She would humor Rachel along. She'd done it before. "Can't you practice without one?" She paused and considered the fact that Rachel might indeed be serious. What would happen she had no idea, but it was vaguely intriguing. One thing you could say about Rachel.

She was never dull. On the contrary her behavior was sometimes startling. This was not, for instance, a Christian undertaking. Rachel, of course, had left the church years ago. Part of the reason Clarissa faithfully checked up on her was in case she needed the last rites. There might be time for her to call Father Donahey.

"Clarissa," Rachel said patiently, "do you enjoy the company of like-minded people?"

"Of course," Clarissa answered in a mollifying voice. "You know that." She paused and added, "I enjoy visiting with you. I have for ten years."

"Nonsense," Rachel said. "How in this world did you make the connection between like-minded people and us? You're no more inclined toward being a witch than you are toward becoming a janitor. I, however, think witches may have something to teach me. My mind is not closed."

Clarissa knew what that meant. "No, I suppose I'm not," she answered feeling hurt from the slam. "A practicing Christian would hardly consider witchcraft an option after all," she stated firmly, thinking she'd better leave soon. That was a mean thing Rachel had said. Clarissa was hungry and she wanted a good soak in the tub to rest her feet. She'd been standing most of the day. "I've got to go," she said and rose, smoothing the wrinkles from the bedspread where she'd been sitting.

"There are no ads here," Rachel said with a sigh, closing the paper. Damn Clarissa. She was so sensitive that the truth was never an option. "I suppose," she said, "this is the wrong place to look. I'll have to go to the library to find some of the magazines or papers where they might advertise."

"Actually, there are quite a few magazines with unusual ads at Cornucopia. I never read them anymore, and I can't be certain there would be anything to do with witches, but I could check tomorrow when I have my break."

"That would be really helpful," Rachel said feeling more sympathetic toward Clarissa again. She rather liked her most of the time, she reminded herself.

During the next week Rachel realized that a coven might be impossible to find. No ads she read even vaguely suggested such a thing existed. Clarissa told her about one back-to-earth magazine from last fall that had advertised a gathering for the full moon. She told Clarissa it was probably a bunch of organic farmers having a square dance.

By then she had finished reading a book about witches, a history by an English scholar. It gave her a better sense of what she was looking for, but she was surprised to learn that witch burnings had resulted in hundreds of thousands of deaths during the Renaissance, a time she had always considered so much more enlightened than the Dark Ages. Some en-**light**-en-ment, she thought, dividing the word by its syllables. "Light" by the burning of human flesh. Grisly thought.

Why had the Catholic Church played such a nasty role in persecuting women? She had no idea, but she did know that Catholicism was not for her. She, herself, was what she jokingly called "a recovering Catholic," and she knew all too well that the church had its faults. Even then the thought of its major role in the deaths of so many people shocked her.

Fond memories of incense and stained glass had a way of softening her condemnation of the church over time. Mass had always seemed so comfortingly harmless. True, she had grown tired of the endless requests for money and Father Donahey's long-winded, pop-eyed sermons that went on too long, but she missed the ritual. Well, perhaps she'd find a new kind–if only she met some witches. What would Father Donahey think about that? Actually, she didn't give a rap.

Since there were no covens advertising, she decided to place an ad of her own. She would invite witches to come together. Perhaps, as the English scholar had described, for the summer solstice–to celebrate the longest day of the year. But where? No room in this tiny apartment surely. She went over the various places she had visited which might be appropriate and realized quickly that her summer house on Lily Island would be ideal. That's it, she told herself, I'll call Ellen and ask her to open the place early. She's probably already begun shingling the roof. I haven't been down in two years. It will be wonderful to go in June.

She pictured the peninsula, the soft pink granite rocks, the pebble beach, the giant spruces and pines. The more she thought about it the more her spirits were buoyed. The idea of quitting her job, taking her retirement money and . . . she dialed and listened to the phone ring three times, then she heard Ellen's cheerful voice at the other end.

"Now here's something, Incy," Grace said aloud to her Siamese cat who perched on the back of her chair. Incy, or Increase as he was called when Grace was scolding him, was her sole companion in a life Grace characterized wryly to herself as ascetic if not asexual. He was asleep and heard only a blend of sound mixed with his own purring. "Widdershins," Grace said and reached over to pluck a one volume encyclopedia on myths from the shelf. She read:

Counterclockwise, the direction of the moon or 'left-hand path' of pagan dances (still prevalent in folk tradition). To open the door of a fairy hill, one must walk three times widdershins. As sacred caves once served as pagan temples, the medieval church forbad their use and claimed that walking or turning one's self widdershins was an indicium of witchcraft.

Grace sat up straighter, but Incy never stirred. Whoever signed the ad "Widdershins" knew the meaning of the word and would perhaps expect the reader who responded to it to know also. It was not a common word like coven. This could be it–the opportunity to write an original case study of witches forming a coven. If I can just become part of it, wherever it is, I'll have a primary source, first-hand evidence of neopaganism.

She felt exultant. Just for an instant she wished for someone to share her excitement. I must answer promptly, she told herself, dismissing her feelings as self-indulgent. There might be a cut-off number for participants. She tossed the paper onto the floor and rose from the arm chair. The Siamese, finally annoyed, opened one eye, closed it again, kneaded the back of the chair twice and returned to purring. Grace, who had not seen him kneading the upholstery, stroked him fondly. "You can come too, Incy–be my familiar."

She paced back and forth before the little fireplace, its cheerful pot of red geraniums flashing on the hearth in place of a wood fire. Along with the yellow and white Rya rug, her one extravagance, it was only bright spot in an otherwise drab apartment.

"What to say?" She quizzed herself, "I'll give myself away. People who know they're under observation change their responses. It could spoil everything." She paused, "Yet it's dishonest not to let them know I'm only interested in witchcraft from a scholarly perspective. Well, I'll tell them the truth afterwards. See how they feel about being included in a study. But what will I do if they refuse–want me to throw out my work?" She was disconsolate with both the thought of losing a great opportunity and having to be dishonest to take advantage of it. She continued to pace in silence for fully five minutes, then went back, snatched up the paper and reread the ad one more time.

She was triumphant. "It doesn't say one has to be a witch," she informed Incy. "It says, 'People interested in forming a coven please contact Widdershins, Box 465, Portland Evening News.' So, I'm interested in how a coven is formed. That's

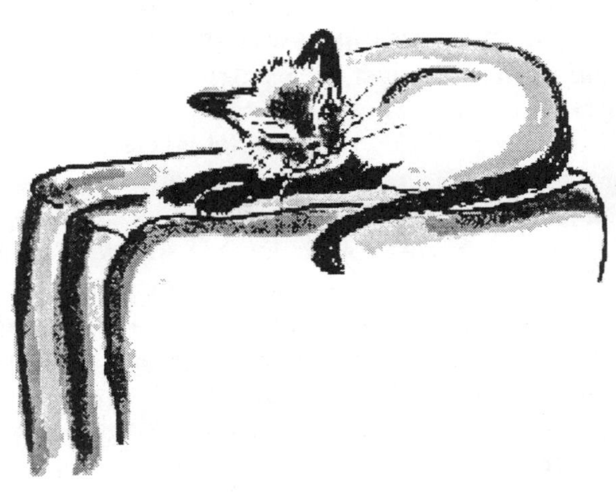

not unethical." She booted up her computer. Using the word processor which had become a lifesaver for the writing of her dissertation, she dashed off a polite reply of interest.

Father Donahey pushed the buzzer, pulled out his pocket watch and counted the seconds it would take her to reach his study door from the kitchen. He felt a twinge of guilt as he listened for her step. Why wasn't he consulting the bishop or at least someone else in a nearby parish? Alison's knock on the door saved him from having to answer.

God, she thought, as she stood waiting for permission to enter, the man is so restless. Can I guess what foolishness it will be this time? There was always some trumped-up errand to run, as if his tiny bowed legs couldn't carry him anymore. True, he was a little frog, had the belly too, but there was nothing wrong with him–just lazy–and unfortunately convinced that she was in love with him. Pitiful, that. He should be hopping off down the street to do his church's bidding.

"Yes, sir," she said in the solemn tone she'd adopted for this part-time job. She'd seen some of the old films that romanticized Catholic priests and their housekeepers–the Barry Fitzgerald syndrome, she called it. She suspected that he'd seen the movies too, because he seemed to like her style. All in all, she was pretty good at placating the man's tremendous ego. He wanted reverence, well, she'd manage it for the time being. This was an additional place to earn money. She had the other part-time job at the courthouse, work experience essential for graduate school. That should be within the next year or so.

"Alison!" He assumed his I-am-the-shepherd-of-this-flock tone which she found amusing. "I've a special project which will need your assistance."

She knew he was giving her the once over. Her sweatsuit bothered him. She really should be wearing something more appropriate for a parish housekeeper, but it seemed a shame to change until after finishing the morning work. Pray, get on with it then, she thought impatiently, and caught herself. She giggled inwardly, hearing an Irish lilt to her inner voice.

"Sit. Sit," he flourished grandly, rising to pull a chair away from a side table and put it before his desk, an unprecedented act.

She was stunned. He'd be asking for something really big this time. Was she prepared?

"I've a favor to ask. It's official business of the church, highly confidential, you understand?" He looked away. "Correspondence which due to its highly secret nature must . . . must . . ." She watched his face carefully for signs of deceit, and then caught sight of his small spatulate fingers, playing with the letter opener, then his rosary, then a pen, and then returning to the letter opener. He jabbed at the telephone cord. He stopped, picked up the rosary again. She waited, unwilling to prompt him. This confusion was a delightful surprise, a change from his usual glib speech.

". . . be delivered elsewhere!" he finished, blurting the last of the sentence in a great rush. He'd lost her. She'd be damned if she knew what he'd said.

"Could you run that by, I mean, repeat it, sir?" She'd forgotten the damned accent. Had he noticed? Apparently not. "I didn't understand, Father," she explained in a falsely humble voice.

He tried again, "I'm expecting a letter, but due to its highly confidential nature, it can't be delivered here. I was wondering if you could, if you would–accept it at your home address?"

So that was it. He had a woman! No wonder he was nervous. He'd never had any secret liaison before that she knew of. All he liked to do was sit here evenings and read those stupid horror stories. No, it could not be a woman. Yet what else would cause him to blush like that? It had to be something on that order.

"Sure, if I can be of service, Father, I'd be glad to do it for you."

"Do what?" She was surprised that her ordinary answer had thrown him off, but then he regained his composure and went on, "Not for me, Alison, for the church," he said reprovingly, fully recovered from his momentary awkwardness. He had her now. "For the church," he repeated piously.

A crock, she thought. "Certainly," she replied, eyes downcast, in case he should suddenly read there what she thought of him. "If that's all then . . . ."

He waved her off with thanks and when she had gone he returned to the letter and signed it with a flourish he thought looked quite feminine. Clovis D. A safe enough name, and certainly sounding a little like a child of the devil. He folded the letter, stuck it in the plain white envelope, and wrote the box number and address of the newspaper on it. In the upper left hand corner he wrote Alison's address.

"So you're really going through with this?" Clarissa said trying to put just the right tone of measured skepticism in her voice. She wanted Rachel to think carefully about the planning of the event, not to cancel it. It was touchy business because Rachel might not invite her. "What's involved?"

"I don't know yet," Rachel answered shortly. Then she relented and added, "I've gotten several letters of response that sound promising and only one kook," she grinned mischievously, "of the 'socks-knocking' type as you so aptly put it. I threw that one out."

"Really, Rach, I only showed you that one ad. I didn't write it. That's not my kind of language."

"Oh, no?" Rachel still had the grin, "Getting prudish, are we? Well, anyway, I don't know how many there will be, but I'd like you to take part if you will."

At last. Clarissa was delighted to accept, not only because she was fascinated with the idea of seeing witches (she tried not to think how shocked Father Donahey would be if he knew she was even considering the possibility), but because she simply shouldn't couldn't let Rachel go off alone on this adventure. Not at her age. What if she took ill? To Rachel, however, Clarissa spoke of more practical matters, "I'm concerned about provisions. Will these people bring their own food or should we supply . . . ?"

Rachel interrupted. "What made you think I'd ask you to bring food for others? If I know you, you're thinking of leftovers from Cornucopia." It was the last thing Rachel wanted to eat—that dry dark bread and horrible bean soup.

"No, not really, although that's always possible where the baked goods are concerned. I just thought bulk rates might be cheaper." She was already concerned about the kind of people who would come to this gathering. Like Rachel, they might well have a vitamin or mineral deficiency.

Rachel was thinking of bulk tofu, stored in Cornucopia's large glass refrigerator. She could see the stuff sitting in its brackish water, flakes of chalky pinkish-gray floating free, unappetizingly reminiscent of wet tissue paper in a toilet bowl. Yuck, she thought. "Bring your own stuff, Clarissa," she said rather more sharply than she'd intended. "I'm telling everyone to bring their own food." She changed the subject quickly. "We'll have to go a day early to the island to open and air the place. Pray for sunshine. It will be hell if the weekend's damp and rainy."

Clarissa refrained from making the obvious comment on hell and witches. She'd managed to read at least part of the history of witchcraft that Rachel recommended. It was truly remarkable to her that anyone would launch a new life as a witch knowing all the facts about persecution. In the old days widowed or single women were particularly suspect, especially if they lived alone. They were vulnerable to accusations and frequently tortured and put to death (at least twice as many women, the author said, as men).

What was Rachel thinking of? Did she have a secret death wish? No, the danger simply never occurred to her. She just wanted to take some time off now that she was retiring. And time off to Rachel meant action of some kind. She'd always been like that.

Rachel was already packing. Clarissa looked at the stuff she'd put in the two small boxes from the corner store, all of it poisoned by additives: two cans of Campbell's mushroom soup, three cans of Chicken of the Sea tuna packed in oil, one box of Ritz crackers, a loaf of lifeless white bread, two cans of fried onion rings, a box of Tuna Helper, and some little tins of ready-to-eat pudding. Not a green in sight.

Rachel was busy with something at the stove. She put five large blocks of paraffin into a big pot. "You making jam, Rach?" Clarissa asked conversationally. It did seem like a lot of wax for a few jars of preserves, but if a food had sugar in it, then Rachel would make a lot. "Isn't that what you use to seal jars?"

"Yes, but I'm making torches, not jam. You can help if you like." Rachel pointed to a bunch of newspapers in the corner. "Here," she said, "You take one end and roll three layers thick–diagonally–like a funnel–see?" She demonstrated.

"Then what?" Clarissa was intrigued. "You pour the wax, right?"

"Clever girl," Rachel said, her tone gentle, "but first you fold over the end and staple it, like so." She took the paper funnel and closed its end. "Then put it in the sink so if it leaks out it won't spill on the floor. You pour just a little in the bottom–allow it to harden first. That forms the base; then you pour in the rest. When the wax begins to harden, you stick one of these down the middle so you'll have something to hold onto." She motioned to a pile of long thin dowels. "Here, hold this one while I pour."

Clarissa, who was essentially conservative by nature, saw torches as an extravagant measure. "Wouldn't a flashlight or a candle do just as well?"

Rachel snorted. "Not really. One thing I'd like to see is a procession down to the shore. I think any coven would agree to that. It's a great spot to watch the moon rise. Maybe we'll have a bonfire too."

God, I hope no one's there to see us, thought Clarissa. A bunch of old people trudging along with huge torches. It would be enough to bring out the worst in many people she knew. If they didn't believe in devil worship before that, the sight of a procession by torchlight would certainly start them thinking along those lines.

"What are you going to wear?" Rachel asked her, looking grumpily at Clarissa in her usual bland corduroys and flannel shirt.

"I didn't realize that clothes mattered." Clarissa replied, deciding to defend herself from what was coming. She had visions of Rachel in a tall hat and flowing veil. Perhaps she should admit to Rachel that she was really only a concerned bystander–(one with a large case of voyeurism). "What would you have me wear, Rachel? You know I have a somewhat limited wardrobe."

"You said it, not me," Rachel said impatiently. "Witches wouldn't be caught dead in L.L. Bean's stuff. Come on, Clarissa. Can't you use a little imagination? You could go to a second-hand clothes place–find something dramatic."

The whole thing was shaping up into a costume party, Clarissa saw. A second childhood for Rachel. Why hadn't she seen that before? Then a thought occurred to her. In the history of witches Rachel had lent her, there were some fairly up-to-date pictures of present day witch covens. The people in the pictures were stark naked. Thank God Rachel had not opted for nudity.

"Who is going to lead this thing?" Clarissa asked hesitantly, worried that someone else might ask them to take off their clothes.

Rachel was irritated. "Do you mean, will I be playing the hostess?"

Misunderstood again, Clarissa shook her head and made a face. She decided not to mention the nude pictures. "I'm just curious about the order of events. I . . . ."

Rachel interrupted, "We'll see when we get there. This may simply turn out to be an organizational meeting. We may not get anyone who has ever led a coven before." She sighed. Clarissa still went to mass regularly. A new ritual might throw her completely. "Don't worry," she said soothingly, "everything will move according to destiny."

That, Clarissa said to herself, was small comfort.

They had one class at UMO together at the end of the day. Then they drove to a local pub for a beer–something a bit quieter than the Bear's Den on campus. Three days during the school week, Bernice, better known as Bernie, left her two sons with her husband, Richard, and joined Ann and Solange for a break from studying.

The pub was nearly empty and they had finished their third round of drinks and popcorn. Their consumption of popcorn bothered the new bartender who had been instructed to provide free munchies with every drink. The boss had not, however, supplied a big enough popper. In an attempt to slow them down, the bartender deliberately over-buttered and over-salted the last batch. His ploy had failed.

Waving the dish at him, Bernie gave him careful instructions for the next round. She was a hard person to refuse. Just today, having made the momentous decision to go to law school, it seemed to her friends that she had picked up even more magnetism, more authority to her voice. The bartender backed off, bowing clownishly, empty dish in hand. He recognized defeat.

Bernie grinned rakishly at his retreating form. She lit a cigarette and turned her attention to her friends. Solange coughed deliberately. Ann and Bernie both smoked and couldn't understand all the fuss. "Everything you eat, breathe, touch or wear is poisonous," Bernie routinely scolded any dissenting non-smoker. "You might as well enjoy your short time here." Solange remained adamant.

"All right, so where were we?" Bernie said, ignoring Solange for the moment. "It's your turn," she said to Ann, reviewing the rules. "Be honest now. Name three parts of your body that you love most. We did it. You can." This was the latest version of a game they played regularly, an offshoot of the consciousness raising they had begun in a women's support group three years ago.

Ann and Bernie were in their mid-thirties, Solange was fifty-five, and they were part of the large non-traditional student population of the university. All three loved learning, expected a great deal from their teachers, studied hard and were inevitably unpopular with some of the younger crowd who engaged in a minimum of scholarly pursuits.

Solange frowned, "I know I've already had my turn, but I'd just like to say that I love my lungs, and I'd like a little respect for my air space." She waved a hand in front of her face and swept back a stray curl of her black hair that had only recently begun to turn grey.

"O.K. O.K.," Ann relented and stubbed her cigarette. "You too, Bernie. She's right, you know." Of the three, Ann who was more conscious of "process" as it was called in her psych classes, was most interested in analyzing their friendship and keeping it strong. She envisioned a career in mediation, perhaps one helping to negotiate settlements between labor and management.

A natural go-between as the oldest child in a large family where there was a lot of in-fighting, she learned early to listen and understood intuitively how people felt. Her siblings gravitated toward her when they needed to blow off steam. Most of the time she let them ventilate, but occasionally she insisted that they reach a peaceable solution. It was satisfying to see a fight turn into a compromise, or, as she was fond of calling it, a no-lose resolution.

"What if we promise to smoke one at a time? Would that work?" Bernie argued doggedly. They'd been over this ground a million times.

"Absolutely not," Solange said. "Then there's smoke in the air all the time."

Bernie grimaced, but put out her cigarette.

"Sorry, Ann. Begin again," Solange prompted. "What part of your body do you like best?"

"You're going to make fun of me, if I say. You'll tell."

"What's this?" Bernie said in mock dismay. "The rules haven't changed, have they? Solange, after we leave here tonight, are you going out to publicize Ann's most private thoughts?"

"Of course," Solange said sarcastically, and Ann grinned sheepishly.

Solange and Ann both loved Bernie's brash woman's repartee, loved her plain face with the ever-present quizzical expression framed by ash-blond hair.

Ann struggled for the courage to talk about something personal and her friends waited respectfully.

"Take five, Annie," Bernie said, "I'll just step outside for a quick one," she patted the cigarette pack and was gone.

Ann sat quietly contemplating what she wanted to talk about. Solange watched her. She was long accustomed to the fact that Ann was a carbon copy of Cagney, of the old Cagney and Lacey show, a sometime handicap when she entered a public place.

"It's scary to reveal yourself," Solange offered tentatively. "You can always pass if you feel uncomfortable."

"That's true, but I'm going to do this, silly as it may seem." She looked out the window at Bernie and motioned to her to come in. "If she doesn't hurry, I'll have to go out myself. I've been having an easier time lately–waiting longer between smokes. Maybe I'll be ready to give it up soon."

"Maybe Bernie will join you." Solange was hopeful.

"In what?" It was Bernie, pulling out her chair and settling back in place again.

"Nothing," Ann said, knowing that Bernie was not about to give up smoking in the near future. "Just about smoking."

"Are you ready, then?"

"Yes." Ann shut her green eyes tightly and slipped down into her chair. "Well," she opened them again, long enough to take a long swig of her beer and began in barely audible tones, "I like my nose. It fits my face–actually I like my whole face, and my hair, but . . . ." She paused again and then plunged on, "it's sometimes embarrassing to be . . . to be," she couldn't finish.

"Beautiful?" Bernie prompted.

"Yeah, I guess, although I wouldn't use that word. There's something heavy about being a look alike–as if you don't have a face of your own." She swallowed and continued, "but that's not it, really. We've talked about that before.

There's something else more serious I wanted to say today. I'm beginning to like . . . my vagina," she blurted it out, then cleared her throat and hurried on, "I'm just discovering it." She broke up then, bending over the table and hiding her face in her arms. Her smothered laughter escaped.

"I can understand that," Bernie said, when they had recovered. "What can I say? If it weren't for my vagina, my two little guys wouldn't have made their way into the big world. They'd still be driving me crazy in utero." She gave her belly a soft pat. "Besides," she added happily, "My vagina is important to me for other reasons. I love Richard, and I love sex. It all goes together." They laughed again and the bartender, who had been eavesdropping, glanced nervously their way.

Solange said, "What would Richard think if he heard you say that?" Her own vagina seemed remote to her. A woman who had had only two love affairs in the last ten years, neither with the potential for anything long range, she had come to terms with the fact that neither having sex nor giving birth would be important parts of her life.

"Hey, the man knows me inside out–no pun intended–he expects this kind of thing from me."

"You're lucky, Bernie." Solange answered. "Do you know that? Finding someone like Richard?"

"We should all be so lucky," Ann said, and then she continued, "I've got something more I want to say about this subject." She fiddled with the ashtray and then shoved it away. "Private parts," she said quietly, "that's what my mother called the vagina, the vulva and–you know, 'down there', she emphasized the words, by pointing, then laughed again. "So it's hard to speak easily, never mind poetically or philosophically when you've been told it's wrong to say anything at all. There's just no language that comes naturally or seems appropriate–unless you are in bed with someone or in a doctor's office–then there are two different languages–neither right for times like now, for . . . just ordinary talk."

"But some of what has come to be ordinary slang is pretty disgusting," Bernie said, grimacing.

"But does it have to be that way? People introduce new words to the language all the time, and old words return to popularity. Couldn't we do that–adopt a word like 'yoni'. That's a word we could use. Do you know it?"

The two shook their heads. "Yoni means entrance of fertility, or place of birth. It also means vulva. It's a sort of all inclusive term from Indian and Tibetan religion where sex was celebrated as a spiritual part of life–the culmination of religious ceremonies in some cases. In those days, sex was not condemned as unhealthy or dirty. And did you know that the vulva is symbolized by the last letter of the Greek alphabet, Omega?"

They listened amazed. Ann was the one who always found new bits of feminist myth and lore. "And also," she continued, "the horseshoe hung over entrances is also the sign of a yoni," she continued, "even to this day." She giggled. "I seriously doubt most farmers hang a horseshoe over the barn door knowing what it really means. They think it stands for good luck."

Solange saw the connection at once. "Well, in the old days, fertility might easily have been synonymous with good luck. Farmers would welcome good luck in breeding their livestock."

"Women having difficulty getting pregnant would also look at it as lucky to become fertile," Bernie said. "Even today."

They poured the last of the beer from the pitcher and sat for a moment feeling impressed and pleased with themselves. "Yoni sounds so much less clinical, not nasty at all," Solange said quietly. "I think I'll use it from now on–that is when it's appropriate." She giggled.

"Me too," Bernie nodded emphatically. I'll teach my boys to say 'yoni' instead of those disgusting terms they're already picking up at school. Maybe they'll start a trend." She laughed.

"Speaking of dirty language," Ann began again, "the root of the word 'cunt' is Cunti, another name for the goddess Kali. It was not a vulgar or sexist word in mythology. The words 'country' and 'kin' are derived from it."

Bernie put down the bowl of popcorn which had just been delivered without salt and butter. "That's an incredible connection, but I can't see myself explaining it to a kid. I mean, can you see me having this discussion, talking over the derivation and meaning of the word 'cunt' with the boys?" The craziness of her suggestion struck them and they laughed wildly.

The bartender turned away so that they would not see his smile.

"It would be difficult I think," Solange said when they had calmed down. "Ann, do you have more you want to say?"

"No. I've said what I wanted, but I am interested in hearing more about the way you feel about your voice and your hands, Solange. You should take voice lessons at the very least."

Solange regarded her solemnly. "But I'd never sing in public. What would be the use?"

"Oh just for your own pleasure, I guess," Ann said, " and mine." She took a helping of popcorn and crammed it into her mouth. When she finished chewing she continued, "I think you have a beautiful voice. And your hands . . . you express yourself with them, more than the average person, you know?" She looked down at her own hands which lay on the table, fingers spread out as if they were about to be traced on paper. "I've studied both my mother's and my father's hands and my kid brothers' and sisters'. My hands don't look a thing like theirs."

"Well, I'll never know what my parents' hands looked like," Solange said a bit wistfully.

There was a lull as the three studied Ann's hands and then Solange's. They were thinking of Solange's remark which had to do with her father's recent death. At seventy-nine, her father had changed her life dramatically by leaving her an inheritance of incredible wealth. For years she had struggled along as a part-time student, full-time secretary at the business office. Now she could do anything she wanted.

"Let's not talk about it, O.K.?" Solange requested, guessing what they were thinking. "I get dizzy thinking about all that money. I need to keep my feet on the ground for a bit."

"Fine. So we'll summarize," Bernie said, backing away from the subject that they had been talking about off and on for the past month. "We have mentioned feet, legs, hands, eyes, chin, hair, brains, nose, voice, skin and last but not least, vagina," she counted them off on her fingers, leaving the little finger of her right hand wagging provocatively.

"What does that say about us?"

"We're still new at this describing and admiring ourselves." Ann offered. "And I certainly did a poor job compared to the two of you."

"This was not a contest," Solange reminded her, kindly, "and besides, it's not easy to talk about yourself, never mind things as intimate as . . . ah, your yoni."

Bernie said, "We also need to learn to go into depth, to explore more of our feelings, and even our spirituality."

Ann nodded vigorously. "Once you become a feminist you're bound to learn more than you ever wanted to. Once you renounce some of the old paternalistic comforts, things other women still want and take for granted, it becomes a whole different world out there. It's not enough to let daddy take care of you, even if it's the biggest daddy of them all up in the sky. There has to be something to replace what we've lost."

Solange nodded vigorously. She took a drink of her club soda. At times like this she felt a little left out of the alcoholic glow. As the only non-drinker of the three, she had to trust that they would hear and remember whatever she shared with them even when they were slightly euphoric. She plunged in. "You know I don't go to church anymore, but I miss it– even though I know some of it's so wrong for me."

Ann brightened visibly. "I know something that might help you. Have you read any of Starhawk's stuff? It has a lot to offer women who feel disenfranchised by Christianity or Judaism."

Bernie nodded in agreement. "Even me. As a Jew, I never have been all that interested in the spiritual side of religion. I do care about Israel, I care about the holocaust, about my heritage, but that seems rooted in reality. Strangely enough, Starhawk's writing intrigues me precisely because it isn't connected to the real world. She directs herself to women who are searching for new ways to explain the mysteries. Some parts of her writing are a bit too . . . ," she left the thought unfinished. "I think I'd be open to trying out new religious rituals."

Ann responded. "Starhawk's on the right track. Women used to be priestesses. There were Goddesses like Kali or The Triple Goddess two thousand years ago, even before the goddesses of the Greeks and Romans. There were dozens of them. Now there's a resurgence of interest in those ancient religions all over the world. People are beginning to revive the pagan rituals involving those deities. I think it's challenging, and I'd like to be part of it."

Solange tore a piece of paper off the menu and wrote "Starhawk" on it and tucked it in her pocket.

"So should we?" Bernie was intense, not wanting the conversation to roam from the topic.

"Wait," Ann was saying, "did you by any chance see the ad from Widdershins in yesterday's paper?" They shook their heads. "Just a minute, then," she began rummaging in her tote bag. "There's a connection, Bernie, I promise," she said, understanding that Bernie wanted to pursue the religion question further.

"Here," her finger was already rapidly tracing down the edge of the personals.

"Aha. So–you've been reduced to looking for romance in the personals again, eh?" Bernie cracked.

Ann bridled. "Personals don't have to be raunchy. I've had some half-way decent dates from this very column. Your use of the word 'reduced' is offensive. Are you going to be fair about this, or shall I forget the ad?"

Solange intervened, "She was only kidding . . . ."

"Solange, ever the peacemaker," Bernie chuckled and grinned. "I certainly was kidding and Annie knew it. She's just touchy on the subject of men these days."

"How could I know you were kidding, Bernie?" Ann asked, but the edge was gone from her voice. "It says here," she spoke slowly and deliberately. "Are you ready?" She smiled at Bernie forgivingly and began to read.

When she had finished the Widdershins ad, the three sat quietly staring at each other and then Bernie said, "What are we waiting for?"

"So, who responded to your ad?" Clarissa felt there was an inordinate amount of secrecy surrounding the upcoming event. Lately, when she dropped in after work, she had the impression that Rachel was not all that glad to see her. I'm the only one she really knows who's going on this trip, for better or for worse, and I could be of help if she'd let me.

Ruefully, Clarissa admitted to herself that Rachel was managing nicely without her. The pouring of the torches had been the extent of her own involvement. She's years older than I am, and she really hasn't slowed down a bit since I first met her. She was sixty-one, then–my age, now, she thought and was swept with a sense of the loss of years.

Clarissa was still hurt from Rachel's response to the latest birthday gift. She had returned the niacin, dumping it unceremoniously into Clarissa's palm, saying in clipped tones, "Clarissa, I get all the vitamins I need in my food. I'm not into megavitamin therapy. I thought you knew that by now."

It was a downright rude response to a caring gesture, and just one more way in which they differed from one another. Clarissa always thanked someone when she received a gift, and she would never think of giving it back. Comparing herself with Rachel always left her feeling uncomfortable. Rachel was independent, liked living alone, went for long walks at night, spent hours in the public library, even attended the Portland Symphony concerts by herself. Clarissa couldn't bring herself to leave the apartment house once she returned from work except to go grocery shopping and to mass. Still she yearned for company–someone she could share a meal with at least.

On Tuesday nights Rachel sometimes went to the little coffeehouse to listen to an amateur group of neighborhood musicians who played rock. She ate the terrible Mexican chili and other hot foods served there. Clarissa accepted Rachel's invitation to go there just once. She could barely hear

Cornucopia's customers asking for their orders the next day, and she had stomach cramps for a week.

Every once in a while on a weekend Rachel walked down the hill to the Old Port district and wandered contentedly over the cobblestones. Clarissa knew she liked to sit on one of the benches on Exchange Street while she ate one of those huge chocolate chip cookies from the bakery. Quite by chance, Clarissa, who sometimes shopped at The Whip and Spoon, (where they carried her favorite Belleweather scone mixes), had first caught sight of Rachel lolling on a bench, watching the varieties of people stroll by. The sight was startling. Rachel, she decided, was usually the actor, not the spectator. It was comforting, somehow, to catch her observing the passers-by in their contrasting outfits–males and females in punk looking spiked, colored hair and leather jackets mixed with the yuppy clean-cut elegance straight from Amaryllis or one of the other elegant little boutiques.

There were other things she and Rachel differed on. Clarissa loved liturgical chants but she also liked country western and blue grass music. That combination of musical preferences, she knew, struck Rachel as uproariously funny. In turn, it seemed mildly humorous to Clarissa that Rachel thought of herself as a Yuppy, only recently modifying the term to Ouppy–an Older-Upwardly-Mobile . . . . Totally silly.

Rachel made friends too quickly, and Clarissa not at all. Rachel entertained occasionally, but seldom did she invite Clarissa. It hurt to be left out, but on the other hand, she had a kind of social life at the Cornucopia unlike the cold, uncaring insurance company where Rachel had toiled, cooped up in a little booth with white sound pouring in over her head.

Cornucopia customers were outgoing, friendly types–organic farmers or gardeners, vegetarians, runners, new age types–people who cared about causes–equal rights for animals, women, gays, and members of the peace and anti-nuclear movements. Some of what they said conflicted with Church teaching, but, and this was a strangely consoling thought, there were always renegade Catholics who supported such groups. Sometimes she overheard bits of their conversation and wanted to join in. Other times they looked right at her and asked her opinion.

When it came to questions about farming she felt she could take part in the discussion freely. Sometimes she even thought of herself as coming from the land. To be honest, she would have to say that her parents had been teachers who hired a tenant farmer to do the actual planting and harvesting. Still she'd grown up in the country, had her own little garden plot. One of her most cherished memories was that of harvest time, especially the digging of new carrots and potatoes; root vegetables were so satisfying. Digging in the soil for hidden treasure–that was it, for treasure that didn't shoot up like lettuce on the first warm day and turn bitter before August, didn't have to be shucked, like beans and corn turning your fingers numb and raw. If properly mulched, carrots would winter over in the ground, and when April came you could dig them up, sweeter than ever.

Then there was the cutting of heads of lettuce, cabbage and broccoli on early summer mornings with beads of dew still glistening on their leaves and the braiding of onions and garlic in late fall or . . . .

"So far," Rachel penetrated Clarissa's daydream, "I know very little about these people. There are only names, all women. I've sent them the ferry schedule which also includes a map in a neat little pamphlet. The map gives the major routes to the terminal from all points in the state." She liked that feature since she was absolutely no good at giving directions, never mind drawing a map. "Oh, and I put a note in telling them what to bring and how to get to the house after they get off the ferry."

"Rachel, what if these people are weird?" Clarissa said boldly, surprising herself. "What protection do we have from them in case they get into something . . . well, drugs . . . or behavior that is not right?"

Rachel laughed sarcastically. "Why do you always expect the worst of people? I mean, thanks a lot. You've just given me a hint of what you really think of me for starting this whole thing . . . warped."

"You're over-reacting, Rachel. You have no idea who these

people will turn out to be. How could we possibly protect ourselves if . . . ."

"I can't believe you're saying this to me," Rachel spat out. "I carry a handgun all the time. How does that sound to you, safe enough?"

"Sickening, that's what. A lie anyway. Furthermore, you're avoiding reality, Rachel, and I don't think I want to be involved."

"Good. Stay home, for all I care." She regretted the words immediately.

Clarissa, however, persisted in the sure knowledge that she was right. She was about to provide Rachel with what she thought was help. A small pencil-like mace gun. It not only incapacitated the attacker, but marked clothing and skin with an indelible orange dye that would later help to identify the criminal if necessary. She really did want to go on this expedition, silly as it might turn out to be, but she wanted protection too. Rachel would undoubtedly refuse the mace. "Rachel, I'm sorry," she said, hoping to salvage her invitation. "I only meant . . . ."

"Meant, meant. You don't know what you meant. First of all you're a scaredy cat." That expression, rising from some childhood name-calling memory-bank, was out before she thought, but it brought her to her senses. "Clarissa, what do you want?" she said without her usual impatience. "I'm sorry if I snapped."

"I would like to go with you, but I want to be prepared for any eventuality–to err on the side of caution isn't the worst offense is it? Things do happen all the time to unsuspecting, innocent people. In a remote place like your island the chances of getting help quickly are not good."

Rachel sighed. "Precisely because the island is remote, it is safer from the kooks of the world. Look, I don't want to get into the whole gun control issue with you. Let it suffice to say that I don't believe individuals should carry weapons. That's the prerogative of the police."

"But you're bringing the people with you, and they are strangers, Rach. You said yourself there are no police on the island."

Rachel acknowledged that that was true. She watched as Clarissa struggled with herself, knew that this was about something more than safety. It was about friendship; sparse as it was, this ten year acquaintance was a kind of friendship, if only by dint of faithfulness. Rachel saw now that it had surely been too one-sided. She would try to be a little kinder.

Clarissa took a deep breath and plunged on, "I brought something with me that I thought might be helpful, an ounce of protection," she hesitated. "Actually it does weigh about an ounce." She smiled tentatively and drew the pen-like object from her pocket.

Under ordinary circumstances, Rachel would have been annoyed, but now, thinking carefully about this as an offering of friendship, she felt both embarrassed and touched. Her ambivalence made her awkward. "Explain it to me," she said as she turned it over in her hand.

"Be careful, Rach," Clarissa warned. "If you pull back on that lever it could spray you. It can hit up to a distance of eight feet, and it's incapacitating for fifteen minutes. Long enough for someone to escape from attack."

"I see," Rachel said attentively, reading the description on the mace. "Where'd you get this–Cornucopia?"

Clarissa nodded. "One of the customers went to the 'Take Back the Night' meeting at City Center. She was giving them away to anybody who wanted one. I took two actually. One for me, one for you."

Rachel saw that this was a time to choose words carefully. "Well, Clarissa," she spoke slowly. "I've always thought of myself as independent. I've lived a long life already, and so far, even in this neighborhood I've felt safe. I've never been afraid of people. I guess I just want to go on doing what I do, without unnecessary, perhaps even paranoid precautions. I can't see how something like this spray thing would be helpful to me. Still," and here she was trying new territory, reaching for something she hadn't quite dealt with before, "I know that there are women and children, and yes, men too, who've been attacked without provocation, who didn't ask for it. Like the witches in the old days," she said, hoping Clarissa saw the connection, "They could have used some mace." She paused, and gathered her strength for the last bit which was the hardest. "I thank you, Clarissa, for thinking of me, and while I probably won't carry it, I want you to know that I appreciate your concern."

Clarissa sighed. She was grateful for the effort that went into Rachel's words. This thank you was some kind of progress, and it made the interchange a kind of draw rather than a loss for either side. Clarissa would carry her own mace even if Rachel refused to carry hers. "It's complicated, Rach," she said appreciatively. "I know that you are a proud, independent woman. Not everyone is as strong as you are."

"I may not be all that strong, but I do like making my own choices . . ." Rachel stood and stretched, turned and began rummaging in the kitchen cupboards, ". . . and I choose to have lunch right about now. Are you hungry? Have a bite with me and I'll tell you about the island. The house is fairly old, 1860s or thereabouts," Rachel began immediately, taking a bite out of her sandwich of Wonderbread, Spam and mustard and shoving the loaf and the can of Spam toward Clarissa.

Clarissa, who politely declined to eat, swished a bag of Tetley's tea quickly through a cup of hot water. Tea was the safest thing to drink in Rachel's apartment. "Can you see the water from the house?" Never having been invited to the island before, she was anxious for details.

"Oh, yes. From most windows. It's a small farmhouse on a peninsula of twenty acres, within walking distance of the harbor."

Clarissa nodded eagerly.

"You've probably heard me say how I've tried to keep it just as it was in the old days," Rachel continued. "No electricity. There are kerosene lamps, a pump at the sink. There's a gas stove and refrigerator, concessions to the 20th century. Oh yes, and there's the outhouse." The outhouse would surely set Clarissa off and running, Rachel thought, gleefully.

Clarissa was unwilling to be baited. "I imagine we'll get along fine. After all, we're only going to be there for two nights, right?"

"Yup, and the outhouse is clean as a whistle. Nobody has used it since I was there. We'll pick up some peat moss and some lime–which helps."

Clarissa couldn't imagine what good peat moss or lime could possibly do. In fact, she could barely imagine using an outhouse. She'd probably be constipated beyond belief.

". . . sleeping bags," Rachel was saying. "I've told them all to bring them . . . ."

"So who did you say they are?" Clarissa said, returning to her original question one more time.

"There's a woman named Clovis from Portland and one called Grace from New Jersey, kind of formal sounding in her request, then three women from the university up at Orono who were more down-to-earth. Their letter came from the business office, actually. One of them works as a secretary there," she said. "They just don't sound like violent types, Clarissa."

Clarissa ignored the last remark. "College kids, I bet," she said smirking. "That's something. I thought witches were your age." She saw the look on Rachel's face. "And mine," she added quickly.

"And what makes you think these women are young?" Rachel shot back. "Secretaries come in all ages–so do students." Rachel was beginning to feel on edge. Clarissa was good to have around in small doses only. What was it she had taken from her pocket to chew on this time–a great chunk of carob? Most people would have thought that impossible to eat, but Clarissa loved it.

"Here," she said riffling through some papers in a kitchen drawer. "These are the responses. Read them yourself. And by the way, you really ought to get some sensible walking shoes. Those sandal things are not safe for rocky places. The island is full of granite ledges and pebble beaches."

Wednesday morning the letter lay on his desk just as if it had arrived with the other mail. Alison had discretely placed it there with whatever had been delivered at the door. The letter, he found, contained a note saying he should bring sleeping bag and food (heavens, who would cook it?) and also a pamphlet with a map to Lily Island, complete with ferry schedule. There were, the little pamphlet said, no public accommodations, no camping on the place, but worse, Father Donahey noted with some alarm, Lily Island was not within his parish by any stretch of the imagination. Still, the ad for the coven had been placed here in Portland. Was a Portland resident behind the ad?

What now? Call the whole thing off? Or could he complete his investigation while taking a long weekend? If so, how would he get there and where would he stay when he arrived? He'd need to keep a low profile, to have privacy, a place where he could don some kind of disguise, certainly a necessary thing if he were to perform an exorcism. No devil would let him approach if it saw his collar. He called a halt to his fantasy. An exorcism was a dangerous presumption. He still had no idea if this was child's play or the real thing. He wouldn't be able to tell till he got to the place and found out who was involved. Perhaps he'd better confer with the Bishop after all. And what if the Bishop ordered him not to go? No, he was going and no bishop would stop him.

With short-lived relief he found the answer to the lack of accommodations on the island. Alison again. But how could he ask her without letting her know too much? This was far more difficult than using her mailing address. What he wanted was her RV. She had a fancy one with real sleeping quarters, a shower, stove and refrigerator. It seemed an extravagant thing for someone in her position, but she had won a lottery contest a year ago and used her winnings to buy it. It was her pride and joy. She would never lend it to him. Perhaps he could rent it. That was it. Why didn't he just rent an RV from an outlet somewhere? No, they might want to know where he was going–or ask his name for insurance purposes or whatever. He could say it was for a vacation, but, some parishioner would find out and there would be talk. Why would a priest need to rent an RV for a vacation, they would ask? Suspicious. Nothing wrong with his car, someone would say. It had just been serviced. People around Portland knew too much about him.

He was not thinking clearly about this thing. He was stepping out of bounds for the first time in his years of service and it made him just a wee bit nervous. Yet, this coven business had him stirred up somehow. If he couldn't explain it to the Bishop, who was in a position of authority over him, perhaps he could tell Alison who was under his own authority. The notion pleased him.

He buzzed for her and she arrived in her jogging suit, sweaty from running again, large unsightly dark spots under her arms and over her chest. He'd have to speak to her about that, but not now. He needed the RV.

He's read the letter, Alison thought, trying hard to look cool. Ten minutes notice and I could have changed. This schedule is killing me. Something has got to give and I suppose it will be my running.

"Thank you for delivering the letter. It has presented me with another more serious dilemma, however." How to say this, he wondered? Could he just ask to rent her RV by the day, plus gas, like any commercial arrangement? What did he owe her by way of explanation? Just more of the same top-secret church business, which after all was what it was. The thing was fraught with complications. Perhaps he should take her into his confidence, but she wasn't a Catholic. (What Catholic would have had the gall to come into his study in a sweat-stained jogging suit?)

He had learned that she was not of the faith after he had tasted her gourmet cooking–when he was already hooked. She had come in as a substitute for one of the parish women who took ill unexpectedly. That one had been an ordinary cook, and she had since gone to her just reward. There had been no one else available except Alison.

It was unheard of, he knew, to have someone outside of the faith working in the parish house, and the parishioners were gossiping. Some said he was too weak to fire Alison once she got a foot in the door. He heard that at a rosary group. Some said he was self-indulgent, cared only for his own culinary satisfaction (that from someone at choir practice). They might be right, but one woman had actually given him to know, in the confession booth no less, that he was taking his housekeeper to bed. Cleverly confessed as gossip, the nasty bit of business had, he understood, been shared first with family and friends. So be it. The gossip was wrong on that score, although he was not beyond understanding how someone could come up with the idea. Alison was obviously fond of him.

"Now, Alison," he began again. "I've a job to do which requires some undercover, er, clandestine, how shall I say it, sleuthing for the church?"

The sweat rolled down Alison's back, but she didn't care. He was wonderfully foolish in the throes of his deception, and she would stay all day, if she only could, to watch. What next, she wondered. Does he want my apartment to meet his lover?"

"Your vehicle. Have you ever lent it out–ever rented it?" he amended, guilty about putting pressure on her to give it outright. He knew she had not.

She had been that close! The van was even better than her apartment. He could get out of town alone. Pick the woman up somewhere and never be seen. The nerve of him asking her for the RV, though. "I don't lend it out," she said, quietly firm. "Besides, it's difficult to maneuver. It has extra gears because it's so heavy. It doesn't have an automatic shift like the church car, you know." She stopped, then added quickly, "Besides, I need it. It's my only means of transportation."

He hadn't thought of that. Still he had a chance. "I'll tell you the truth, Alison," he began. "There's an island where this church business is being conducted, and there are no motels. With a van I could park in someone's driveway for a few days, have a place to stay without intruding upon anyone."

Alison was intrigued. His voice sounded less shaky for some reason. This might be the truth, in part anyway. The woman probably lived on the island and she couldn't get away. He wanted to visit her and he needed a place to entertain her. But why all the secrecy about the mail? Of course. He hadn't told the woman he was a priest. Then where had he met her? He always wore his collar. She was befuddled. I don't follow him around, she thought crossly. What do I know? He could easily switch clothes if necessary. Maybe the woman's blind. This caused her to smile inwardly. Whoever this lover was, she had missed seeing the object of her affection for what he was–a frog. Hell, this is so silly, Alison thought. But such fun. Most people have affairs without these complications, but Christians, and in particular Catholics, carry all the baggage of sin and guilt. A priest, paragon of virtue that he's supposed to be, carries the heaviest baggage of all. What madness.

"Why do you need the van, Father?" she probed. If he was uncomfortable with her being so forward, she already had him hooked. He would not fire her now. He might even believe she would blackmail him. What did he know about her except that she wasn't a Catholic? She knew quite a bit about him, and the big thing was that he had taken leave of his senses. He was obsessed with some woman. Yet, she was not quite sure. Ah, then maybe it was a man. That would make it even more complex, more perilous for him.

Suddenly she heard his voice sounding clear and strong. "I need it because I'm investigating a possible case of devil worship. This is strictly confidential, Alison," he warned. "Word must not get out. I can't use the church's vehicle for obvious reasons."

Now this was the old Father Donahey. She was surprised, after all the secrecy. If this was not the truth, he was doing far better at masking his deceit than he had before.

"There is to be a meeting on that island. I need to go, need a place to stay in hiding–out of sight. I have to approach carefully. It could be dangerous." He was speaking confidently, but she could also sense his excitement. It was an adventure for him, the poor clod. He was bored with his job.

He noticed her face soften. The truth had done wonders, he believed. He could work things out with her yet. Who said you could not trust a non-believer? This girl had a childish, really harmless crush on him and he could use that to the benefit of the church and for her as well. Perhaps he could even convert her. He had never even asked her what her religion was. No matter. He went on, "Now if I could . . . ."

She interrupted him with as much courtesy as she could gather, "But Father Donahey, you don't drive regular shift, and this is truly a big van, not easy to manipulate." He was too short to reach the pedals, but she couldn't tell him that. Besides, she realized unexpectedly, I want in on this caper.

"Then you drive, Alison," he said earnestly. "I'll pay time and a half. We'll close the house here for the weekend. I'll get Father Greene to say mass for me. He's a newly retired priest over in South Portland. He'll jump at the chance. When we get to the island we'll find a way somehow to provide proper sleeping arrangements." He said all this as if he'd read her thoughts. "No one will know anything other than that I'm off for a holiday weekend."

What parishioners would think, he knew, would be an extension of what they already thought. He'd cope later. They might want to retire him earlier than he'd like but perhaps if he were successful in breaking up a ring of devil worshipers, even in performing an exorcism, that would balance the unfair accusations. A troubling thought occurred. He might never be allowed to reveal the details of his triumph publicly. He'd report to the Bishop later and see. All of this, he recognized with a start, was presuming that there would be a triumph.

"Will you drive for me?" It was a question this time, more diplomatic in tone, and with just a note of anxiety. She could refuse.

"Yes, Father," she said, in her obedient Irish voice again. She was delighted. No matter which way it turned out—woman, man, or fantasy lover, she herself was off for the weekend, and with a firsthand opportunity to observe how a Catholic priest followed his obsession to a conclusion. If only Father Donahey knew, she thought bubbling inside, what I know.

Palisades Avenue. Union City. Sometimes Grace thought she could not face the loneliness of the place one more day, even if the rent was cheap and the view from her window a postcard of the New York skyline. Even if commuting to school via Lincoln Tunnel, two blocks away, was quick and easy. Most of her neighbors spoke only Spanish. They were olive-skinned and short and viewed her, a tall broad-shouldered woman as an enigma.

The first few times she'd gone to the corner store the conversation had ceased and people viewed her peripherally, curious but unable to ask how she'd got into their neighborhood. She was unable to tell them. They'd found a word for her since: giantess. In Spanish it was "giganta." She'd looked it up once after she overheard it and knew they were referring to her. It felt better somehow than "gringo". She was touched by their need to give her a name. Now she was more comfortable with the people and their warm smiles, and certainly the streets in the immediate New Jersey neighborhood were safer than New York.

She was simply not cut out for the huge crowds of the city itself, the dirty air, and all that ceaseless traffic. As she turned from the sidewalk to walk through the wrought iron gate guarding the entrance to her apartment building, she looked forward to the mail. Her newspaper lay on the floor of the lobby in a clutter of letters. It was the one in which she'd found the Widdershins ad, and a reassuring reminder that a less frenetic, friendlier life existed back home. Usually she was annoyed by the postman's cavalier treatment of oversize mail. He tossed whatever didn't fit in the slot, where it landed on the floor where anybody could, and sometimes did, take his pick. No one, however, seemed to want a Portland, Maine paper except her. Today it looked awfully good.

The newspaper represented her past in more ways than one. It was a reminder of her job in the features department which she herself had helped put to bed for two years. She had ended up being the assistant editor dealing with intriguing subjects; in fact, one assignment had led her to the realization that she wanted to move on. She loved research. And research was leading her finally to her doctorate, not in journalism as she had initially envisioned, but in sociology. For all of that she had her grandmother to thank. The small allowance, given in lieu of an inheritance (her grandmother was alive and feisty as ever) had allowed her to embark on her studies. It paid her rent and tuition and left enough for food and just occasionally something extra.

Her first big success with the paper had been an assigned article on Mary Dyer, a Quaker who was hanged at Boston Common for daring to preach in Massachusetts after she had been banished from that state. Grace had gone to visit the descendants of Mary, who lived in Benton Falls, Maine and listened to their anecdotes, even examined a letter written by Mary in 1659, the year before she was hanged. Grace wrote the article carefully interweaving what she could find on Mary at the University of Southern Maine's two libraries, one in Portland, one out at Gorham. Neither had as much as she would have liked. The story got accolades, however, from the editors and even two letters from readers, almost unheard of about anything that was not a present-day scandal. As a result of this piece she became interested in other persecuted witches, a subject which the newspaper was not keen on having her pursue right away.

She had begun research on the Salem witch trials on her own time. The behavior of people during the trials fascinated her so much that she eventually decided she wanted to go back to school to learn more about mass persecution and how it came about, which eventually led her to graduate school and to New Jersey. Now, ironically, she might be returning to Maine in pursuit of her work. To study a coven! Coincidence or magic? She wasn't sure any more. She was going home to Maine anyway.

She unlocked the door of the building, walked up three flights, and when she opened her own apartment door, found Increase, who immediately slithered around her ankles. He was a namesake of Increase Mather, one of the many strange voices of Salem history, a man who seemed to make sense when he said that it would be better to let twelve witches go free than put to death one innocent person. Hardly anyone had listened to him.

As a tomcat, Increase had his ways of getting even for being kept in an apartment after years of traveling the city neighborhood in Portland. Looking at him now she knew instantly that he was guilty of doing something forbidden. She made a brief inspection tour, walking through the kitchen into the living room. There she glanced down at the carpet and froze. Her prize Rya rug, the only touch of elegance she permitted herself, was ruined. A great hunk of it lay in a pile of shreds.

"You are impossible," she screamed at the cat's retreating form.

"If it had been this old thing," she waved at the second-hand sofa bed she slept on, "I might have forgiven you, but you are wantonly destructive. It's the last time, my friend, you are going to do this kind of thing. You won't go to Maine. You're going to the veterinarian–to be de-clawed."

The Siamese, sensing danger, leaped to security on the high part of the armchair–his usual perch.

"Get off there," she cried fiercely. He bolted, then slowed to a dignified walk, tail high, circling behind her into the kitchen where he disappeared under the table.

Grace picked up the ruins and sat down at her desk. She fingered the ragged threads, wondering where she could possibly get the rug repaired and whether she could afford the price. She pushed the thought aside as she saw the only other piece of mail she had received with the newspaper. It was from "Widdershins." Fascinated, she read the pamphlet on the island ferry schedule and the accompanying note. It would be easy enough to get there–although a long drive. But what would come of it all? In a way, it could be problematic if she were stuck out there on an island in an unproductive–even dangerous–situation. Any number of scenarios flitted through her mind. She wanted to know more about who was in the coven–who was Widdershins? Probably someone who was practicing witchcraft. That much was encouraging, but even as a reporter she had never walked into something with so little information about the situation she was facing or the people she would be meeting. She reassured herself that the directions were clear. The handwriting of Widdershins, whoever that was, looked sensible and sane. She brought herself up short. When did I become an expert in handwriting analysis, she asked herself?

She was going to go, knowing full well that it was simply an excuse to be in Maine–to go home again. This was the only time she'd have before the summer session began. She turned to the ever-present practical matters: cost, mileage, time. If this is a joke, she told herself, I can still tour the island. There are three afternoon departures of the ferry to the mainland. If I get there early in the morning I can check things out and if there's nothing really going on I'll easily have a few hours for sightseeing. I'm going.

Grace contemplated what she would need for the adventure. She'd need her tape recorder and some blank cassettes, a notebook, extra pens, her sleeping bag, some hiker's mix, some of her favorite falafel mix, also perhaps some tofu. She would stop at the New Day health food store in Portland instead of carrying all that stuff from here. Then she could get fresh veggies. She would need her flashlight, a change of clothes, soap and towel. Should I take the tent? She decided not. That should do it–except for one more item. She pulled a large case from the closet, marched into the kitchen and placed it on the floor with its hinged top open.

"First things first," she announced loudly, flinging back the tablecloth. Increase was pressed up against the wall on the far side of the table. She reached out and drew him gently but firmly towards his destiny.

"Solange, how are you feeling about the money? You haven't talked about it lately." Bernie was in the front seat of Ann's

Subaru station wagon. She looked back at Solange as Ann drove. "It must be incredible to realize you're an heiress. I mean, I'm not used to the idea, so I can't believe you are."

Solange was stretched out, a copy of Starhawk's book on her lap. She smiled and shook her head in wonder. She had never had close friends as a child growing up, nor as a young adult. The truth was after spending her childhood in a kind of poverty of the soul, she had simply moved on to an expanded version. She isolated herself from relationships with people in general. This friendship with Bernie and Ann had been her salvation. She had walked into their rather casual lives, totally disarmed by their ability to accept her, an older, reserved woman, as a friend. She was intrigued by the rich variety of events in their days and relished the endless bantering that came as part of their companionship. She found herself opening up, able at last to talk about her feelings. She couldn't imagine life without spending at least a few hours every week with them, time spent discussing some incident, trivial or momentous, couldn't imagine a life devoid of their reactions to classroom discussions, to books, to news on the campus and to the world. She loved planning with them the latest agreed-upon conquest of unknown territory (whether of people or experience) and then carrying out that conquest–just as they were doing today. She was having her childhood after all, she told them.

Thus Bernie's question about money was not an invasion of privacy. She and Ann always asked intimate questions that expected honest answers. Solange was used to that now. What was so stupefying was that a stranger she knew only through rare messages signed "Father" had died and left her a fortune, made her the sole beneficiary of his estate, and as a result, wealthy beyond her present power to comprehend. It put her into a strange emotional state when she tried to figure out how this much money could possibly, finally, fit into her life.

As a middle-aged woman she was long toughened to frugality, a life of pinching pennies. She seldom caught herself longing for the frivolous or the extravagant. A secretary's salary covered the rent of a small apartment in a neighborhood within walking distance of the college campus, and left enough for food and sometimes new clothing and certainly books. The college paid her tuition. Taking one or two courses a semester she had slowly closed in on a degree in liberal arts. She contemplated graduate school like some people contemplated a vacation. Studying was such a joy to her that she sometimes contemplated becoming a professional student.

But the inheritance was changing everything. There was some kind of responsibility, she saw immediately, that went with it, a thundering kind of responsibility in fact. She would heed that thunder eventually, but could she also hold onto all that she cherished about her present life? There was no way yet to know.

"Something may get lost," she answered enigmatically. "Oh, I really don't know how I feel yet," she added. "I'm sure I'll start feeling something one of these days–disappointment maybe that this money comes without a face, without a personality, without an opportunity either to thank or curse my father for it.

"You know what? I found myself wondering for the first time in a long time about my mother. Why didn't he reveal her name, if not his, at least tell me where she lived? Maybe she's dead. Maybe she's been dead all along. After all I'm 55. Lots of people my age have already lost their parents. I do think about her. I'd like to know why she gave me up.

"My foster parents were so lacking in loving-kindness that there was never a moment when I felt as if I belonged in their family. Let's face it. I knew I wasn't part of the family. They were paid good money to take care of me and they did what they perceived to be a good job by providing me with a bed to sleep in, clothes, food–but it was a job, not a labor of love, and they let me know that."

"So how are you feeling about having all that money?" Ann pressed, sure there had to be some kind of reaction on its way. She knew Solange. This might be the calm before the explosion.

"At this point, nothing feels any different," Solange insisted. "It's not real. I haven't had time to really think . . . ." She gave a little shrug. "I know you want me to be expansive and spend my money extravagantly on some wild and wonderful spree, but I'm not sure I'll be able to do that." She paused and then chuckled. "No, that's not entirely true. I did get an American Express card last week with no trouble at all. They couldn't wait to give one to me. Ever hear of a card without a limit?" She chuckled. "Only kidding, but talk about a limit that exceeds my wildest fantasy! I haven't put anything on it yet, you understand, but I could, couldn't I?" She grinned wickedly and they all laughed.

"Do it. Splurge. You've been living off a secretary's salary for how many years is it? You could quit working and go to school full time," Bernie said, waving a hand as if she were a magician about to make something appear.

"You could buy the school now," Ann added, an idea which delighted them all.

"After we bought it, who would we fire?" Solange asked. She sat upright in the seat, queen for a day.

"That creep who tries to get his women students to sleep with him." Bernie said.

"Right, and the cook in the cafeteria who serves all that pale glop."

"And the Pillsbury Doughboy who works in the bookstore—the one who tried to copy Solange's term paper." Bernie, almost unconsciously pulled out a cigarette and lit it. Then, remembering, she rolled down the window. "I'll blow the smoke out, honest. I promise," she said to Solange in a pleading voice.

Solange reluctantly consented. "Now," she said getting back into the fantasy again, "who else?"

"How about the dean of students?" Ann suggested. "You can never get to see him, and when you do he never follows through."

"Him too. Off with their heads. All of them." Solange cried.

Out of breath with laughter, each woman yielded to her own vision of the future. Bernie knew damn well what she'd do if she had the money. Go to law school. Get a full time nanny. Give Richard money to start his own business. That would be wonderful. Ann was not so sure how she would spend a fortune, but she knew she'd save some, put it aside for bad times. Some of it would have to go toward her graduate degree–then all her brothers and sisters would need an education too. Oh, she could spend it easily, if it were hers. No doubt about it.

Solange continued as if she were reading their minds, "You know that I will help you guys out with your education. We'll work on this together–whatever your needs."

It was quiet for a moment and then she spoke again. "Maybe I'll take singing lessons, and piano too." She looked down at her hands and said softly, "Remember?" They remembered.

Ann was driving easily within the speed limit but they were making good time. I95 was essentially boring but the quickest way to get anywhere without entering an endurance contest with bumper-to-bumper tourists. This was not a part of Maine that was particularly beautiful. Once they got on the other side of Bangor and headed toward the coast there would be more green and less of the shopping mall infestations that cluttered this part of the state. Solange and Bernie had voted for getting to the island as quickly as possible. "We'll set up the tent and then do some exploring of the island. If it turns out the whole thing is a sham, at least we'll have a day of sunshine," Bernie suggested.

"So what do we know about witches?" Bernie asked after they'd been on the road for an hour and a half. "Has everybody done their homework?"

"Sure," Ann said "I was the one who recommended Starhawk, remember? Listen, we've had our little ceremonies together–the three of us–that could be called witchcraft, you know?" She paused and glanced over her shoulder at Solange, "How are you doing with Starhawk–had a chance to read any of it yet?"

Solange had curled up. *Dreaming the Dark* lay by her side. She picked it up and leafed to the place where she'd left off, "Yes. She talks about creating your own rituals, gives samples in the back, just like you said, but it's the initiation rites in the beginning of the book that put me off. If that's what you have to go through to become a witch, count me out."

"You're referring to the part where she goes howling like a banshee through the canyons and the caves, right? A lot of that stuff reminds me of Native American rites of passage–peyote-induced travel. I feel that kind of thing belongs to a specific culture, is more fitting in context. We don't have to adopt rites or rituals that don't suit us," Bernie said. "If it doesn't feel comfortable, then we don't do it," she grinned and Solange, visibly relieved, smiled back.

"So we're not going to make this an initiation of some kind?" Ann said.

"Well, who knows what the others have in mind? We'll have to see who they are and what experience they've had."

"That's a bit worrisome to me," Solange said. "I've always liked the idea of our having some kind of spiritual experience of our own to share, just the three of us. We've always been spontaneous. Things change when they get repetitive, when they're expected and formalized. That's one of the things I don't like about church. After a while it becomes obligatory. You become a sinner if you don't take part–an outcast. I'm not sure I'm all that keen on joining with strangers either." There it was, sounding like an afterthought, but they all knew it was a basic concern.

Bernie pounced on it, "Solange, this is a fine time to be saying it. We decided together to do this, remember?"

"Well, I was sort of swept up in the moment, there at the bar. We were having such good fun–a spontaneous decision seemed right at the time."

"Yes, but then we've talked about it since, planned all along on going. You never expressed any reservations until now." Bernie was becoming aware of her own hesitation but didn't want the other two to know. "It's a bit late to turn back, don't you think? We're half way there."

Ann, sensible as ever, pulled the car over to the side of the road, and turned in her seat to face both of them. "Wait just a minute. I'm willing to do what the group wants here. Shall we have a little consensus meeting? We certainly can go home again, if we wish. This is not a law we're following here. It's a whim, and if it's not going to be fun, or spiritual or whatever, then we can return to school, or, or the pub." She looked inquiringly at Bernie and then at Solange. "Maybe we should go to a resort somewhere and just have a fun weekend?" She sounded wistful, like a child who had hoped for a snow day so that school would be canceled.

"Of course not," Solange said, becoming practical when she saw that the other two had turned indecisive. "I vote we go find out about the coven, but that we have a signal–a password. If one of us uses that password and there are other people around, it means we want out of there, and without discussion. It means cut bait and reconvene where we can talk in private. I want that password to be accepted by each of us as sacred and to mean we all abide by it, that we re-group by ourselves and then we can decide what's next." She looked earnestly at the other two. "I want a safety net."

"Absolutely." Ann said feeling much better. "I can go with that real easy. How about you, Bernie?"

"Yup," Bernie was visibly relieved.

"We've got an hour to the ferry. Anybody hungry?" Ann asked. They had escaped from I95 and were just outside of Brewer. "I need to stop for gas now, and I want a cigarette. I don't know if there's gas on the island. We don't want to run out."

"Just a moment," Solange said urgently. "We've forgotten something–the password."

"So you choose it. It was your idea. You get to pick," Bernie said indulgently.

"Don't say that. Now I can't think of a thing," Solange answered.

"That's O.K. Take your time," Ann said.

"There. There's a place now," Bernie called out seeing a gas station. "There's a grocery store next door."

"Groceries." Solange said.

"What?" Ann asked. "Do we need something? I thought we got what we needed at home?"

"No," Solange said, "I mean, yes, we did, but groceries will be the password."

"Great," Bernie was feeling triumphant. We're on course, she thought. We're together. She reached over and patted Solange on the arm. "Groceries," she repeated and Ann did too. "Let's get some gas," she said.

"Pump," Rachel said sternly to Clarissa. "Pump. Pump. Pump. Steady now. That's it. Keep the rhythm."

Clarissa pumped, but the handle of the stupid thing was giving no resistance and here was Rachel pouring water down its throat by the gallon–just the opposite of what was supposed to be happening. "How long does this go on?" she asked, imagining their putting four or five more buckets of water into the pump before it started delivering. Might as well walk to the well whenever you needed water. She said as much to Rachel who managed to remain patient.

"Just pump. It takes a while. What we're trying to do here is create a vacuum so that the water in the well will come up through the pipe. Don't stop now. Never mind the floor. We can wipe it up later."

Clarissa watched the little stream of water trickle down the side of the cabinet onto the floor near her shoes. "It's making a mess, that's all, and besides my arm is getting tired," she added. Rachel always assumed she was incompetent. But then in fairness to Rachel she asked herself how many times like this had there actually been. She should count her blessings. She was here at last on this beautiful island in this wonderful old house. She'd never stayed on an island, let alone in a house without electricity. A pain shot from her elbow to her shoulder. She said nothing.

"It's linoleum, Clarissa. That's what it's for," Rachel said, her patience beginning to wane as the pump remained unresponsive, "and we can wipe it up later. Here. Switch with me. I'll take a turn at the handle."

Rachel felt as if a slight amount of pressure might be building. She pumped harder. Clarissa was such a wimp, never got any exercise. Seemed tired. So much for health food. The other thing was she was totally unprepared to rough it, words she had used to describe a YWCA outing she'd been on as a child. This was one and the same person who bragged about growing up on a farm. Incredible. She'd certainly be learning a thing or two here. Good enough for her.

A woman appeared on the back steps. Looking in through the kitchen screen, she watched the scene, amused. "Hello in there," she called. "Welcome back." She pushed open the screen and stepped inside.

Rachel turned and smiled, but continued to pump the handle. "Hi, Ellen," she said, "I'll feel better about being back when I get this thing going." She nodded her head then towards Clarissa and introduced the two.

Ellen, Clarissa noted, was pale with blond, tightly curled hair. A straw hat hung by a draw string on her back. She wore work clothes: painter's pants and a workman's shirt, and her eyes were incredibly brown in contrast to her hair. There was an air of maturity and calm about her which Clarissa liked. Rachel had told Clarissa that this woman was a student of Italian architecture and that she had spent years in Italy. What was she doing on a Maine island then, Clarissa had asked. Rachel replied that Ellen was staying with an elderly aunt who was recuperating from surgery. Ellen could find work anywhere. Although she was a scholar and a writer, carpentry was her hobby, and she was good at it.

"I don't want to distract you. A pump can be a pesky thing," Ellen said. "Does it need a new leather?"

"No," Rachel replied. "It's just dry."

"That's a little bit easier to fix," Ellen commiserated. "Well, I wanted to let you know that I'll be working on the house tomorrow while you're here. I'm repairing a few of the clapboards on the west side. The nails have popped. Then I'll start shingling the roof. Hope it won't be too noisy for you? I was hoping to do it before you got here."

"Not at all," Rachel said smiling. "I'm only grateful that you can find time to do the work." She felt the water rising in the pump now. Clarissa had just switched to the last bucket, creating a small flood on the floor, and they would have to go to the well again if this didn't do it. She pumped rapidly, giving it her best effort, and then she yelled at Clarissa, "Quick now, put the bucket under the spout, and we'll fill it

up again. We're going to need water to do dishes. There," she cried triumphantly, as the water flowed. "That wasn't so bad, was it?"

Clarissa kept her opinion to herself. If this was camping she could let it pass. You could push a switch or turn a handle at home with instant results and no sore muscles.

Rachel kept on pumping until the bucket filled. "Now," she said firmly, and Clarissa mentally steeled herself for a lecture. "Don't ever leave the pump handle up," Rachel said, and added her arm's weight to it although it was already down. "If you do, we'll lose the prime and have to start all over again."

Clarissa nodded solemnly, then busied herself with mopping the floor. That was one piece of advice she would take seriously.

Ellen chuckled. "We've got a pump in our kitchen too. Wouldn't change it for the world, although Auntie Eve put electricity in years ago, as well as regular faucets in the bathroom. There's something about a pump that feels comforting."

"I know, but it can be irritating getting it started. I imagine you don't have that problem."

"No. Auntie has never gone away long enough to shut down the water."

"Have a cup of coffee, Ellen?" Rachel invited.

"We deserve a break after that," Clarissa agreed. "Do sit." She pulled out a chair from the table for Ellen.

"Why not? I have a minute." Ellen said. "I'll join you."

The three women sat at the kitchen table, their yellow and blue mugs steamed with Clarissa's cranberry tea and Rachel's and Ellen's coffee. An unlit black metal kerosene lamp was suspended over the middle of the round pine table. There was a drop of oil in the center of the yellow plaid plastic table cloth. Rachel absently wiped it up.

"Doesn't that ever drip into the food?" Clarissa inquired warily.

"Could, I suppose." Rachel was unwilling to make false assurances.

Clarissa wrinkled her nose and then, conscious of Ellen's presence, changed the subject. "How do you like the island? It must be awfully different from Italy."

"Ah, yes, it certainly is," Ellen said, feeling nostalgic. "Rachel told you of my interest in Roman architecture?"

Clarissa nodded.

"There are things about Rome that are impressive and things that annoyed me. The art, however, is superb. I enjoyed my stay, but this place has gotten into my blood." She turned to Rachel, "I did all the research for my book in Italy, but I'm progressing nicely with the writing of it right here. I've decided to stay permanently, Rachel. My aunt is fully recovered, by the way."

"I'm really happy to hear that." Rachel reached over and patted Ellen's hand. "And I'm sorry I didn't inquire immediately after her health."

"Oh, her surgery made a remarkable difference. When I first got here a year and a half ago, she was practically starving to death because of her gall bladder attacks. Now she is back to a healthy weight, can eat all the foods she loved in the past. In short, life is worth living again."

"That is good news."

"Yes, and the other good news is I am beginning to get just enough carpentry work to keep me busy when I am not writing. A nice balance."

"Are there houses like this everywhere on the island needing repair?" Clarissa asked.

"A few. This is one of the oldest. The kitchen was added in the early twenties, but the rest of the house was built sometime in the 1850s. The wide floorboards and the granite foundation give it away. Another thing. If we were to do major reconstruction we'd probably find that the house is a product of lunch-box carpentry. Builders took odd pieces of lumber left over from the jobs they were doing elsewhere and put them into their own houses. There are a number of houses on the island like that."

Clarissa nodded. "Should have called them patchwork quilt houses." She was thinking how much she liked the kitchen, a very summery place with shells, sand dollars and sea urchins (Rachel had given her their names) on the window sills. There was an appliqued map of the island hanging over the refrigerator–the sea was a background of blue muslin, the island in white sail cloth. There were five windows and each a little bit off balance. The whole house was like that, and it gave it a curious but charmingly lopsided look. Except for the picture window which Rachel had installed a few years ago, the windows had six-over-six panes and she could see the ripples in the old glass. Rachel had put up no curtains, and the kitchen was bright with outdoor light. A kite made of flowered cotton hung from the ceiling in one corner, its blue satin tail tacked along one wall. "Those two pieces over there, Rach," she said, "did you do those?" She indicated a drift wood branch nailed to the wall on the left of the sink that served as a cup rack and another longer piece neatly suspended above the stove. An assortment of baskets hung from pieces of rope looped up and over the branch.

"An island friend, Susan, did those. She knew how limited storage space is in this house. All I have are three kitchen cupboards to store things in. They are big, as you can see–go all the way to the ceiling, but there isn't a single closet in the place."

Ellen said, "But the house isn't cluttered. It looks spacious."

"No, I am not one of those people who can't throw anything away, and I do have the apartment, after all, and it has excellent places to tuck things away."

"This is one of the most cheerful kitchens I have ever been in," Clarissa announced. "Not many people would chose to paint their kitchen chairs and table bright blue and their cupboards, walls and ceiling yellow."

Rachel warmed to the compliment. "Well, these walls and the ceiling were natural matchboard birch and they had darkened a lot by the time I bought the house. They were actually a dirty brown. I had to do something to brighten up the place."

"I love the picture over there–" Ellen said pointing to an old fashioned framed print on the wall next to the sink, "all those children in sailor hats and bloomers dancing around in the waves. I'd like to join them."

"That was in the house when I bought it," Rachel said, "and I love it, too. I think I could get used to living here year round. It's a homey place–just the two rooms downstairs and two up. Easy to care for and cozy,"

"But cold in the winter. No insulation," Ellen said. "I don't know how the original people stood the cold. Even with the kerosene stoves they must have had."

"The harbor freezes over sometimes. The coast guard has to clear a path to the mainland. Some days the ferry doesn't run at all," Rachel told Clarissa.

"What do people do all winter?" Clarissa asked.

"People hole up in their houses," Ellen explained. "The women do the usual housekeeping chores. Some have hobbies–knitting and quilting–that kind of thing. They cook and care for the kids. There are always committee meetings and church. The men do odd jobs. They mend their traps or make new ones. A few old timers knit bait bags. Nobody fishes in the winter and there are only a few hardy souls who clam in the freezing mud.

"I guess for the most part we're just like everybody else. We have our share of problems, along with the rest of the state. Right now, for instance, we are dealing with developers who have no conscience. They are buying up the island, not to settle here themselves, but to sell at a higher profit shortly. They may change the quiet atmosphere and push up the taxes without a thought for those who are already here." She sighed and stirred her coffee. "I'm afraid I've gotten caught up in the politics of it somewhat. I try to be of help where I can, but I don't have much clout. I'm not sure the islanders approve of my getting involved. They still see me as a city woman. Someone 'from away.' " She smiled ruefully.

"Even though your aunt is a native–born and brought up here?" Rachel shook her head. She stood and rummaged in the cupboard for something to eat. She pulled out a package of sugar donuts and emptied the box onto a plate.

Clarissa refrained from her usual lecture about refined sugar as she watched Ellen and Rachel help themselves.

Ellen continued, "It takes time to win their trust, but I'm willing to hang in here. It's worth it."

"Who are these particular developers, anyway?" Rachel asked crossly. "Developers seem as attracted to this state as flies are to flypaper." She knew that the whole state was attracting new industry and that a building boom was in progress, but she had thought the island, because it was remote, would escape somehow.

"And why this island?" Clarissa inquired.

"Well, it seems like someone's master plan to develop every rural nook and cranny–anything pristine and unpolluted is fair game when there's money to be made," Ellen said angrily.

"It's happening all over New England, wherever the land is attractive and unspoiled. And Lily Island is rather unspoiled, compared to most of the quaint towns–no night clubs, no pubs–no liquor in fact. Nothing to attract the faster, swinging types. The other thing is there are a great many little coves, private spots where the view is unique. Some have dark volcanic rock and deep water, crashing against the shore, and an open view to the ocean. Others have shallow water, mud flats good for clamming, and there are little islands just off shore. Some places are easily accessible for boating or swimming. There are fields that run right down to the shore where there are all kinds of rocks and pebbles. Everybody collects the stones here. And there are two or three places where there are actually white sandy beaches. It was inevitable that real estate here would be considered rare and thus expensive. Have you had a chance to look around yet?"

"We got in late yesterday afternoon," Rachel said, "but I took her over to the harbor and the lighthouse and then to The Carry . . ."

"Where the Penobscots carried their canoes to open water," Clarissa finished. "I even saw a shell heap, left over from their clambakes. Funny, most people don't know, and I certainly didn't know, that the Indians came here to camp–for their summers," she added, pleased with the idea. The history of the island beckoned intriguingly to her and she was looking forward to an opportunity to explore. Perhaps she could sneak away sometime during the afternoon.

Ellen was smiling at her, wiping her fingers clean of the sticky sugar from the donut she had just finished. "I shouldn't be burdening you with island real estate problems. You're here for a break from all that, I'm sure. That's why people come here in the first place. So tell me. What are your plans while you're here? Going to do some walking? Some folks have already started swimming, mostly in the quarry; the ocean is always a bit chilly."

"Actually," Rachel began, and Clarissa knew when the word came out of her mouth, that witchcraft would be the subject that followed. This, in spite of the fact that Rachel had sworn she would not talk about it outside of the yet-to-be formed coven.

So much for secrets, Clarissa thought disgustedly.

Ellen took in the announcement calmly, a studious and attentive look on her face. "Why the word 'widdershins'?" she inquired when Rachel had finished.

"I guess I liked the sound of it, and the meaning, of course. Widdershins means counterclockwise as in the path of the moon. I am a woman who has always done things counter to the accepted way–I never married, always earned my way in the world. I left the church because I couldn't accept some of the teachings . . . and I refused to retire from work when I was supposed to. I've always been independent–from the very beginning of my adult life until now. Widdershins sounds like me."

"And there **are** witches?" Ellen asked.

"Oh, yes," Rachel continued, "I certainly hope some witches will be here this afternoon. Maybe we'll be able to cast a spell on the island developers, make them go away." She is only partly joking, Ellen thought.

"I don't know how many there are yet, but there are five people arriving. We'll be celebrating the summer solstice, the longest day of the year, tomorrow."

Ellen nodded, her expression serious. "What do you think these witches will be like?"

"Well, my knowledge so far is limited to what I've read," Rachel worked at explaining, "but I think I can safely say that witchcraft is a kind of spiritual experience, involving healing sometimes, herbal medicine perhaps, and magic. Witches have been maligned by society for centuries. Actually they were mostly older women, like us," she gestured to Clarissa and herself, "living alone but called upon to attend a death or a birth. They were just widows or spinsters who had no connection to anything vaguely resembling evil."

After a moment Ellen nodded her head, impressed with the amount of knowledge Rachel had at her fingertips; she did not seem irrational at all. "Do you have a set number of people invited or would one more be all right? I'm fascinated with the whole idea. I'd like to be here, at least for part of it.

I'm going to attend a planning board meeting tonight, but your solstice celebration is tomorrow, am I correct?"

Rachel nodded. "Yes, please do join us. We won't begin probably until dark, but come for supper at 6:30 if you can."

"Well, I'll see how this evening goes." Ellen rose to go. "We've got a very powerful group arriving here for the meeting tonight, and they are asking for changes in the island land use regulations and the building codes. They're arriving by yacht at the far end of the island and expect us to pick them up. As if we ran a taxi business!

"I'll be back anyway, today, to work on the house," she said cheerfully, and was out the door as they wished her good luck.

"Damn," Rachel said. "Wish I could do something to help."

"Ha," Clarissa said, clearing the table of cups. "That would be biting off more than you can chew. You've got your hands full right here this weekend. You don't have to take on the whole island."

That's the first sensible thing Clarissa has said since she's arrived, Rachel thought. "All right, then, let's get to it. We've got to get the refrigerator started, so you can put your foolish tofu away." She stuck out her foot and caught the front hatch at the bottom of the refrigerator and pushed it aside. "It runs on gas just like the stove. Here, let me show you." She gestured to a little knob at the bottom of the refrigerator. "That's a by-pass to the pilot light. You lie on the floor, push that knob in with one hand, hold this little wire with the other," she picked up a piece of copper wire tubing. "You light it and hold the flame to the burner until it stays on by itself."

"Oh no, not me!" Clarissa envisioned an explosion. "I'll do something else. Anything. I've had enough of the kitchen for a while. I'll dust the living room and sweep the floors." She moved quickly into the living room to hide her guilt. She knew it would hurt Rachel's arthritic knees to get down on the floor, but she couldn't help it. It was Rachel's house. Let her cope as best she could.

Rachel half-admired Clarissa for having the spunk to refuse. I'll get the damn thing lit with a blow torch if I have to, she told herself, remembering the year when the gas man had done just that. She knelt stiffly, her knees aching painfully, a box of wooden matches in one hand. She slid down flat on her stomach and lay looking into the dusty recesses of the refrigerator.

All the many green shades of spring shone out at them from the shore. Lily Island, rock-bound like so much of the Maine coast, lay just ahead. The land curved gently in and out and brilliant water dappled with white caps finished up with a flourish again and again around its edges. Above the shoreline they could see white houses tucked in among the pine and spruce trees. The dwellings seemed delicately balanced on gentle hillsides; a few had steeply pitched roofs reminiscent of churches.

Near the ferry slip, perhaps a hundred yards away (how would you measure it in nautical terms, Bernie wondered?), were three Boston Whalers, a small sloop named *Pandora,* and a lobster boat, with its gray stay sail keeping her steady. The word *Mistress* was painted on the neat yellow stern. Bernie scanned the shoreline and then out at several smaller islands which seemed to be uninhabited except for cormorants and seals. She handed the binoculars to Ann and retreated into a kind of dreamy state, feeling the damp wind against her face. She wondered how Richard and the boys were spending their day without her.

The ferry bumped against the slip, and Bernie almost lost her balance. Ann thrust the binoculars into her hand and returned to the car. A deck hand slung back the big chain that blocked the end of the ferry and stood waiting for the ramp to come down. "You're gonna have to move," he announced matter-of-factly to Bernie, but then he grinned and said, "You don't wanna be run over, do ya? Cars disembark first."

She slid into her seat as Ann started the motor. As they drove down the causeway they saw two women standing on the steps of the terminal. The older one flagged them with her shawl.

"You answer the ad?" Rachel shouted when Ann rolled down the window.

"That's us," Ann replied, smiling happily. "You must be Widdershins."

The old woman, obviously delighted, nodded and called out directions, "Turn right up there and drive to the end of the road. We'll follow shortly." She was already waving at the next car. Another member of the coven, undoubtedly, they told each other. Perhaps the woman with the New Jersey license plate and the yowling cat.

Old F.D., Alison thought of calling him now that they were traveling together in her RV. It stood for Old Fuddy Duddy as well as Father Donahey, she decided. Surprising how your own vehicle was like your castle, gave you a sense of power, and after all, she was in the driver's seat in her own RV now. Somehow that freed her up to call him anything she wanted, at least in her own mind.

The man was such a sketch in drag, sitting there beside her dozing away, and so thrilled with himself for embarking on his parody of an exorcism. She hadn't the heart to tell him that there would be no coven. He'd shown her the letter finally, had confided in her fully. She giggled, delighted that she would be there to meet these people. Some of them might be serious about learning the Craft. In that case . . . .

He opened his eyes momentarily, having heard her laugh, then returned to his reverie, looking for all the world like Toad dressed up as the Washerwoman in *The Wind In the Willows.* That was who she'd been reminded of all along. She suppressed her urge to laugh aloud again. Why was it that when men dressed up in women's clothes everyone thought it hilarious? Was it that no "real" man would seriously want to dress as a woman, to be taken for a woman, even for a

minute? That couldn't be it, otherwise why did priests like Father Donahey actually wear skirts when carrying out their highest duties–and other men, too–judges who sat on the high court wore robes, and lawyers and dons in England. Some even wore ridiculous wigs with ratty curls. What made a man in a skirt so solemn sometimes and so silly others?

Think of the kings, the popes, the archbishops–all that finery. No one laughed then. Well, almost no one. These men were given permission to break the taboos, so to speak, and that changed the meaning somehow. The more power a man wanted to display, the finer his skirts or robes.

There was something she'd read once about men usurping a woman's power by this means. Even the word "djellaba", the robe men wore in the Middle East, was translated to mean "imitation woman." Ah, and there even the commonest of men had complete dominion over women. So whatever magic lay in the woman's dress had to be left-over from the old days when there was a matriarchy. Some scholars maintained there never was a true matriarchy, but the myths were there. People created stories to suit their needs or the needs of the society. It seemed to her that the historical connection between ritual and dress was something to think about. She couldn't remember where she'd read that business about the djellaba. She'd have to try to find it again.

She glanced at the priest sitting next to her. He trusted her. How touching, she thought elated. (The way to a man's heart was certainly not through skirts. Oh no. It was good cooking that made magic in that domain–the man's castle–his home.)

He was innocent looking, half asleep on the way to his greatest adventure, an adventure he seemed to be playing by ear. He'd done no planning that she knew of except to bring a heavy tome with the ritual for exorcism in it, and his usual holy paraphernalia he carried on home and hospital visits. If she had anything to say about it, his role would be insignificant. Certainly he would come to no harm. No one would. Alison was committed to that as part of her creed. If he wanted the thrill of a plot like Stephen King's *The Shining* or *The Stand,* she was not about to help him. Anyone who answered that ad was probably the furthest thing from a satanist. On the other hand they were not witches either. And there was a great difference between the two.

The Toad (he had such potential for nicknames) was not capable of hurting anyone, not deliberately. He could cause a great deal of alarm and confusion, certainly. Better that he be waylaid somehow. She would see to that later.

"Father, are you going to sleep?" she asked him now. "Don't we need to coordinate our efforts? Are you at all concerned about what may happen when you get there?"

"Leave that to me, my dear," he said fuzzily. Such a good chance for a nap, and she'd interrupted it. But he saw that she wanted to be part of the work, and he had promised himself he would set an example, allow her to see the importance of his work. He glanced at his outfit. It didn't exactly enhance his position of authority.

"This costume was leftover from the Christmas play, Alison," he said seriously, "I took what I could find that fit me." She could see him preening just a bit, even while pretending he was joking, just as Toad would. She looked out the side window so he wouldn't see her smile.

"It's authentic, however," he added. "I do look like an older, er . . . woman, who comes from a rather shabby but respectable background–yes?"

"Yes, Father," she said trying to hold back the grin, but he sensed that she was laughing inwardly.

"Well, then, will it work? Are you thinking it won't fool anyone?"

"Not exactly, Father. I just think you ought to wait until nighttime to make your appearance. It will be more convincing. They won't have any ceremony or ritual until the moon rises anyway. This is the Solstice, you know?" Or did he know? He hadn't bothered to read up on witches that she knew of. She was willing to bet he revelled in the demonic version of EVIL personified and really believed that was what witchcraft was all about.

"What makes you think there will be a need for exorcism, Father?"

"Where there's a call for a coven, I suspect," he said weightily, "there are evil doings. This is not a Christian activity, after all, my dear. That is all I need to know. By the way, you don't attend mass, do you?" He knew it of course, but it was a way to begin talking about her faith.

"No, Father, I'm a fallen Catholic. I haven't been to Mass for years."

"But you're a mere babe. It can't have been that many years, now, can it?"

"It seems that way, Your Holiness," she said putting on the Irish lilt. Two could get into role playing, she thought, and then too she might need to distract him if he was going to proselytize.

Father Donahey was suddenly alert. She had made an error no Catholic should have made. "Your Holiness" was a term reserved for the Pope. Even the youngest Catholic learned that.

"What took its place, my dear?" he said eyeing her curiously, and deciding to let her play out her hand. "You must have some faith to carry you through the hard times. And we all have hard times."

"Oh, I believe in the Golden Rule. I try to be kind and honest when I can and," she hesitated, "and, mostly, in doing no harm." That's true, she told herself. Beyond that he'd learn soon enough.

"Now," she said brightly, steering him away from discussion of her faith, or lack of it, "what will you do when we get there?"

"We need a place to park and for me to stay in until dark. You, if you'd be so good, can look around for me and report back. Meet the people. Find out what they're planning, if you will. I'll need to know the grounds, the house, whatever looks suspicious." He was getting into his sleuth's role now.

"What might be suspicious, Father?"

"Oh, bones, blood, signs of sacrifice . . . ah, well, ah, perhaps nothing that obvious, but there could be some subtle signs of torture, violence, and some sacrilegious books, pictures, statues–things of the Dark Side," his mind flooded with various stimulating descriptions of books that he'd read--all awesomely gory. "Check the cellar if you can," he continued. All would unfold in due time. He would move along under the protection of Heaven, and the Devil beware!

Alison was amused, but also a bit concerned about the extreme dimensions of his fantasy. He was a mass of contradictions and certainly he wouldn't be worried about what happened to her in the cellar. "What if there's nothing like that?" she asked. He knew only what he'd read about, never having met a devil in his life. Was it always like that, she wondered, people imagining frightful things, getting carried away and then having to make up some hocus-pocus to make the scary things disappear? Even in medicine diagnoses proved baffling sometimes and doctors had been known to turn to spiritual means of healing when all else failed. She had spoken to a child psychiatrist recently who described a child of four with medically inexplicable convulsions. A psychiatrist called in to consult on the case was dumbfounded as to possible treatment. By chance, he mentioned the case to another psychiatrist who, it happened, was also a Catholic priest. Together, they decided there could be no harm in trying an exorcism. The psychiatrist/priest performed the ritual and the child stopped convulsing. Although astonishing as a case, there was no doubt in Alison's mind that this one-time occurrence proved little. Some other dramatic event might have worked equally well to still the child. Perhaps she would have stopped at that moment no matter what happened to her. No one could know for certain. Three months later the child's convulsions had begun again.

Whatever, Old F.D. was a goner for the gory, and she was almost certain there would be none of that here. Still he wanted his adventure. Somehow, she'd have to give him a little scare. Enough to keep him satisfied. Nature would take care of the rest.

"What will I say when I meet the people? They'll want to know where you are. Will you eat dinner with them?"

"No, no, I shouldn't do that. I'll stay in hiding until dark. But you can tell them some of the truth. Tell them I'm elderly. That's no lie. Tell them I'm resting. I will. I'll rest. Then there'll be no deception. I'll take a nice nap, and you can bring me a bite to eat. Surely you'll be doing the cooking, for them all, eh?" he asked slyly.

"I couldn't presume, Father. They will have made their plans. We should provide for ourselves. I packed a casserole and some eggs for an omelet. If they have oven space, I'll pop the casserole in and offer to share some. Otherwise it will heat up nicely over the stove here in the RV. I also brought some bread and the makings for a salad. That should take care of our meals nicely. And your favorite apple pie." He smiled contentedly. Dinner would be nice, and then the exorcism.

"In the evening," she was interrupting his thoughts again, "what do you plan on doing?" He was surprised that she was so inquisitive, but then again she was a great little organizer. She was trying to keep him on one of her schedules. It wouldn't hurt him to share with her what he had decided to do.

"I'd like to observe a bit before joining. If I could find the way to where they'll have their coven meeting, I might be able to stand back in the shadows and watch a while. Then at the right moment I can step in."

"I see," Alison said, realizing that he hadn't needed to plan. Not from his point of view. He was simply using his horror story formula. He was bound to be seen along the way. Someone would speak to him. Then what would he do? Let him go his way. It would be amusing to see how people reacted to his disguise. Perhaps they really would think he was an old woman. Or a witch. She laughed out loud.

"What is it?" He was alarmed by her laughter.

"I just realized," she lied, "that I may have to do some explaining myself. I have no story, except that I came as your driver. Who am I, anyway?"

"Try to stick as close to the truth as you can, my dear," he said in his priestly function once more. "It'll be better that way. 'Oh what a tangled web we weave, when first we practice to deceive . . . .' Remember, that's from Shakespeare and it's a quote that has always served me well. Besides it's a sin to lie. Just say you are a cook."

Ah, he was so full of self-deception. There was no way she could excuse him on that count. "I'll do what you suggest, Father. I'll tell them the truth then," she said smoothly. She turned and looked out at the scenery and grinned. They were going to catch the scheduled four-thirty ferry. It was the longest day of the year and the sun would not set until nearly nine. There would still be time to enjoy the beauty of the island.

"Welcome, welcome to Lily Point," Rachel beamed. She and Clarissa had returned to the house to find Ann, Solange and Bernie getting out of their car. "Here's one more, right behind us," she turned their attention to another car proceeding slowly down the curved dirt road and into the yard.

There was a round of introductions as the women greeted each other and everyone fell to unpacking their cars.

"Ah, this is so exciting," Rachel said. "You have no idea how delighted I am to see you all here, and with such perfect weather. We'll have an opportunity to find out about so much."

"This is an ideal spot for our weekend," Grace said carefully, not sure which of the two older women was Widdershins.

"Look at those roses," Ann said. "The bushes are tree-sized and you can smell them all the way over here."

"Rugosas. They're hearty and they spread. If you like, you can take some back with you," Rachel said.

"I'm afraid in my apartment they wouldn't last long. I'll take a rain check though. Maybe someday I'll have a place in the country."

"You've got it," Rachel said. "You're all welcome to take cuttings," she said. "Please, do make yourself at home and enjoy the day. There's a lot to do and see before the evening events begin."

"At some point we'll need to put up our tent, if that's all right?" Bernie said to Rachel.

"I have a platform down on the shore. The path is just beyond the shed." Rachel gestured toward a small out building by the kitchen door. "Why don't you have a little lunch with us first, then take your things on down and settle in. After that the rest of the day is yours to explore the island." She turned to Grace, who had been standing some distance apart from the others listening intently, "You're welcome to sleep in the house unless you also have a tent. We've plenty of room. The couch in the living room is really a bed."

"Thank you. I thought about bringing my tent, and then at the last moment, with the confusion about my cat . . ." she paused and turned back to the car. "I forgot to ask you. I hope it's all right that I brought my cat?"

"Of course. Of course," Rachel said heartily.

"Well, he'll be in the cage, at least for now, and he shouldn't be any bother. He was supposed to go to the vets to be declawed but they couldn't take him at the last minute."

Clarissa loved cats and had never been able to have one in her apartment. She went immediately to the car and looked into the carrying case. "Don't you worry," she said in a soft wheedling voice. "We'll give you lots of treats, poor baby."

In answer, Increase emitted a mournful meow.

"He's not used to being caged, but I can't let him out right away. He might run away," Grace said apologetically.

"We'll find a place for him where he'll feel safe and where he can watch what's going on. He'll calm down in a little while," Clarissa said comfortingly.

Grace opened the hatchback of her car and slid the case out onto the ground.

"Over here," Rachel said. "Under the big pine. It's shady and he'll be able to see us coming and going. What's his name?"

Grace told the story of Increase's name.

The newcomers unloaded their food in little heaps, everywhere it seemed to Clarissa, who immediately began clearing spaces, tucking things into corners. Amused, Rachel said, "That's all right, Clarissa. We'll make do."

When they were seated, Clarissa, who had volunteered to serve lunch, handed around big yellow bowls of her homemade pea soup, a rich, vegetable pudding, so thick it was. On a plate carefully positioned to the side of the overhanging kerosene lamp (in case it dripped), she placed a small basket of hot scones wrapped in a blue cloth napkin. Beside it she set one of Rachel's green depression glass dishes filled with raspberry jam. Even Rachel was forced to admit that the food was delicious.

"I love this room," Ann said, "it has the look of a *New Yorker* cover–one of those ethereal summer paintings all light and delicate lines filled with nostalgia and old-time ambience."

"Well, the house was built in the mid eighteen hundreds. It could easily serve as a model for a *New Yorker* cover," Rachel said proudly. "I've left it pretty much the way it was."

"You really do use kerosene lamps for light?" Solange asked, observing a small table that held six lamps.

"Yes, I clean the soot from the chimneys every other day or so, trim the wicks when they get burnt, and I fill the lamps once a week. The best part is that there is never an electricity bill from Central Maine. The cost of these lamps is cheap by comparison."

Bernie carried backpacks and Solange struggled with her suitcase along the narrow path to the shore. "I see now why you have those things," Solange muttered.

"What things?" Ann called back over her shoulder.

"Backpacks. I bet I don't have any more stuff than you, and look at me. It's so cumbersome dragging a case this size through the woods."

Bernie laughed. "You've got a hundred feet to go, Solly. You'll survive."

Ann reached the tent platform. "Look at the site!" she exclaimed. She was surrounded by a small wooded area of scrub pine and white birches. The ground cover was a soft green matting of hair cap moss and fringy grasses. "What a view you get of the cove and the other islands." She slid out of her pack and lowered it to the rocks. She proceeded directly to a rope hammock suspended between two spruce trees and looked back at the other two. "I'm putting my dibs on this right now. Never mind the rest of the world. Never mind witchcraft! I'm settling in for the duration. You may have the tent. I'll sleep here."

"Come on," Bernie groaned. "You don't get off that easy, even if you don't sleep in the tent."

"Certainly, Bernie," Ann offered serenely from her nest. "What do you want?"

"I want help. I can't remember how the tent works. The last two times Richard and I went camping, he put the thing up."

"That's reverse sexism, letting him do all the physical work. Didn't you even volunteer to help?" Solange kidded her.

Bernie was offhand. "Richard wanted to prove one person could do it alone in ten minutes or less, so I let him."

"You didn't learn anything from that," Solange badgered.

"Sure I did. I found out he could put up a tent in twenty minutes all by himself."

Ann laughed. "O.K. Solange. Let's watch Bernie put the tent up . . ." she pushed the hammock back, lay down across it and let go. The hammock rocked gently forward, then back, ". . . in twenty minutes."

Solange dropped her bag and came to the hammock. "This is a two-person hammock. I'll watch from here. Move over."

"Enjoy yourselves," Bernie said in mock bitterness. "I'm going back for the tent. You'd better be rested and prepared to help when I return." She thumbed her nose and went up the trail to the house.

"Let's hide," Ann said mischievously.

Extracting themselves from the hammock, they followed what appeared to be a deer trail into the woods. "Such an incredibly lovely spot to have a summer place!" Solange said enviously.

"Mmm," Ann answered. "Everywhere you look there's something beautiful. Remember *Summer Island* by Eliot Porter? This is it, isn't it?"

"Must be. Look at those–are they bunchberries–those little white flowers with four petals, and their neat little matching leaves."

"That's right."

"And these?"

"Starflowers."

"How do you know?"

"I've got a wild flower book, and I walk the woods inland. Some of the flowers are the same. We've got starflowers and those," she gestured, "bluets or quaker ladies, right along the edge of the campus." Ann reached down and brushed her hand over a small patch of tiny blue-white flowers.

"I remember seeing them now."

"What do you think of Rachel and Clarissa?" Ann asked.

"So far? Very different from each other, I'd say. Rachel is striking, in command, knows exactly what she wants, almost powerful," Solange said, "but I like her wry humor, and her friendliness shines through too. Clarissa is more reticent. Less sure of herself. She's almost a 'sixties' person, isn't she? But not quite self-sufficient. I like them both. What do you think?"

"I feel intrigued by Rachel in particular, as I do a lot of older women. It's tough to be old in our society, especially if you're a woman so full of ideas and energy." She paused and stood looking out at the sea. "I'm not certain why, but I used to be afraid to be around older people. Maybe I thought age would rub off on me, or that I might have to witness a death."

"I know what you mean. But neither of these women act old."

"I liked our talk around the table at lunch. Grace is really interesting too, but she didn't say much. She's a scholar, huh?"

"I think so. A writer maybe?"

"I felt as if we were all on an equal footing. I respect their experience, their opinions. Somehow this doesn't seem like witchcraft . Know what I mean?"

"Well, except for Bernie, nobody said all that much about witchcraft."

"Do you think she's a witch?"

"Which?"

"Which one's a witch?"

They both giggled. "Who's on first?" Ann said and fell silent for a minute, stopping to untangle a branch caught in her sweater.

"Where are we going?" Solange said. "Isn't this far enough?"

"Almost. Let's go over there."

"So?"

"So, no. I don't think any of them is a witch, but would I know one if I saw one anyway? What do you think a modern witch is supposed to look like?"

"What does Starhawk look like?"

"Don't know. Never saw a picture of her. Watch your footing here. There's a hole of some kind. Animal, maybe."

"Let's sit." Ann pointed at a flat expanse of rock, between two higher rocks. "Made to order for us," she said. "Looks like a couch."

"Listen. That's Bernie."

"O.K. . . . you guys. I'm coming after you, ready or not. I know you're hiding." Bernie was thrashing through the trees. "You've had your little joke, but I have the food for tonight."

"What's that supposed to mean?" Solange whispered.

"That if we don't work, we don't eat," Ann whispered back. "But the food is in the kitchen. Shall we placate her?"

"Fine with me. I'm benign. I have nothing but good will towards the whole world. It's the salt air, I think. Look at the surf over on that point. Would you like to go for a swim?"

"Are you crazy? This water kills." Ann shuddered involuntarily.

"Nonsense."

Bernie was almost there. They gave up all pretense of hiding and talked aloud.

"Oh, hello there," Ann called as she sighted Bernie huffing from the exertion of her short cut through some fairly resistant juniper.

"Fancy meeting you here."

"God, is this fantastic or what?" Bernie said in good humor. "I'm so glad we came."

"Me too," Solange cried happily. "Why don't we look for some property while we're here. I might buy some land where we could put up a tent and spend time each summer. A reunion place."

"Honest?" Bernie was wide eyed.

"Why not? You said I should spend some money."

Ann said seriously, "Don't forget what Rachel said at lunch about developers. The price is probably way out of reason. Then too the island could be spoiled soon–condos and all."

"They won't let that happen." Solange was incredulous at the thought.

"Who's they?"

"The people who live here."

"I hope not. I think it's a wonderful idea to look at property. Will we have time?"

"Maybe," Bernie said, and then, "So. What were you guys talking about while I was gone? Favorite body parts?"

"Of course." Ann reached up and tugged at Bernie's sleeve. "Sit down here on our couch for a minute. The tent can wait. Don't be so task-oriented."

Solange said. "Actually, we were talking about swimming. Do you want to go in? I will, if you will."

"Here? Now?"

"Where else? No one's around. Let's skinny dip."

"It's cold," Bernie said tentatively and then throwing caution to the wind, she pulled her sweat shirt over her head, and her shorts off in one quick movement.

"All right. Last one in is . . ."

"Count me out," Ann said. "I'll keep watch."

"For what? There's nobody within five miles of here. Even if there is, I'll be in the water." With a giant splash she landed in a bed of dancing sea weed, water foaming around her. She raked her way through the bed walking deeper in until she was up to her shoulders. "Yikes! It's cold," she called back. "It takes your breath away, and there are clam shells or something sharp . . . ."

Solange left her clothes in a neat pile and climbed carefully down over the rocks. Hopping over the edge of one final ledge, she stepped daintily into the water. She let out a little scream and ducked, swimming furiously as if her life depended on it. Ann watched from the safety and warmth of the rock couch.

After thirty seconds of swimming, both women were tingling with the cold. Ann called to them, "Come on out. I'll go back and get your towels. You're turning bluer than the water."

"We're late, aren't we?" Father Donahey said accusingly. He pushed up the cuff of his lace silk blouse to check his digital watch. They were entering a town.

"Not really," Alison said reassuringly. "There are two more boats. It's better that we come late. Less time for problems to arise." It would certainly be easier for her to keep him out of sight.

"How much longer," he asked, "before the next boat?"

"About an hour, and we'll be there in forty-five minutes, I should say."

"This is an ugly street," Father Donahey remarked, sniffing critically. He looked at the vast sea of advertising that lined either side of the main road.

"It's Route 1, after all," Alison reminded him, "but you're right, it's about as bad as it can get. Even with the billboard legislation removing the big stuff, it's still unsightly."

"Well, I'm glad Portland is not like this," he sighed.

"It'll get that way if the big boom lasts," Alison said. Amazing, she thought, we're having a normal conversation. F. D., however, had slipped into a snooze. Alison drove on. The traffic was getting heavier.

How quickly the roads filled up in spring. All the out-of-staters hurry back too soon, she thought. I don't enjoy the crowding. She turned on the stereo tape deck. Chris Williamson's voice rang out. The song was one of the classics of the women's movement–the lyrics so universal, one would expect anybody could empathize. Yet her music was seldom heard on the big stations.

Father Donahey stirred. "Who's singing?" he asked. "It's quite nice. I like the lines about the drops of water on the stone, and the stone wearing away. That's the way I feel when I give the sermon some Sundays. My words are just drops of water on that stony congregation."

Not exactly what Chris had in mind, Alison smiled inwardly, but people brought their own meaning to lyrics, and there are so many different perspectives. How then could women's music be so bad, so dangerous when it spoke of oppression and the universal need for love? She smiled serenely ahead at the traffic. "It's a wonderful song," she agreed. "I'm glad you like it. The voice is Chris Williamson's. She's not well known. Perhaps the next time she's in Portland, you'd like to go to a concert."

"Pretend you're asleep now. Turn this way. Pull the shawl over your head. Good." Alison was about to leave the ferry and drive up the island causeway. She had no idea who might see them or if there would be anybody waiting at the terminal. Best to be careful. There was no traffic.

She remembered the directions. Turn left and follow the dirt road. She drove until she reached a patch of woods where the road went downhill. From the curve of the land visible when they arrived on the ferry, she suspected the shore could not be far away and that the road would end shortly. She pulled the RV into a little clearing in a wooded area by the side of the road and parked. She would walk in.

"Stay here, as we planned," she reminded him. "Pretend you're asleep if someone comes. I'll be back as soon as I can."

She hopped down from the driver's seat and strolled along the grassy middle of the road. Ahead there was an opening in the woods. Another hundred yards, she thought, ought to bring her there. The white house stood out, its bright red door gleaming, its windows showing clearly through to windows on the other side, and to the sea beyond. On her right, a vegetable plot lay unplowed and unplanted except for a persistent rhubarb, already quite tall. There were roses blooming along the other side of the house, as high as the roof. Their perfume filled the air; mixed with the smell of freshly cut grass, it was heady stuff.

On the roof over one wing of the house a woman in white painter's pants and a plaid shirt was ripping shingles off and throwing them down onto the lawn. She looked down at Alison, waved, then continued with her work.

Alison approached that end of the house and called up, "Anyone home?"

"Yes," the carpenter replied. "You here for the solstice?"

It sounded so natural that Alison thought for a moment she might be talking to one of The Craft. "Yes," she answered, "as a matter of fact I am."

"I'm Ellen. Rachel and Clarissa are in the kitchen. The rest, I believe, are hiking somewhere along the shore. They'll be back soon."

"I'm Alison. I hope I'll see you again."

"I'll be there tonight."

That sounded hopeful. At least there was one woman who looked competent and, if you could say that on such short notice, the right kind of person to celebrate with.

As she turned and walked toward the kitchen she heard an eerie mournful cry coming from under a large pine. Bending down, she spotted a carrying cage for pets and looked inside. A most striking cat of beige and brown peered back at her. "Poor thing, you don't like it there, do you? I can't let you out. Whoever put you in wouldn't appreciate it." She put her fingers through the cage sensing that the cat was friendly. Immediately, he began to purr, moving his head close to her hand so that she could stroke him.

"I can't stay all day," she said. She stood up abruptly and

walked to the kitchen door. The cat began his lonely howling again.

"I see you've met Increase," said a voice from the kitchen door.

Alison looked up. "Increase? Had a lot of kittens, has she?" She smiled and walked up the steps.

"Fathered a lot actually. Named for his prolific parenting skills. Also for Increase Mather, a minister from Salem in the days of the witch trials."

Alison was delighted. "Really? How clever. My name is Alison. Clovis and I just arrived on the ferry. You are expecting Clovis?" She paused uncertainly. Had Father Donahey been taken in by a prankster?

Rachel smiled and nodded. "Of course."

Alison continued then, "I'm her driver, housekeeper and cook, but I'd also like to be part of the solstice celebration if that's possible."

"By all means. And Clovis is . . . ?"

"Elderly and napping in the RV. We plan to stay there so we won't be a burden on your hospitality."

"Please. Come in," Rachel opened the door, and Alison moved into the kitchen.

"How nice this is, such a sunny room. What a great old table," she touched the soft mellow pine surface, turned and walked to one window and then another, "and the view from the windows wherever you look is magnificent."

"Yes. Inspiring isn't it? I feel fortunate to have found it. I'm Rachel, by the way, but you probably know me as Widdershins. That's the way I signed my little ad in the paper."

Alison smiled and said, "Yes, indeed. I'm happy to meet you." She was relieved in fact. If this was Widdershins, so far so good. The woman looked fragile but strong–a natural crone, a term that new witches were using to designate their elder women of status. It would be interesting to see how much she knew about The Craft and what she expected from the solstice.

"Hello. Another arrival?" Clarissa came down the one step from the living room into the kitchen. Rachel introduced the two, suggesting that Clarissa give Alison a tour of the house and grounds.

"I'd love that," Alison said, "but I also need to know how many of us there are and what the plans are for the evening. I'll have to report back shortly to Clovis (the name felt artificial on her tongue), plus take care of supper and all that."

"Oh," Rachel said, "join us for supper. Clarissa, fill her in, will you? I want to finish up here, and then I'll be with you." Rachel turned to the large cast iron sink where there were two basins, one heaped with pans and dishes, the other with rinse water. An empty dish rack sat beside it. This was compulsive, she knew, washing every dish in the house, but it was a kind of beginning-summer ritual she went through re-familiarizing herself with the plates, the bowls, the cup and glasses, all old friends whose colors and personalities she loved.

"If you need to use the refrigerator or the oven, by all means bring your food here. I've got the fridge going now and it's good and cold," she called after Alison who was already in the living room.

"Thanks, I'd like to use the oven for a casserole to share with everyone."

"How nice," Clarissa said, hoping that it was something all vegetable. "I've some extra Tofu if you need any," she added.

Tofu was the password for vegetarians, Rachel thought, wrinkling up her nose. It separated the vegans, or whatever silly name it was they called themselves, from the dairy-food eaters.

Rachel did not catch Alison's reply, because the two women had gone upstairs. Shortly, as they came down the stairs, she heard Clarissa's voice again.

"Will your friend, ah, Clovis, is it, join us for dinner?"

"I'm not sure yet about Clovis. It's hard for her to get around. And the others, are they all here?" Alison continued quickly to avoid conversation about "Clovis" if possible.

"They are all here. There is a woman named Grace from New Jersey. She's staying here in the house. She's the one with the cat."

"Yes, I met him out in the yard." Alison said.

Clarissa continued, "Three others are from the University. Bernie, Ann and Solange. They've put a tent up down on the shore."

Alison decided to probe a little, "Are you a friend of Rachel's?"

Clarissa nodded, "Ten years we've been neighbors in the same apartment house in Portland, and we're close friends, both living alone as we do. I like to keep an eye on her. She's seventy-three, you know, and suddenly she's got this idea of being a witch. I don't know what to think." She shook her head. The young woman looked sensible enough. Really it was a relief to find that all of the women who had come were normal looking. This one had red hair and striking amber eyes. Quite attractive. She looked fit. Might be a runner, what with her jogging suit and running shoes.

As if reading her mind, Alison said, "I'm going to run later on today. Is there anyone else here who's into fitness?"

"I think Bernice runs," Clarissa said, then abruptly changed the subject to what was on her mind, "What do you do?"

"I have a couple of jobs. I'm a part-time cook and housekeeper at a parish house, and a student. I also work at the court house."

"Oh. You must be busy. Are you Catholic?"

A warning bell went off in Alison's head. It could be that Clarissa might actually know the old priest–go to mass at his parish. She decided to be circumspect.

"No. Clovis is Catholic."

"Well, I can't believe she's serious about this business then." Clarissa lowered her voice so that it would not carry to the kitchen, "Actually, I'm sort of like you are. I'm not here for myself. I drove Rachel down here to help out. Witchcraft is not my, ah, hobby, but I assure you this is not really witchcraft anyway." Immediately, she regretted her disloyalty. She attempted to amend her statement. "Rachel is very interested in the subject, but as far as I know she's never been involved in anything serious, that is, until now. I'd hardly call this serious. Rachel used to be a Catholic herself, same parish as I belong to." She paused and remembered then, "Which parish house did you say you cook for?"

"Actually, I didn't. Are the other people down by the water? I'd like to meet them." Alison moved quickly towards the little hall off the living room. "This is a pleasant work space, full of books," she said seeing the desk and the shelves behind it. She reached over and ran her fingers along the spines, checking titles, not for Father Donahey, but for herself. Not a single title that signified knowledge of witchcraft. All were light summer reading.

She called over her shoulder to Clarissa as she went out the front door, "Thanks for the tour. I can find the rest of the way myself. See you shortly."

Strange, Clarissa thought. She didn't answer my question.

"So you're a grad student at NYU?" Bernie asked Grace. Along with Solange and Ann she sprawled in a tangled bed of haircap moss and cranberry leaves that covered the ground at the tip of the peninsula. "I want to go to law school, myself. What are you studying?"

"Sociology. Scapegoating to be more precise; that is, how it happens that certain groups of people are perceived unfairly, and how prejudices affect behavior in society." Grace was relieved not to have to lie. It seemed most likely that these women had answered the ad for the same reason as she–to study witchcraft.

"Great," Ann said eagerly. "I'm interested in behavior too. One of the things I want to do is take courses in negotiation skills and problem solving. I want to help people change their negative perceptions of each other–help them work out their differences successfully."

"That sounds challenging," Grace said. So Ann, too, was a student of human behavior. "I don't know many people who are skilled in problem solving techniques. We could all use a session now and then."

"Well there are a few programs available that specialize in communication skills. I hope to enroll in one at Boston University shortly. I've applied anyway."

"I haven't felt so relaxed in ages," Grace said, rolling over and sitting up, "but I tend to stick to myself too much. I need to socialize. I've been excusing my solitary lifestyle for so long, saying that the city encourages isolation, but I'm not sure New York is all to blame. I'm fairly structured and very driven. I have class first thing in the morning. I teach two undergraduate units in Sociology 101, do my research at the library and then I go home to write. Later I feed the cat, and go to bed. I haven't made a single close friend at NYU, unless I count my advisor."

The women nodded sympathetically, and Bernie said, "Well, anybody can get engrossed in her work. I know I hole up every weekend studying for at least seven or eight hours and it takes everything my husband and kids can do to drag me out into the sunshine."

"Well, I'm glad you all got here this weekend," Grace said sincerely. "It's so good to meet people again. It may sound like a generalization, but I'm convinced that Mainers are never as cold and distant as New Yorkers."

She turned to Solange. "Your name sounds Spanish. I live in a Spanish-speaking district; in fact, I'm surrounded by Puerto Ricans. Do you speak Spanish?"

"No, I never learned. My father was Spanish, but I never knew him. I was brought up in Portland. My name is the only Spanish word I know except for a few greetings. Solange means 'sun angel'."

"Nice," Grace said, "I like that," she said repeating the name. "I used to live in Portland too. I hope to move back one day."

She looked at Ann and Bernie, "And you are old friends. Do you go to school together?"

"Yes, all three of us, but Ann is the one who saw the ad and talked us into taking this trip. We've spent a lot of time talking together about women's issues. The business about witch persecution means more to us than simply a description of an incident or two in history. We're interested in women's spirituality." Bernie said. "We've pretty much decided that most religions turn us off because of their sexist attitudes. Witchcraft–well, it's more woman-oriented."

Grace hoped the women, once started, would continue to describe their beliefs, but she sensed she would have to say something to keep the conversation going. "Yes, I think you are right that neopaganism may be more woman-oriented. Originally, however, I think paganism included men and women, young and old. But as paganism was dying out and Christianity was gaining a foothold, events that occurred created some misperceptions that are still alive today. The early Christian church used paganism as a scapegoat because the church was powerless to do anything about the problems of crop failure, the plague and other natural catastrophes. They decided to blame someone instead and then punish that someone–actually eradicate them from the population. That someone, as most people know today, turned out to be mostly women–old defenseless women. They were called witches although it's doubtful if any of them considered themselves to be witches."

Two gulls went wheeling by, the first holding something in its mouth, the second screaming in pursuit.

"So you're saying paganism was not what people think of as witchcraft today?"

Grace nodded.

"But the old paganism had something that the new religions lacked," Ann said. "Paganism taught that life and death were part of a natural cycle, that all things were dependent upon the earth and the sun, the air and the water. Paganists understood their connection to the universe. Their gods and goddesses were the real powers–beings who caused the wind to blow, rain to fall, fire to burn and the land to be rich or barren. These are the spirits whose works show themselves in all of our lives. People today have neglected them, wasted the resources of this planet carelessly and now it is as if the gods and goddesses are angry."

Grace sat back, her hands pressed into the spongy cranberry leaves. She was touched by Ann's words. Still she was curious about people's need to settle the big questions once and for all–to connect fire with a god or goddess, for instance, saying that this or that god or goddess was angry. It seemed human beings had a low tolerance for ambiguity.

They didn't want to admit there might be some things they could never fully understand. Why was it so pressing for them, she wondered, to find finite answers for infinite mysteries, or on the other hand to invent mysteries to answer the unanswerable?

Another behavior that fascinated her was that once someone became a true believer it was almost impossible for them to admit to sharing something in common with the faithful in other religions. So much proselytizing went on, and so many expectations that other groups would finally see the light and fall into line, if not to their knees. She wondered if these women would like to convert her to their way of believing.

Grace smiled at the three women enigmatically. "Think of all the intelligent people who have pondered the questions of the universe, wanting to know what we are doing here–what the purpose of life is? Yet no one knows for certain."

Alison spotted the four women on the point–one, tall, dark, and rather stately, was climbing to her feet, a backdrop of sparkling water and little islands in the distance behind her. This was a big woman, larger, she guessed than the other, equally dark but older woman, who sat dangling her legs over the side of a small ledge. Her hair was wet. Evidently she and the woman with the cropped hair and wiry build had been swimming. A fourth sat beside her on the rocks. She had the classical features that Americans usually considered beauty pageant material.

Alison grimaced as she caught herself classifying women by their looks. People did it to her all the time. How irritating to be called "Red" or "Fiery," or told that she should have a sense of kinship for other redheads. What nonsense. When she was younger she'd thought of dyeing her hair just to be rid of the cute remarks. But no other color suited her as well.

She approached, unnoticed for the moment, listening to their voices, watching their body language. The tall woman stood apart from the group, formal, a bit nervous, maybe a loner. Perhaps, she was the one who owned the cat. The other three seemed connected. She decided to put the tall one at ease if she could. It would be the beginning.

"Hi. I just spoke to Increase," she called across the short distance now separating them. The women looked startled, squinting up at her in the sun, but Grace responded quickly. "And what did he say?"

"He told me to tell Grace he wants out," she laughed. "My name's Alison and you must be Grace."

Grace stuck out her hand, liking the easy humor of the introduction. She did the introductions for the others. "Increase has no choice, I'm afraid," she said. "I don't dare release him. He might take off in the woods. He's not an outdoor cat. Not anymore. His days of wandering lust are over."

The women laughed easily. "Is this all of us then–" Bernie inquired of Alison, introducing herself and the others. "Or are there others up at the house?"

"I brought someone with me–Clovis–an older woman. She's resting in my RV," Alison said.

"I remember now. That's it then. We are all here." Ann said with a sense of relief at knowing who would be involved in the venture.

Bernie added, "But there's also a woman named Ellen, I believe. She's joining us tonight. She an interesting person–a student of Italian architecture. She also does carpentry. She's working on Rachel's house."

Alison nodded. "I just met her. She's on the roof. Did she answer the ad?"

"No, she lives on the island. She decided at the last minute that she'd like to join us."

"What will it be like, I wonder?" Solange said then, and everyone suddenly realized that this was the question which had been on everyone's mind.

"Thank god," Bernie laughed, "I thought no one would ever ask."

"Why me? You could have asked." Solange said.

"What–let people see me in all my ignorance, my vulnerable, frightened state?"

"Of course," Solange put her arm around Bernie's shoulders, "You look so good when you're weak-kneed and trembling."

"Who has done this kind of thing before?" Grace heard

herself ask. If she started the others talking, perhaps it wouldn't get back to her.

"None of us," Ann replied gesturing to Bernie and Solange. "We just decided that we'd like to learn more, and also we're feminists and wanted to see if this coven would include the kinds of things Starhawk speaks of. We like her ceremonies and her philosophy. What about you?" she asked Grace.

My turn after all, Grace thought, and then saw her way out. "I've read Starhawk," she said, her first white lie. She had only seen it lying on the counter in Rachel's kitchen and picked it up for a moment's cursory examination. "I'm interested in learning more." She paused and turned to Alison to indicate that it was her turn.

Alison caught the evasiveness in the answer but decided not to press Grace. It would be unkind, given Grace's fear of exposure, which Alison had recognized at once. She might have alleviated Grace's discomfort by using humor, but suddenly she felt ready to change the climate. She sat down beside them and said, "Yes."

There was a short silence as everyone waited for her to continue. Finally Bernie blurted, "Yes?"

"Yes." Alison said quietly again, making them feel awkward. "Listen." They listened for her voice and heard instead the sound of the tide rushing smoothly on its way in, a gentle sound, not the rhythmic pounding of an open ocean shore. They listened and heard the gulls on one of the outer islands squabbling over nesting space, and the growl of a male seal. They listened and heard a crow in a nearby tree calling to another crow in the woods. "You'll be listening now for a while. You'll be watching. Look." She pointed. The rockweed danced back and forth in shallows where the water shimmered. A small school of minnows flashed by, and a crab sidled into the weeds and disappeared. "Look," she said and they saw the moss hanging from the spruces, the white birches gleaming in the darker parts of the woods.

"You've come for the solstice and this is it, a sharpening of the senses, a growing love of all the living forms you find around you. This is the day to celebrate the sun and the earth. No other day is like this one. No other light."

They sat for a moment looking out at the water, each appreciating the sights and sounds. Alison broke the spell. "It's time for us to return to the house. Rachel said dinner would be at six-thirty, and there's just enough time for a good run. Anyone join me?"

"Sure," Bernie said. From the moment Alison introduced herself she knew the woman was a natural leader, not weird at all, in spite of her mind-reading tricks. She'll teach us something, or lead, if there is any leading to be done.

"Not necessary to lead," Alison murmured to her, looking directly into her eyes.

"How the hell did you do that?" Bernie asked.

"What?" Grace had noticed the quick change in tone and pace of voices. Then she understood. Alison had answered Bernie's unspoken thoughts, but it was done casually, without any pretense or ceremony. Did that mean she was a witch or just someone who was good at guesswork?

"No guesswork," Alison said to Grace looking intently at her.

"I don't understand," Ann said. "I've missed something, I think."

"In a little while," Alison said in a soft voice to put Ann at ease, "we'll be sharing a meal and then an evening of celebration. You'll understand then. I want to run at least three miles if I can. Also I want to wait until we're all together before I begin."

Solange said, "Begin the solstice?"

"No, the solstice is now. It's all around you. We are part of it. I meant before we begin our work."

Ann shivered at the words. She turned to connect with Bernie and Solange, then Grace. They were all staring at Alison.

Alison climbed into the RV to find Father Donahey spooning up some cracker crumbs she'd prepared to sprinkle over the top of the casserole she'd brought for the evening meal. She grabbed a wedge of cheese from the refrigerator, quickly sliced some and put it on a plate for him. "I'll take that spoon and the crumbs," she said and he handed them over.

"I thought you'd never get back. What's happening?" he asked, anxious now as he watched her wash her hands at the little kitchen sink.

"Nothing much. People have been outside enjoying the day and the beauty of the island. It doesn't look to me like there are any evil spirits here at all. No sign of anything you described, although I must admit I didn't go through each book on their shelves."

"So who are they? What do they look like?"

"My guess is . . . ," Alison paused and pulled the casserole out of the refrigerator. She took the tinfoil off and began to shake the crumbs over its surface. "My guess is that we have three school girls and two old women," (for Father Donahey, who had no idea he was sexist as well as ageist, calling them "girls" and "old women" would take away their power) "and," she continued, "one scholar around my age." She was guessing about Grace's age. "Oh, yes, and there's a carpenter also."

"What's he like?" Father Donahey asked, thinking that this must be the one to watch out for.

"Jesus was a carpenter," Alison admonished him and then realized that she had answered a thought, not a spoken statement. She hurried on to cover her tracks. "Actually, he's a she, and also a scholar of Italian architecture."

By the heavens, Father Donahey said to himself, searching his vest pocket for the security of his beads. A woman carpenter. Italy. Scholar. A woman aping a man, doing his work. Surely this was a dangerous combination.

"Surely not," Alison said aloud before she realized that she'd done it again. She would have to watch herself. "She lives here on the island, didn't even know there was a meeting taking place until the woman who wrote the 'Widdershins' ad told her."

Father Donahey missed the first part of her answer and assumed he had spoken aloud.

"Oh," he said, visibly disappointed. "Well then, what about this Widdershins?"

Remembering the conversation about Catholicism with Clarissa, Alison decided to be caution about giving names. Rachel might also be connected in some way with Father Donahey. "An old lady, like yourself." She couldn't help herself, laughing out loud at his scowl. "Not an evil bone in her body," she finished, to give him a sop.

"The scholar, then? Is he, ah, suspicious looking, trying to, ah, get to the women? How do you know he's a scholar?"

"How do you know it's a man?" Alison said crossly, in spite of herself. Outside of motherhood and cooking, Father Donahey apparently could not picture women possessing any skills or knowledge. She sighed and told him that Grace was the "other" scholar, but that she wasn't sure what area of scholarship it was. "She certainly isn't trying to control anyone."

"Probably not," he said. He was growing morose. There had to be something to keep him entertained for the evening. She did not want him at the ceremony.

"I'll go back and pop the casserole in," she said, "I'll check around the ground for signs of anything suspicious. Then I want to run. I'll let you know."

"Good girl, Alison." he said considerably cheered. "Keep up the good work."

"Groceries," Ann said, sitting in the kitchen after Alison left for the RV.

Clarissa inquired, "Are you short of something–for your supper?"

Bernie glanced at Ann quickly, then at Solange. "No. Just need to check the car to make sure we have everything."

"Cigarettes." She patted her pockets. "Is there a local store open?"

"Yes, but they close shortly. I have to tell you, I don't allow smoking in the house. Dangerous with kerosene lamps and all," Rachel said firmly, and then gave them directions.

They passed Alison on the road carrying her casserole. "We'll be right back," Bernie shouted out the window. "I do want to run with you. We still have time."

Alison nodded and waved.

"All right. What happened back there on the rocks?" Ann said as she drove rapidly down the road to the store.

"Yes," Solange added. "I want to know too. Did she really read your mind, Bernie?"

"I'm sure she did. You're not frightened, are you?" Bernie asked, looking from Ann to Solange and back. She, herself, felt exhilarated. It seemed like this might be the real thing at last.

"It happened so fast," Ann said and stopped to gather her thoughts. "Yes, actually I'm a bit uncomfortable with it. I mean first we were just joking around. She was–Alison, that is. And we were too. Then, out of nowhere she sort of took over, not exactly hypnotized us, but something . . . something happened there."

Solange nodded, "Yes. I felt momentarily out of control, but I wasn't frightened. I liked her guided fantasy using the senses to make us more aware. Still, I think it's good we're having this opportunity to touch bases." She was glad she'd insisted upon a code word. "So, are we going on with this? Or what? Was this a false alarm?"

Bernie looked to Ann. "It's your move, Annie. Whatever you say goes."

"I guess I'm O.K.," Ann said, "as long as you know I'm feeling a bit uncertain, and we still have the code word to use if necessary."

"Right." Solange said. "I'm for going on."

"Great," Bernie said. "I want to see what 'opening a circle' brings. Starhawk describes several ways to do it. It'll be fascinating watching Alison's ceremonial techniques."

"She might not do any of that, you know," Solange said. "She might not be a witch, after all."

"That could be," Bernie acknowledged. "So Annie, are you O.K.?" She reached out and put her arm around Ann.

Ann nodded. "Yes," she let out a deep sigh. "It's funny. Solange needed the code word, and you were talking about having an attack of fear and trembling, but I'm the one who actually panicked."

"Oh, I think we've all had our share of uncertainty. That's why we agreed to the word in the first place," Bernie reminded her.

They nodded solemnly. "Should we change it now–the word?" Solange asked.

"Maybe." Ann said. "They might catch on if we're endlessly yelling 'groceries' at each other and then bolting."

They roared at the picture of themselves. "Hopefully we won't have to do that," Ann said when the laughter subsided, just a note of wariness creeping into her voice. She continued. "Let's just keep things the way they are. We don't need any more confusion here. Right?"

"Right." Solange concurred.

"Well, we can go back now, then," Ann said.

"That's right," Bernie said. "I have a whole carton of cigarettes in back."

They were half way home when they remembered the RV they passed parked along the driveway to Rachel's house.

"Clovis!" The word exploded from Ann. "We didn't even think of her. Did you see anybody in that RV?"

"I didn't look."

"Me either," Solange said. "We were so busy talking. What are you thinking?"

"Isn't it a little strange that this mystery woman hasn't made an appearance yet?" Bernie asked.

"Resting, is what Alison told us," Ann said, the tone of her voice accusing. "Hey, what if Clovis is the devil and Alison is her servant?"

"What is the matter with you?" Bernie asked, annoyed. "You've been seeing too many Geraldo shows."

"Look, let's stop on our way back and visit her. That should help put to rest any suspicions we might have," Solange suggested.

"Or feed them," Ann said.

"Oh, God, you two," Bernie said. "Keep it up and we'll be in a panic before nightfall."

Two minutes later they approached the RV they had seen parked in a grove of pines at the side of the road. They could just make out an old woman on the passenger's side in the front. She appeared to be sleeping.

"Knock," Ann said insistently. "We need to meet Clovis–to know who she is."

Bernie knocked loudly on the window next to the woman. She jumped. Her shawl which was pulled down over her forehead was askew and she had a rather rakish look.

Ann was suddenly swept with guilt for waking an old woman, especially if she were going to join them later in the evening. It probably took all her strength to stay up late for such a night as this.

"Hello," Bernie called loudly. "Could we speak to you?"

"Of course, of course," came the hoarse reply.

Wonders never cease, Bernie thought as she looked at the strange woman who fumbled with the window with odd flat fingers, sliding it partially open.

"Yes?"

Ann thought, she has a cold. It seemed foolish for her to be here.

The old woman eyed them now, alert and curious.

"Now who might you be, my dears? The students Alison has told me about?"

They were relieved. Apparently she was harmless.

"What are three nice ladies like you doing . . . ," the old woman stopped suddenly changing her mind about what she wanted to say, but it was too late.

Bernie finished for her, "at a witch's coven, you mean?" It seemed an odd thing for someone to ask who had answered the Widdershins ad. "The same thing you're doing, perhaps."

"Ah," the old woman's eyes popped ever more brightly. "You think I'm a witch, then?"

"Why not?" Ann said, feeling annoyed with the attempt at artifice. "There's nothing wrong with that. We came to meet witches who could perform the ritual." She felt a need to continue the conversation to find out who Clovis was.

"Yes, yes. Certainly." Father Donahey said soothingly. These girls looked a little old to be going off on their own. Where were their husbands, he wondered. The blond beauty was just the type whose body was ripe for possession. He thrilled to the thought. "I'll try to come to the ceremony tonight," he continued, his voice trailing off. "But now, you go and find Alison and tell her I need my supper. Be careful," he added before he could stop himself, but managed to restrain himself from giving them his blessing. He squeezed his rosary tightly in his hand as they walked away from him to their car and began to pray. "Father, they will come to no good here," but somehow the prayer got interrupted by thoughts of Alison and food. He needed to talk to her about how she could protect these women from the others. Still, he admitted, he didn't know who the others were yet. They could all be harmless . . . . He reached behind him to find his bag. I should prepare myself. I'll need all the help I can get.

Alison and Bernie ran comfortably together, rounding a curve in the road which passed a beautiful crescent cove and starting uphill. The air was perfect with just enough breeze to cool them as they ran. Alison said, "You're a senior at the university? Do you have plans for next year?"

Bernie replied, "Plans, yes, but I'm not going on to grad school till the following year. Law school. If I get in, that is."

"You will," Alison said, then added, "if you want to."

"How do you know? Are you a psychic?"

"Sure. I have extrasensory perception. But so do you. We all have what is called the gift of foresight. I've just allowed mine the freedom to develop."

"Is there such a thing as magic?" Bernie asked.

"Yes, but it's not what most people think of as magic. We'll do some tonight. We need a reason, however. There should always be a serious purpose. That's why we must meet and talk before we begin."

Bernie was impressed with Alison, and the whole trip was, she saw now, turning out to be more exciting than she had thought. Not even Ann would deny that. They rounded another bend and struck out on a dirt road. Rachel had given them directions for roads that connected. They would eventually come full circle.

The kitchen filled with a grand mixture of aromas: Alison's "Mystery Casserole" baked in the oven; Rachel's tuna fish with tuna helper and onion rings sat bubbling on the back of the stove along with the baked beans and hot dogs contributed by Ann, Bernie and Solange. Both Grace and Clarissa had brought tofu which they combined with a package of falafel so that there would be enough of both to go around. The golden balls of falafel and tofu sizzled in peanut oil adding a middle-Eastern zest to the bouquet.

While Clarissa fried, Grace shredded lettuce and chopped tomatoes and onions. Tucked inside pita bread, the salad makings along with a salad dressing of mayonnaise and yogurt would complement the falafel.

Rachel set the round table with paper plates, cups and plastic forks for a buffet. When it was time to eat, she instructed, people would take their food to sit at the picnic table on the lawn overlooking the water.

"I've eaten at home, but I wanted you to have these," Ellen said, arriving with three loaves of homemade whole wheat bread just out of her oven. She put them on the table and sat down to watch the others at work.

"God, the smell is heavenly," Bernie observed. She was fresh from the shower, wrapped in a beach towel, her hair dripping. "That solar bag beats an indoor shower hands down," she told Rachel, grinning through the screen. "I think I'll get one for when we go camping."

"Can you imagine standing there under the trees, the sun shining on you, the ocean as your view? What a way to wash the sweat off," she said to Ann and Solange. "Richard and the boys would love something like that. It's fabulous! There's enough water out there for one more person," she added. "Want to try it, Annie?"

"No thanks."

"Then I'm next," Alison volunteered. "I've got a shower in the RV, but the water hasn't heated up yet."

"Do hurry," Rachel said, bustling around the table, fingering the dishes and silverware. "You have fifteen minutes before your casserole comes out of the oven. We should eat then or the rest of the food will have to be reheated."

"How is Clovis going to feel eating supper all alone out there? That doesn't seem right somehow," Solange said sympathetically to Alison.

"Clovis knows she's welcome to eat with the rest of us. She chooses to stay put for the time being," Alison replied, then excused herself and went out to take her shower. She was beginning to be sick of covering for Father Donahey. She couldn't imagine what he would do with his evening. He had worked himself into such a lather over his role in the so-called exorcism that when she'd returned from running he told her that he must call the Bishop immediately. He wanted her to drive him to a public phone.

"It's almost dinner time," she had dissuaded him, matter-of-factly. "I asked Clarissa to turn on the casserole ten minutes ago. I'm going down there to ask if I can take an outdoor shower, and then I'll be back with some of the casserole for you. Besides," she added, trying to see things from his perspective, "what have you done that's wrong? So far nothing. The Bishop can't fault you for being concerned about the possibility of a devil's cult." The words were strange in her mouth, the possibility of a devil foreign to her way of thinking.

To calm Father Donahey she had soothed him with extra hors d'oeuvres: Lebanese spinach turnovers, home-made cheddar cheese crackers with a creamy dip of chives, apples, and raisins, plus his sure-to-pacify favorite–curried stuffed eggs. While she was gone he could indulge the rest of his appetite, one that included Scotch and soda.

She did not explain to the other women that one of the major reasons Clovis chose not to join them for dinner was Scotch. Scotch whiskey, as far as she could see, was another form of communion, a ritual which she believed gave him as much pleasure as his priestly functions. He kept his bottle in a leather case with a little silver shot glass for its top. With this he measured out his drinks with a great flourish – just the right amount for two doubles before dinner, and one after. That was during the week. She was sure he allowed himself more on weekends.

With glass in hand, he become a peremptory questioner, demanding to know if she'd found anything suspicious in her inspection of the house and people.

"Not really. Everything is pretty casual. No plans seem to have been made for tonight as yet," she had told him calmly. He gave her a strange look. How soon would he understand that a witch had wended her way into his very household, had been under his nose all along, casting her spell through her cooking? How would he handle the revelation when it came? The fates would decide about their dubious partnership. She would accept whatever she must. To her that was part of The Craft.

Alison returned to the kitchen just as the casserole was removed from the oven. She took a small plate, filling it with Father Donahey's portion. "I'll be right back. Please don't wait for me." Fixing him a place at the little table beside a window, she saw that he was already mellow and not the least interested in anything other than what he was about to put into his mouth. She left him with the understanding that she would be back as soon as she had anything of importance to tell him.

Back in the kitchen, Ellen said to the group, "I probably shouldn't be here. I'm in the foulest mood. Before I came over I got a phone call from Martin, the chairman of the planning board. He's called another meeting of the planning board tonight. Jack Russell is bringing two developers who are going to do a lot of fancy building along the shore. They didn't show up last night and now they have the audacity to phone from their yacht and ask the town to meet with them again–on Saturday night to boot! Evidently they ran aground last night on their way here and couldn't get their phone or their engine to work. They were stuck off a small uninhabited island with no rescue in sight." She scowled and turned to look out the window. "Well, I guess that was not their fault, and I should be sympathetic, but I'm not. If they had known how to read a chart they wouldn't have been stranded in the first place. The other thing is that we're at their beck and call. I served as taxi driver last night, waited at their landing place for an hour. Then I sat at the stalled planning board for another hour while they tried to figure out whether to cancel the meeting. It's maddening. And guess who is taxi driver for tonight?"

Rachel interrupted, not unkindly. She put a hand on Ellen's shoulder. "Try not to think about it for now. Help yourself to food and move out to the picnic table. Enjoy it while it's hot. The conversation can continue out there," she added politely. Her mouth watered for a taste of her own tuna casserole with the new tuna helper. Always suspicious of herbs, she hoped there wouldn't be too many in the mix. She glanced at the other food on the table and swallowed. Baked beans and hot dogs were no problem. The extra salad that Grace had separated from the falafel-pita sandwiches was a blessing, but to eat the falafel itself would take courage. And goodness knew what was in Alison's dish. She often refused Clarissa's offers of food, but this was different. It would not do to offend guests.

Rachel put the negative thoughts of food behind her as she left the kitchen. Balancing her heavily-laden plate carefully, she followed Alison to the picnic table. The sight of her guests happily arranging themselves at the table transformed her. She saw this occasion, a lovely gathering of friendly people, was her doing, something she had engineered with a simple ad in the paper. Momentarily, she lost sight of the group's reason for being–and then she turned back to the conversation.

Alison and Ellen were still talking about the developers. "You sound as if you are opposed to further land development," Alison said.

"Not at all," Ellen answered her strongly. "I'm sorry if I gave that impression. I'm against poor planning for use of the land anywhere on the island. Developers should be subject to laws that protect the total island environment and the people who have always lived here."

"So, who has the real clout in this situation?" Ann asked.

"The committee is advisory only, but many islanders support the concept of planning and protecting the environment. In the end, it's the board of selectmen that has the final say. That's where the island power is. I don't know, though, if island power can stand up to this onslaught of big money."

"So how do you think things are going?" Rachel inquired politely, not altogether happy with the seriousness of the conversation.

"It's too early to say. This company, Logan-Russell, is a collection of wheelers and dealers of the worst possible sort. They have very convincing come-ons, a lot of fancy talk and promises. But there are no guarantees they'll do anything they say. They're looking for land fill for the swampy areas of the land they're selling, and also permission to build roads some of which abut on other people's property, people who don't want to see the changes envisioned by Logan-Russell.

"There are all kinds of problems associated with what they are doing. For one thing they've called in a private company of soil test engineers to check for appropriate drainage on their land. We know for a fact that this company has given approval to a number of septic systems which wouldn't pass state standards. Too much ledge makes for poor drainage and we've got a lot of ledge out here. It could be disastrous if they get permission to put drainage fields in the wrong places, and equally problematic if they decide they should pump their sewage right into the cove," she said waving an arm to indicate the water that edged Rachel's property. "That could happen."

"But aren't there laws?" Ann cried.

"You have a right to go to court on issues like that," Bernie said.

"I had no idea," Rachel said, boiling with anger at the possibility of the beautiful cove being spoiled by sewage.

"I hope you make your feelings known to Winner," Ellen said. "You are a taxpayer, after all." She turned to the others, "Winner is our equivalent to a mayor. He's the oldest selectman."

"I certainly will," Rachel said. "I might sue that company."

"I'm glad that you feel strongly enough about the issue to consider filing suit, but you're dealing with a firm that has its own legal staff on board. Anyone who has full-time lawyers working as permanent employees can afford endless litigation. Better be prepared for a long haul."

"That sounds so bleak," Clarissa said. "I hate to think of this beautiful place destroyed."

"It's absolutely criminal," Solange added.

"How do the islanders feel about this?" Ann asked.

"Some are upset. Some call it progress. What's happened is complicated. Those islanders who live on fixed incomes, like my aunt, want to be sure land values don't skyrocket. If that happens, older people and low income families who have enjoyed their own bit of shoreline or view of the water will have to beg, borrow, or steal to pay their taxes. Some will sell and move inland where an acre is cheap because there is nothing but slash to look at. Worse and inconceivable to most of them, they could be forced to move off island.

"This house, for instance, could be revalued at, say, two hundred and fifty thousand because it's on a private peninsula of fifteen acres." Instantly, Ellen looked contrite, but the words were out of her mouth. "I'm sorry, Rachel," she said.

Rachel felt physically ill from the news. She had no idea that the value of her property could suddenly rise because of land development on the far side of the island. She had not been able to afford what was called "modern conveniences," but she hadn't minded roughing it, and there had been an added benefit. Her outhouse, she was fond of saying, served as an insurance policy against raised taxes. Her tax bill had hardly changed from the year she bought the property at a song some thirty-five years ago.

"It's all right. I should have known," Rachel said, struggling to regain her composure.

"Then, too," Ellen continued, hoping to put Rachel's predicament into perspective, "there are people who are unemployed most of the year. This is not exactly a bustling business community. People scrape bottom too often. They need jobs. They see the building boom as providing all kinds of employment. Lots of young struggling families here are strapped for cash. They hate the idea of losing their island to a wealthy few who come here only when the weather is beautiful, but they try not to think about it too much."

"What is the island's next move then, Ellen?" asked Alison.

"I really can't say for sure. Members of the planning board feel hamstrung, at least from what I hear. They go over the same material each time they meet. They hash it out. They say it's wrong for things to go the way they are. They repeat their concerns to the selectmen. Then the next month they go over the same ground again. In some cases, land owners have been known to go ahead and do what they want anyway, no matter what the committee says. A building is built too close to the water, a septic system gets installed where drainage will spill out over onto someone else's land, too many trees get cut down too close to the shoreline causing blowdowns and erosion. Once done–that kind of thing can't be undone." She sighed, and her eyes looked tired.

"Actually we have good building codes and zoning laws, probably some of the best in the state, but we can't enforce them, you see."

"I see, all too clearly," Rachel said, mournful at the thought of sewage washing up on her shore. Now she pulled herself up to command attention. She was half serious, half facetious as she said, "I have a suggestion. If witchcraft has any power at all, then we should put it to work, put the whammy on the developers."

"Here, here," Bernie said enthusiastically, followed by Solange and Ann. Grace nodded her head politely. Ellen gave a chuckle and looked skeptical.

"Be sensible, Rach," Clarissa said. "What you're suggesting is childish."

"I do not mean a spiritual whammy, Clarissa. I mean a real, practical, down-to-earth whammy."

"Then that is not witchcraft, but it probably is illegal," Clarissa said distractedly, as if it didn't matter anyway. She helped herself to more of Alison's delicious Mystery Casserole, thinking Rachel might be going off the deep end. She determined to enjoy Alison's cooking no matter what.

Maybe Clarissa was right, Rachel thought. It was beginning to look like witchcraft was an ostrich's reaction, just one more place to bury your head and forget the threat of danger, just one more religion that you lifted from a box on special days, only to return it shortly, and never, never put it to any practical use in the real world. Witchcraft had seemed different from other religions, at first, seemed open to change, but then again, maybe she was just imagining it. She remembered Lolly Willowes who became a witch so that she could have a life of her own. She, Rachel, expected something even more than that.

Watching these women fence verbally, Grace felt wrapped in sociability and good humor. She knew it was only temporary stay against the loneliness she had so regularly endured, but that fact did not make it less delightful. The two hostesses, Rachel and Clarissa, were disarmingly frank with one another, their bickering touching as well as amusing. Affection for all the women overwhelmed her. They had included her as if she were an old friend, made her feel more comfortable as a woman among women than she had for years. Now she wanted to help Clarissa and Rachel to understand that they could find a peaceful resolution to their differences through witchcraft. To do so, might change the value of her study. It would be a form of personal intervention and thus unscientific–it would skew their responses. Well, damn that, she thought, irritably, she could do nothing about it now. Nevertheless, she held her tongue.

Solange miraculously came to the rescue, "From what I've read recently of witchcraft I understand that spells might be interpreted to be wishes followed by action. Witches call for their strength from the elements, but they are not averse to using whatever resources they have at their command to effect change."

Ann nodded her head vigorously. "That's what I was thinking. Anyway, we don't have to be witches to believe that we could do something to help. Any group can generate creative power. It's called synergy. The whole is worth more than the sum of its individual parts."

"Power in numbers. Is that what you're saying?" Clarissa asked, almost hopefully.

"More than that," Rachel corrected her, suddenly happy again. "What you can do as a group is more than what each person could do separately."

"Right. Synergy," Ann repeated.

"Power in numbers," Clarissa repeated obstinately.

"What, by the way, is in your Mystery Casserole, Alison?" Ellen inquired with a view to changing the subject. It seemed futile to her, this fantasy of changing things by synergy.

Alison smiled, "I hate to tell you because you've all been enjoying it so much." she paused, "Or have you?"

"Very much so," Grace said. "I think I know what's in it though, and I happen to like it."

"So out with it," Rachel demanded. "No secrets in this coven."

"It's eggplant," Grace said confidently. "I know the recipe. It's called 'Eggplant For Those Who Hate Eggplant.' "

Rachel was flabbergasted. "I hate eggplant," she said, "and I loved this."

"Exactly," Alison said and she and Grace burst into laughter.

Father Donahey had already gone over the events leading to the trip too many times. The whole thing was turning topsy-turvy. All he could do was sit here. He didn't want to go down there and tell them he was a Catholic priest. That would spoil everything. He'd answered the ad, after all, just like the rest of them. He'd been deceitful, signing another name. And furthermore, he'd gotten carried away with the disguise which was the most foolish thing he'd ever done in his life. Or was it? Keeping Alison on as cook, he berated himself, might be the most foolish of all. The woman didn't have a crush on him. She was using him, enjoying this little trip, putting him on the spot. He was a victim of his own appetite. Or should he say appetites. He loved her cooking, but he also loved her red hair. Otherwise he would never have tolerated her nasty sweat suits for a minute. He was lusting in his heart–like Jimmy Carter, but he would never make a fool of himself publicly, like Carter. He, as a Catholic, could go to confession. Never mind letting the whole world know. He'd confess to another priest at some point.

Alison had suggested he wait till dark before he moved out, but maybe that would be too late. He should go down there now and see what he could learn for himself. He paced the floor of the RV, went into the tiny cubicle bathroom and looked into the mirror. "Not a pretty sight," he said messing with the curls of the hot and itchy wig. He adjusted his shawl, washed his hands, then went to look in the refrigerator. He found a bunch of grapes and one more stuffed egg and ate them while he paced the floor. He gave himself a mental pep talk. Do it, he said. Get out there and find out for yourself what's going on. He went to the mirror and adjusted his shawl one more time–the blasted thing had a way of falling off his shoulders all the time. All right, he said to the walls of the RV. I'm off.

Rounding the corner of the house stealthily, he approached the kitchen, and stood to one side under cover of a large blooming shrub. If he was caught, at least he was in disguise. He could always say he had decided to join them.

Through the window he saw that no one was in the kitchen. Where were they? Then he heard voices coming from the back of the house. He contained his panic and did not run. Spotting a small shed fifteen feet from the back door of the kitchen, he moved quickly across the open space and around to the rear of the shed and found himself standing safely in a makeshift shower stall. A half filled container of water, resembling an enema bag, hung over his head from what looked like a gallows. The bag leaked steadily, wetting one curl on his forehead. The water dripped down his nose. He was going to sneeze. He pressed viciously on his upper lip and the sneeze died away. The water continued to drip, so, with an impatient swipe at his forehead, he moved closer to the lathe fence which made up one side of the shower stall and provided privacy from potential viewers in the kitchen and on the lawn. It was all that protected him now from the women whose voices he could hear quite well. He noticed that there was one section where the lathes in the fence were loose. He pushed a little and one shifted slightly. He squeezed a finger through and pressed on one side gently to see if it would give. It did, but he could not see the women who were apparently eating some distance from the fence. Still it would have to do. If he had to, he could move into the woods behind him to escape quickly. He concentrated carefully and listened. Heavenly Father, they were talking recipes. That should have been comforting, but it wasn't. Their meal was probably all but over. He'd probably missed the most important conversation. For women, however, sometimes the most important thing was a recipe. Certainly Alison's recipes were worth getting. He would request that she write them all down shortly. Then fire her. He would rid himself totally of temptation.

Clarissa could see that Rachel was annoyed with her about her last remark. "Let me clean up here," she said in an effort to make amends. "I'll do up whatever dishes there are, and you people start the meeting without me." The voice sounded vaguely familiar to Father Donahey.

Damn martyr, Rachel thought. "You'll do no such thing." she said sharply. "There aren't that many dishes and they can certainly wait till tomorrow." This was, she realized, the first

show of temper she had had in front of the other women. It would be too bad to spoil things now. She gave a quick smile.

"Fine," Clarissa said properly and thought to herself, don't say I didn't volunteer. She stood and gathered as many plates and serving dishes as she could carry and moved towards the kitchen.

"Ten minutes to stretch, or go to the outhouse, and then we meet in the living room," Rachel said, her irritation with Clarissa evaporating immediately. She could hardly contain herself with joy. Perhaps they could do something to help the island. They could certainly try.

Father Donahey was puzzled. This other voice also had a familiar ring to it. He just couldn't place either of them yet. "Where's the shower, anyway?" asked Solange. "I heard that it was really cleverly arranged."

Alarmed, Father Donahey moved quickly, catching his foot on the drain platform, but regained his balance without falling. He stepped carefully into the bushes to the side of the shed away from the house.

"Over here," he heard Alison call. He nearly choked when, from his uncomfortable crouch, he caught sight of her feet within arm's length. His knees were killing him. If he had to stay this way too much longer he'd collapse.

"Convenient, isn't it?" Alison was saying to another pair of feet. "And what a lovely way to shower with the sun shining on your skin."

"It can be chilling when it rains," said one of the familiar voices on her way to the kitchen. "I'll put the kettle on for coffee." The voice moved beyond the shed, and he heard her footsteps mounting the steps. The screen door slammed. More feet on the steps. The door slammed again. Then he heard voices in the kitchen and also, closer, Alison and someone else talking as they moved from the shower presumably towards the outhouse that seemed to be located in the woods on the north side of the shed. Their voices faded away and then there was silence.

Father Donahey was momentarily disoriented. He could feel his heart thumping. He took a breath and exhaled slowly trying to relax. He would wait until traffic to and from the outhouse subsided. Then, when it was safe, he could move in on them.

Finally they were all together in the living room, comfortably seated in wicker chairs filled with plump pillows or on the two couches that faced each other across the room. Coffee steamed from their cups. The room was light and airy, with three of the windows looking out on the cove. Two others gave a view of the drive and the garden. The sky was turning gold and pink. If they had thought about it, they probably would have believed that Clovis was still in the RV, but they would have been wrong. Clovis crouched amidst sprouting day lilies under the window behind one of the couches and listened as one person said she was sorry Clovis could not be with them.

Father Donahey flushed, and felt stupid squatting in a flower bed with a skirt tugging awkwardly at his knees. Knees that were used to kneeling, but would never last in this position. He gave in almost immediately and knelt. More comfortable, he regained his sense of mission. He knew he was about to discover what was really going on.

Alison was speaking, "I should tell you about Clovis before we begin." He was stricken. Was she about to reveal his true identity? Would they come storming out of the house up to the RV to discover that he had left, was in fact down here hiding in the bushes. How embarrassing that would be. As much as he wanted to bolt, he forced himself to stay on his knees and learn what it was she would say. "Clovis will not be joining us at all. She simply is not up to it." Alison saw the looks of concern on their faces and reassured them, "No, no. She's not ill, just tired. But the other part of it is, she's changed her mind. She's just decided that witchcraft is not something she wishes to pursue at this time." She smiled politely and then went on, "I, however, am delighted to be here, to have this opportunity to meet you all." She turned to Rachel. "Please, I think you, as our hostess, should open our gathering."

Rachel had changed into her new floor-length skirt–made of real patchwork quilt in many colors. Her long sleeved white silk blouse showed off her bangle bracelets, cloisonné of blue and red and the others of silver. Then there were her new white sandals, both comfortable and attractive. It was the moment she had envisioned from the beginning–the opening of a circle, or so she thought of it. Rachel began, "Welcome. I'd like to thank you all for coming." She was exhilarated by the faces looking at her, at the idea that together they might experience something new. "I've looked forward to our coming together, and I am full of hope that we can find our way together into the mysteries of witchcraft." She waved a hand outward as if to include the whole world in her greeting. "I have to say my little piece, then I'll ask each of you in turn to do the same. A few ground rules, first. I believe it would be helpful if we don't interrupt each other's initial remarks, and if we allow each other whatever it is we need to say without contradiction. We can always ask questions afterward. We will go on to our make our plan for the solstice, after everyone has had a turn to speak."

The room was quiet and each person settled into her place. "I've always welcomed change in my life," Rachel began. "I'm a single woman. I've lived my life alone, but for the most part happily so. At seventy-three, I thought it seemed as good a time as any to reaffirm my independence, to be free of bosses at last, and of schedules and unproductive, uncreative work. I want," she gazed out of the window at the glittering sea, and paused for a moment. "I want the opposite of retirement. I want involvement, but on my own terms. I want to exercise my own power." She felt proud saying those words and she glanced at the young faces around her, smiling back at her. Even Clarissa looked sympathetic. Her presence in the group suddenly seemed all right.

"I suppose it might look strange to you younger women, that someone my age would be striking out into new territory, but that is how I feel."

Ann and Solange simultaneously assured her that it was not strange at all, but impressive, and then apologized for interrupting. She thanked them and went on. "I've done a lot of reading, and from what I can determine, some of the witches today have fashioned an interesting blend of the old paganistic reverence for this planet and the new feminism. They make choices for themselves and take responsibility for their choices. They work cooperatively, joining their powers with the power of nature to do good things. I hope to find such a group of witches and join them. I want to learn The Craft. I don't know very much about non-rational belief systems, except for Catholicism, and that has never worked for me."

In the lily bed, Father Donahey winced. That voice was right at the edge of his memory and he still could not put a face or name to it. Just the fact that the speaker might belong to a member of his own parish confirmed the rightness of his being here.

Rachel was silent for a moment looking down at her hands. Then she looked to Solange who sat on her right. The circle was opening, she thought, and so it should go widdershins, not in the usual direction. "I should explain to those of you who do not know what 'widdershins' means." When she had finished she nodded to Solange who began to speak, "I've had trouble finding a support system all my life. I was abandoned by my mother and my father as a baby, put in a foster home. My father was very wealthy. He left me a fortune when he died recently. Yet money, I find upon suddenly acquiring it in large sums, can be troublesome. I find it hard to talk about it, even now," she shrugged. "It is not quite the miracle it seems like it should be." She ran her fingers through her hair. "I am a middle aged woman, someone who has just recently returned to school after years of working in a mill. I have learned to live without much money quite well. I guess that now I'll have to live with it."

She sighed and continued on, "One thing I do know; I have two younger friends, here, who have given me the love I needed to survive and to flourish in college. I had never expected to feel so enriched or so hopeful about my future until I met them. They have given me back my youth, and because of them I no longer feel abandoned."

She was a radiant woman, Rachel thought, and there was something about her dark hair and skin that was naggingly familiar . . . and what was it she had just said about her father?

Solange concluded, "I hope that we three can join with all of you to build a spiritual support system of some sort." She was floundering now for lack of words. "I'd like to be of help to other abandoned people, both children and adults. Perhaps to prevent abandonment. I have power now that I never dreamed I'd have. I want to learn how to use it wisely, and not just for myself." She felt as she said those words the sense of herself changing and becoming. It was something she had not expected, yet she sensed a rising self-confidence. She hoped fervently that the feeling would last.

Rachel was incredulous. This woman might have been her own daughter given up for adoption so long ago. The age was right. She felt her face flush and she gripped the arm of the sofa. Her heart raced uncomfortably in her chest. How could she possibly deal with such a revelation at this late date in her life? No, she told herself sensibly, don't be a sentimental ass. It's simply one of those crazy reminders of how often life stories have similar plots.

She rejected the thought firmly, but her eyes stole back to Solange's face again for clues. The dark hair and eyes could have been his, but it was all so long ago she was not sure how accurate her vision of him could be. Yet there was the Spanish name Solange. Could it have been possible that the child's father was allowed to know about the baby's whereabouts when she was not? And all those years . . . . The thought was unsettling. She'd have to stop fantasizing or she'd ruin the evening. She forced her attention back to the opening ritual.

Solange turned to Ann who sat on her right, indicating with a smile that it was her turn to speak.

"I'm a student and unmarried," Ann began. "I know what I want to do with my life. I'll be graduating shortly and I want to go to graduate school to get the training I need to become a negotiator. I want to help resolve human problems. I'm here because I believe there is a higher power, a magic, if you will, that resides in all of us. When we put our magic together it becomes a kind of supreme collective. I love group work. I'm at my best in situations where people have to work something out."

She leaned back on the couch pillows and gazed out the window for a moment and then remembered one of the reasons she was here. "When I first read the ad, I didn't act on it. Not until the three of us got together did I see the possibility of answering the ad. We had been talking about the lack of a spiritual haven for women in a patriarchal society. Surely there's religion, but the authority of Christianity and Judaism has always rested in men. Men make the decisions. They officiate in their high places, using their power to their own advantage. We women hold the religion together by being in the congregation, by bringing up our children in the faith, by upholding the tenets of faith, by believing that somehow things will be better for our prayers and our good works, all the while following the lead of the males in our lives, fathers, husbands, sons and lovers. Unfortunately that tends to work against us. And as the saying goes, the more things change the more they stay the same.

"The world is constantly at war because the big decisions are too often made by men who believe that violence is not the last resort, but the only one. They may use peaceful words but they seem to need power over others to be truly fulfilled." She lapsed into silence and everyone in the room waited expectantly.

"Sorry , I don't get to make speeches very often. Or let off steam, either. It feels good. Anyway, the three of us decided we wanted to see if witchcraft would be a different way of expressing power positively and non-violently." She had finished and there was another quiet interval in the room, a kind of waiting for someone to begin.

Bernie took up the thread, "The business about religion that Ann spoke of concerns me too. I'm a student, but also a wife and a mother. I'm very fortunate to have a supportive, caring husband who shares equally with me the parenting responsibilities of our two spunky little boys. Richard and I both want our kids to grow up with a value system that has practical use, that makes sense in the real world. We want them to feel secure, not fearful of a nuclear holocaust. The churches and the synagogues seem to support the status quo. How many, for instance, stand firmly in opposition to the government's buildup of nuclear waste?

"It's simply not enough for me to hear someone preach, 'Thou shalt not kill,' when he speaks of abortion, as if life in utero were the only sacred kind. I expect the rule to apply everywhere, as a reverence for life, if it is to be truly religious, truly honest and just. The death penalty, war, chemical pollution in the air, oil spills like the one in Alaska–nuclear waste–all of those things kill. I find it very odd that abortion is such a hot issue," she reiterated. "That's just one more way of putting the onus on women, as if they were the killers in this world."

Father Donahey grimaced in the bushes. How much more of this naively wrongheaded, certainly blasphemous thinking could he possibly take? He might give himself away in sheer rage. He must speak to these women somehow. They had no idea how wrong they were. It amazed him how ordinary and unsophisticated the devil could be using these weak women to work his evil.

There was a look of amazement on Clarissa's face. She had never heard such talk in her life. Perhaps she should get up and leave right now? Was she the only Christian here, the only one who opposed abortion? Evidently so. Not one person spoke up. Clarissa decided to wait until her turn. Then she would say something.

Rachel glanced at Clarissa and knew what she was thinking. She felt a flash of sympathy for her. She herself had often felt the way this woman felt, but never could she have said so as boldly or articulately. It had to be hard on poor Clarissa. She glanced at Solange again. Whose nose, whose eyes, whose shoulders went into her genetic makeup? Were there body feature's that she shared with this woman? A characteristic gesture? Anything at all? She just didn't know.

Grace spoke next. "I have to be honest. I was going to ride this through. On a broomstick?" she chuckled and was immediately annoyed for having made light of the subject. The group, however, joined her laughter. She continued more soberly, "I can't. You're good people. I'm learning so much from your truthfulness. It's terribly important for me to be honest too." She took a deep breath and plunged on, "I'm a researcher, not in search of a faith or a craft, or of witches per se, but in search of understanding about how people act on their perceptions. I chose to study witchcraft because of the persecution of witches. Years ago I did an article on witchcraft for a Maine paper when I lived in Portland–*The Evening Press.* They liked it so much that I was inspired to go on studying about witches. After I got into the subject I understood there was an incredible phenomenon of scape-goating of women as witches along with mass hysteria at the times in our history when so many women were cruelly and needlessly executed. I wanted to understand why these things happened." She stopped short, looked around the room and her eyes filled with tears. "When I came here I expected to be objective, removed, and scientific, and it turns out that I'm enjoying myself immensely. I like you all . . . ," she stopped and fumbled for a tissue to wipe her eyes. Bernie reached over and put her hand on Grace's hand.

"I've been so isolated," Grace continued, "living in Jersey in a community where the people can't even understand me when I go into the grocery store. Until today, I didn't know how much I needed friends. I've been so involved in my studies. This is the first fun I've had in three years. And now I've blown it." She wept silently for a minute.

Bernie stroked Grace's shoulder awkwardly until her weeping subsided. "It's OK." Bernie said. "We're all entitled to our say, remember?"

Grace continued, "I wanted to find a primary source–a real coven of witches to study. I was going to deceive you, if necessary, let you believe I, too, was in search of a coven for spiritual reasons, but I can't do that. I can't honestly take advantage of you all. It's just not ethical."

The women made sounds of protest in an attempt to comfort her. She cut them short. "Please. Don't say anything for a moment. First of all I've changed the flow, the climate here. That's unforgivable, but the sharing I've longed for was suddenly available, was right in front of me." She looked around at the faces. "I have no right to spoil the group with my own agenda. I'll be glad to leave if people are uncomfortable knowing that I was going to use your coven as a case study." She'd finished.

A scream split the air. Increase, who had up until now resigned himself to his limited surroundings, decided that he had been captive long enough. His weird and pitiful cry emanated from the cage outside the back door. Grace was stricken. "He must have heard my voice," she told the group. "Another damn thing I did wrong. He's been in that cage for hours."

Rachel was immediately understanding. "Let him out. Bring him inside."

"Would that be all right ?" Grace asked.

Rachel said, "By all means. Go and set the poor thing loose."

Father Donahey had heard the inhuman sound of Increase's cry, but he heard no more. He'd been concentrating on the incredible confession of the only innocent woman in the room. Not a cultist, she was apologizing to women who were. In his outrage he was totally unprepared for the sound that came from the bowels of a huge tree around the corner. He lunged from the bed of lilies and struggled across the lawn away from the noise. There he slumped on the ground out of breath, his heart pounding, his shawl caught in the thorns of a massive rugosa bush.

He was sweating profusely under the wig. Beads of moisture stood out on his forehead. I can't take this, he thought. They must have attacked the poor woman, and I haven't the strength to go in there now. What was I thinking of? His hands trembled as he tried to wrench the shawl free of the thorns, ripping it as he did so. The blouse had come out of the skirt and he was unable to get it back inside. The best he could do was to hold his familiar rosary beads for comfort until his heart slowed down. When he heard the kitchen door slam, he didn't have the strength to move away from his barely adequate hiding place to seek a better one. It slammed again and all was quiet.

Grace returned to the living room, Increase in her arms.

She let him loose and he streaked up the stairs disappearing out of sight on the top landing.

"That's all right," Rachel assured Grace as she started up the stairs to get him. "Let him get familiar with his surroundings. He'll come down in his own good time."

Rachel looked around the room after Grace had returned to her seat. She simply could not tell by their faces how they felt about Grace's revelation. It was true that she had asked everyone to refrain from comment on other people's statements, but this seemed to be the exception.

"Grace, would you like to hear from the others?" she asked.

"Very much so," Grace said.

Rachel saw that those few moments while Grace was rescuing her cat had given her the time she needed to compose herself. "I would appreciate knowing how you feel. I will respect whatever you say."

"Are there people here who object to Grace using us as a case study then?" Rachel asked.

Ellen said, "I'm not awfully keen on having my name used in something that's going to be published unless I have a chance to see it first."

"I can't blame you for that," Grace replied. "There's no reason to use anyone's name in what I'm writing. I'd be more than happy to let you read what I've written before it is submitted to anyone else; in fact, I'd welcome your feedback."

"Anyone else?" Rachel waited.

"I have no objections to being part of a study," said Ann.

"Nor I," added Solange.

"Fine with me," Bernie said

"I do object," Clarissa said firmly. She blushed. "I have nothing against you personally, Grace. I just don't feel comfortable with the idea of being included in a study of witchcraft."

Rachel was stung, but said nothing.

Grace nodded. "That's certainly your right."

Father Donahey who had resumed his place in the lilies had heard Clarissa's statement. He listened triumphantly. A sensible voice at last and one he was sure he would recognize if he could just hear a little more. In some way that voice belonged to a kindred spirit. She was undoubtedly in danger now that she had revealed herself as opposed to a connection with witchcraft in any way.

"Do you object?" Alison said to Rachel.

"No, I certainly don't. I think it's great that she wants to do the research. It's much needed. I feel honored to help her out."

Father Donahey started. The other familiar voice again—this time sounding like an enemy of the church. He was sure he would recognize it soon.

"And so do I," affirmed Alison seeing that everyone had now had an opportunity to speak.

Aha, Father Donahey said to himself, angrily. She's having herself one grand time, is Alison. She must think it's a lark to be part of a study and a coven, both. She doesn't know that I'm listening. Wait till she sees the price tag for her fun.

"That's all of us then. It sounds to me like your project is acceptable," Rachel concluded. Everyone except Clarissa joined in a round of applause.

"Thank you," Grace said visibly relieved and her eyes shone with unspilled tears.

"Shall we continue?" Rachel said feeling some apprehension, since Clarissa's views would shortly be forthcoming. Ellen, however, would be next to speak, so there would be a moment or two to think of how to handle Clarissa.

"I'll be frank with you all," Ellen began, "I'm a skeptic—particularly where mysticism is concerned. I also think that religions of all kinds seem to have a way of dividing people from each other. As far as I can tell witchcraft, benign or otherwise, is just another attempt to organize a group around a set of beliefs." She examined their faces for a response to what she was saying. Finding none she seemed to muster her courage to go on.

"Now, for the good news. I'm not as worried as I might have been about your gathering since I can see you're not about to get carried away in an orgy of devil worship, so my original reason for being here tonight—to protect Rachel from a bunch of crazies—has gone by the board.

"I've never met anyone who was interested in pagan spiritualism before, and you have to admit that witches have not exactly received a good press, so I just couldn't picture a group of intelligent women gathering together to re-create an ancient religion. But . . ." and here she stopped and gazed over their heads in embarrassment, the blush in her cheeks making her look younger, "you're good folks. I feel free to be myself, to say what I need to say–not something that happens in all groups . . . ." She smiled a gently self-reproving smile. "I'm having problems, as you well know, since I've gotten involved in island politics. And I'm not alone. The whole island is involved to one extent or another. You might say that I empathize with the abandoned, as you call them . . ." she turned to look at Solange, "in this case, the overtaxed, or the under or unemployed of the island–all of our futures depends to some degree upon the whims of a particularly powerful group of developers. So . . . I'm your first real opportunity to see if witchcraft works." She laughed again, amiably, although there was still doubt in her voice. She finished, "I really don't see how meeting in the moonlight, or whatever you're going to do here, will change anything for the better–except by creating some good feelings among new friends and some appreciation of the beauty of the night. I'm certainly for that.

"Oh, and by the way if we're going to do anything we've got to start pretty soon. I've got to go and pick up those incredibly inconsiderate developers at ten."

Which developers, Father Donahey wondered vaguely? This woman was a fool if she truly believed the devil was not at work here and that this group was anything less than evil. He moved uncomfortably in the lilies. Time to kneel again. He shifted from the squat position and his knees cracked painfully. He wondered if the sound carried through the window above his head. Perhaps he should rise and enter the house now and expose them all for what they were. Another idea hit him. What if they (or the devil) knew that he was hiding here? What if they (or it), waited for him to make the next move? It was a terrifying thought. For the first time, Father Donahey wondered if he might be outnumbered.

Rachel was both sobered and comforted by Ellen's words. She remembered her own dismissal of Clarissa for sharing similar concerns and yet, now, listening to Ellen express her earlier doubts about the wisdom of Rachel's plan it seemed possible for the first time that the ad might actually have attracted some dangerous types of people. It was true there were occasional serial murders, hints of living sacrifices and sadomasochistic sex all allegedly connected to devil worship. She dismissed those recent news stories, telling herself that that kind of thing was always going on in decadent private circles, usually but not always induced by drugs. People had done weird things since the beginning of time.

She was, however, convinced people inevitably sought out and victimized their own kind, gave their own private signals and avoided the uninitiated–unless (and she realized suddenly that it was an awful "unless") the victims were very young or very old.

Dismissing these troubling ideas, she gave thanks mentally to Ellen for joining the gathering and then she scanned the faces of her new-found acquaintances, absolutely reassured that there were no degenerates or drug-addicted people in the group. She felt certain that something good would come of their time together.

Clarissa was the fly in the ointment here. It was pitiful to see her rise so readily and in blind conviction to the defense of Catholicism. Damn, Rachel thought grimly, I should have left her in Portland. Why hadn't she refused to come if she was determined to be so touchy? Clarissa was a constant reminder that, for some people, once they passed the age of sixty, there was no such thing as pure unalloyed pleasure. Well, she amended, never mind sixty. There were some people she knew who hadn't allowed themselves any joy since the age of six.

She returned from her ramblings to hear Clarissa saying, "If you don't mind I need to collect my thoughts. I'd like to take a break."

Gather your dynamite, you mean, Rachel thought angrily. You'll rip this group apart yet.

The women stood, stretched, and talked in twos. "Just a moment," Alison spoke detaching herself from the comfortable chatter. "Before we break I'd like to ask Ellen if she'd consider a change in her plans." She turned to Ellen. "I think it would be good if you did not go to pick those people up."

Ellen was startled. "You mean I should be late? I can't refuse to go. I agreed to do the job."

"When the time comes, someone else will go in your place," Alison said quietly, something compelling in her voice prevented Ellen from challenging her.

She gave Alison a perplexed look, "You obviously have something in mind . . . ." She paused and thought for a moment. ". . . but you realize that my not going will probably only delay things momentarily."

"Actually, I don't have anything more than a delay in mind at the moment. The rest will come," Alison finished mysteriously.

Ellen gave a little grunt of misgiving, thought for a moment and relented. "O.K. I have to give you your chance to make whatever you have in mind work. Sure, I'll wait. I hope it won't be too much later."

The women poured themselves more coffee from the thermos pitcher on the wicker table in the center of the room. Clarissa went alone into the kitchen for a drink of water. She took her glass to the kitchen table, where she sat, her face covered by her hands, and silently prayed for guidance. It seemed to her, she told God, that there were all kinds of people here and none were wicked, just misled. Two of them were not even part of the witch-business at all but had come for their own reasons. Just as she had. They had not withdrawn. They had calmly and candidly stated their positions. Shouldn't she do the same? Must she make a speech? It seemed kind of melodramatic in view of the others. She thought about the abortion issue that Bernie had brought up. That was upsetting and yet there were Catholics who felt a woman who was pregnant should have the right to choose for herself. Then there was the whole issue of women who had been raped or who were victims of incest. How awful . . . . Her head was spinning.

Rachel is my friend, after all, she decided after a moment more. I am in her home. Besides, she'll be furious if I try to put a stop to this. I could leave it up to the group–just as Grace did. She wondered fleetingly what Father Donahey would tell her to do. Upstairs there was a crash. Clarissa heard a cry from Grace in the living room.

"Oh, damn, it's Increase. He's probably broken something." Grace rushed up the stairs to find a small window screen, the sort that fits under a raised window, lying on the floor. The window was open, the cat was gone.

"Of all the things to happen right now," Grace said aloud to herself.

"What is it?" Rachel called starting up the stairs.

Grace picked up the screen and reinserted it into the window. "The cat got out. He knocked the screen down as he jumped. That's all. Didn't break anything."

Rachel arrived in the room. "Those little screens don't stay in securely. I'm not surprised it fell, only that it didn't go out the window with him."

"He has a way of pulling on things rather than pushing," Grace explained apologetically. "It's a good reason why I need to get him de-clawed. I'm sorry, Rachel. I'm afraid I should go look for him."

"Why don't you let him go until he gets hungry. You have until tomorrow afternoon, after all. If he doesn't show by then, I can always bring him back with me to Portland and keep him till you can come and pick him up. I love cats, and it would give you an excuse to visit Portland again." She smiled.

"I'm sure he'll hang around here," Grace said, knowing Rachel meant what she said. "I guess it's all right, then, to just let him prowl. He's so accustomed to being inside these days, I can't believe he won't be wailing to get back in within five minutes."

Father Donahey had felt the full force of the Devil's heavy body on his head, the claws tearing away at his wig which came down over his face in a suffocating and blinding moment. Then there was a thud and some scrabbling in the rose bushes. All that was left was the wig, impaled on some thorns. There was no clue as to the Devil's whereabouts.

Father Donahey, snatched the wig and crawled away as rapidly as his poor knees would allow, no longer concerned about discovery. Minutes later, when he had composed himself and could breath without gasping, he realized that no further attack was imminent. They had won this round. Standing just inside the protection of a wooded area at the edge of the lawn, sweaty and trembling, he saw the need to seek cover. He began to run unsteadily in the general direction of the RV, holding his skirt in one hand, clutching his shawl with the other. He turned his ankle and cursed his women's shoes as he stumbled on.

He had sustained several wounds on his forehead from the attack and was bleeding profusely. His shawl, already ruined from the rose briars, caught again, this time in a pile of dead twigs and branches. He snatched at it impatiently, leaving threads behind. He saw that the thing had begun to unravel.

Rachel and Grace returned downstairs to find everyone settled into their places. When she saw they were seated, Clarissa began tentatively, "I am a Catholic. I believe that witchcraft is evil, especially if practiced knowingly. I see that you've misunderstood what Christianity is all about, and I can't really think you mean to do harm personally; still, I think it's my duty to tell you. Paganism is destructive, not helpful. Wicked. If you try to use magic, or whatever it is witches do, you'll end up being very sorry."

She looked deeply troubled, Rachel thought, and was suddenly swept with compassion for her friend. It was not her fault that she believed the way she did. Each person had to make her own spiritual journey with or without the sanction of society. She, herself, since the loss of her child, had always been a renegade, always chosen a different path. Leaving home and her parents behind as she had, and choosing to remain single in a world of couples had both been important and difficult choices. With a little twinge of pity for herself and Clarissa she realized that both of them had long endured the attitudes of people who looked at unmarried women over fifty as old maids or spinsters. We do have some things in common, she granted. Clarissa was doing what she thought right even though it was unpopular in this group. That took courage. Just as much as it took for Rachel, herself, to become a witch. If only she could explain that to Clarissa.

Clarissa continued falteringly. "I'm sort of a captive in a sense–as a guest of Rachel's, but it's also true I knew what she was planning when we came here. At first I was concerned and then, well, I just sort of dismissed the idea that it could become serious. I hadn't really thought it through–that is, how people involved in witchcraft might think or behave. I mean I've been warned by the church to watch for Satan, and there are cults I'm sure, but when Rachel explained to me about the women who were accused of witchcraft in the early days, and how easily a woman could be misidentified as a witch, that was the way I began to think of it, as a misunderstanding of sorts.

"And truthfully, I just thought this would be another little adventure of Rachel's. Rach is always having adventures," she added, not without affection. She smiled weakly then solemnly persevered with her task. "But, I can't say I've thought about the business of capital punishment and war and environmental issues in the same light as abortion." She hesitated. "I do know I can't possibly agree with what's been said about Christianity here tonight. Catholicism's been a positive and peaceful force in my life and I don't know what I'd do without it. I couldn't deny God, the Father, as you have done here." She gestured with a trembling hand.

The group watched her and listened intently. No one, she knew, would argue with her, and that knowledge was a great consolation. Her trembling subsided. Rachel, she thought thankfully, had set the guide lines for good manners. That was something of a miracle and to Rachel's credit.

She recalled the meal they had just eaten together, also a point in Rachel's favor. She had brought them altogether to break bread, to share good, healthy food (even Rachel admitted that the eggplant was delicious). How could people who knew about proper diet, who nurtured their bodies, so neglect their souls? It didn't make sense. They'd eaten the tofu and loved it. She looked at their faces and simply could not see any harm in the expressions there. She knew it was a sign of weakness, her need for friendship, but somehow the fact that these women shared a meal with her, a good meal, made them better people, not really Godless, after all. And Rachel. Well, Rachel was Rachel. She'd get through this one somehow. She had before . . . .

"If you want me to leave, I will. I would like you to decide as you did for Grace. I can't partake in any ceremony you might have, but I can stay and . . . and observe if that's all right with everyone."

Alison caught Clarissa's inner thoughts. It was easy to understand how food had become a measure of all things important in her life. There were so many ways of starving to death spiritually. The magic of good food worked to bridge distances, to provide time and space and ceremony as well as sustenance of the most important kind. It could serve as salvation from loss of face as well as loss of life. Think of all the ceremonial meals shared by diplomats and heads of state—an indispensable part of all great peace treaties, and wedding feasts, even wakes for the dead—the Last Supper. Food was evidence that life went on. Catholicism used bread and wine as communion to bridge the gap between god and humanity. Clarissa used her health food.

"Does anyone object to Clarissa's staying on to observe our work?" Alison asked gently, breaking the silence.

"Clarissa, I want you to stay," Rachel said persuasively firm, and then turned to the others. "She's been a great help to me on this trip. I really couldn't have done it without her. She is my old friend after all, and although she has never approved my scheme from the beginning she went along, because of her concern for me. I understand now that this asks too much of her.

"I hope, Clarissa," she said and looked her friend in the eyes, "that you will join us if and when you feel you can." She felt a lump in her throat and stopped talking.

Clarissa nodded her head gratefully, relieved that Rachel had not lashed out at her.

Bernie hurried to add her support. "Hey, I think that if Rachel is comfortable, the rest of us certainly ought to be. We can all have differences about important issues like abortion."

"Right," Ann said, and Solange echoed her.

"I feel happy that you are willing to stay on. You certainly have a right to your own beliefs," Grace said to Clarissa, who felt the generosity of each woman's words as a great gift.

Almost an after thought, Ellen added her vote. "I'm sure you must know it's okay with me. You've already heard how I feel about all this."

Alison was the remaining voice to be heard. She felt the group had finally arrived at a stopping place where they could now focus on the initial reasons for being together. "Clarissa, we welcome you here as a witness to the fact that we will harm no one. We have broken bread together, shared our food. You are right that is it a way of knowing about people."

Clarissa was astounded at the accuracy of that statement. In fact, she had never put it in quite that way herself, but it was something she would have liked to have said. How wonderful to be understood without needing to say anything at all.

Alison continued, "None of us here is evil–nor misled, just misunderstood. You, as a representative of the Catholic Church, can attest to what happens here tonight. Perhaps you will better understand after we have finished that there are many ways to do good work, and that we are, in fact, only human, not in any way possessed by some fiendish cabalistic force. I would like you to stay."

Clarissa understood that what Alison said was not a request, but an expectation. Strangely, she felt soothed by the knowledge that she would stay. "I will," she answered and knew that she had said enough. She looked around the room and every woman was smiling at her.

"That's settled, thank goodness," Rachel declared happily and nodded at Clarissa.

There was a silence that Alison allowed to build into suspense as everyone waited for her to begin her own introduction. "I am thirty-five years old and a single woman. I have begun a career in arbitration at the district courthouse part time. To supplement my income, I also cook, as you know, for Clovis–

do some housekeeping for her. I am working to earn enough money to go to law school." She paused and then said softly, "It may seem incongruous to you, but I am, above all, a witch. Since you've come to find out about witchcraft I will help you learn. Some of you may have made some assumptions about witches–based on the stereotypical witch of fairy tales and films. I would like to expand a bit, shed a little light if I can–in particular, on the myths about witches as evil beings who sell their souls to a devil. There are cults where that kind of thing might be attempted, but it is not the neopaganism of which I am a part.

"The witches I work with are recreating religion in new forms even while honoring what has gone before. They learn what they can from the past. Depending on who the practitioners are, all possibilities exist for positive experiences. Tonight there will be women building bonfires or erecting moonhuts all over the countryside, women creating new symbols for their work, or preparing to present new music or poetry to celebrate the Summer Solstice. In many covens there are men, and sometimes children, who join them, who cooperate to bring about beneficial changes on the earth. These people do not in any way resemble characters you may have seen or read about in horror movies or novels, nor do they resemble people who gather together to torture other people or animals in the name of the devil. None of that has anything to do with neopaganism as I know it. As a witch, I am here to demonstrate what the Craft is really like."

The women were riveted to their seats. One of them sighed and it was as if everyone sighed collectively.

"About the search for a coven. There is no coven here. Tonight, you will enter what is known as a 'grove.' Generally, only initiated witches are admitted to a coven. If you are interested there will be time for that later. The most important thing for you to know is that witches join together in veneration and love of nature. The earth is the manifestation of the Goddess–or the mother of god, if you wish. Witches are rooted in the earth, concerned about the environment. In contrast to the Judeo-Christian ethic that all too often allows its practitioners to look the other way when people exploit our planet, and which sets men and women against nature and against each other, we work to get in touch with our own biological rhythms and with other natural rhythms of the cosmos. One more thing. To those of you with a scientific mind set, it may be difficult to conceive of magic as anything but sham or child's play. In witchcraft, magic has more than one function. The first is mystical in nature, the second, equally important, is a kind of dynamic synthesis of all a group's positive energy focused on a task.

"That is, brainpower, both affective and cognitive, incorporated with the spiritual to do good works. We call on the skills as well as the knowledge of our members. The Craft is as practical as carpentry, nursing, gardening, engineering, teaching . . . .

"Sometimes it works. Sometimes it doesn't. But all talents, all the creativity of the persons involved are incorporated into our work. Witchcraft is not limited to circles in the moonlight. That is part of it–a ritual for showing our respect for the four elements: earth, air, water, fire, and for announcing our intentions, and for centering ourselves so that we can move out into the world. Our goals are to prevent harm if we can, to heal what has been damaged if we can't prevent the damage, to preserve and nourish the riches of the earth, and finally to create new positive ways of sharing and being fully present in the moment."

She paused to take in each woman's wide-eyed wonder, understanding that they were under the sway, not of The Craft, but of their own misperceptions of it as well as their own mystical hunger. Most probably they believed she was weaving a spell, and in a way she was. If she were to describe what was happening, in psychological terms, tell them of the power of their expectations, they would be intrigued, perhaps, but disappointed. That was understandable. They longed for the mystery in their lives again. Their own religion had somehow failed them. Otherwise they would not be in search of something to take its place.

"Join with me tonight," she entreated them, "and we will focus our energies, use all the creativity given us by the Goddess, the Earth Mother." She stood gracefully, her red hair seemed brighter in the now darkening room. She spoke softly, "It's time to begin. The moon is rising. Let me have an hour alone by the water first. Then follow me. Bring whatever you like and come to the shore. Use your torches to light the way. They will invoke the power of the east. May it be well with you."

They understood that she was blessing them and they watched as she turned and left through the little hall and out the front door. Rachel had said nothing about torches, but she was beyond questioning how Alison could know. She simply went to the kitchen and pulled them out of the shopping bag where she had stored them behind the door.

Bernie found matches and the group filed outside, curiously silent to sit on the lawn, murmuring to each other in the darkness. There was no sign of the moon.

Eventually Solange suggested that they light the torches. "How appropriate that the Sun Angel should be the one to preside," Ann said caught up in the ceremony as Solange struck a match and went from wick to wick.

Rachel replied enigmatically, "Yes. Perhaps more than you realize."

Ann shot her a curious look, but Rachel's face, only dimly illuminated by the fire of the torches, offered nothing more. She motioned to the women to walk, and calling over her shoulder, "This way, down the path beside the roses," she began the procession.

"We'll go out to the very edge of the peninsula–along the beach–the easiest way," she told Bernie who was next in line, and they passed long rows of cord wood stashed between trees, walked through a field of wild blueberries and eventually stepped down onto the beach. The water was still and silent. Not a ripple was visible on its dark glass surface. They could see no lights on the distant shore; the skyline was barely perceptible over the water. They neared the point of land where huge granite rocks jutted upward, seeming to float in black water. Suddenly a fire blazed upward in front of them. The formation of tree limbs and branches piled together showed as the light spread through them, and then there was only the fire itself and its mirror image spreading towards them on the water. To the side, standing on the shore, Alison waited.

"Stake your torches in a large circle and then join hands inside that circle."

People experimented with the placement of their torches in the sand until each one stood independently. It was an impressive sight. The women moved inside of the moving light and joined hands.

"Look," Ellen said, glancing back over her shoulder towards the island. "The moon."

It was huge, a deep yellow, bigger than their bonfire, bigger than any light and it was sitting on the top of white pines and birches as if someone had planned it for their amazement.

"Alison," Ann said unable to hide her thoughts, "you did that. You put the moon up there." There was a great gust of laughter releasing them from what seemed almost a stereotypical Halloween setting for witches. Ann's joke made them comfortable again, gave them the freedom to express whatever came to mind.

Alison walked behind them on the outside of the circle. She sprinkled salt and water as she went, murmuring incantations that they could not quite catch. That completed, she stooped and picked up wreaths of sweet pea vines, placed one on her head, and carrying the others in her arms, she stopped and placed one on Rachel's head solemnly then moved on until she had crowned each of the women.

Only Clarissa remained outside the circle. Rejecting her wreath, she sat on a rounded granite rock.

There was a moment of silence as the women looked at each other, the light of the torches slanting across their faces.

"Face west," Alison said, and the women turned toward the water and the small outer islands, beyond which lay an invisible mainland. As they did so, Alison raised her arms, crying out, "May the power of this water, the sea before us, be with us tonight. May the tides turn to help us."

Bernie felt dramatic and giddy and said, "Ho."

Clarissa, stolid on her rock, wondered what "Ho" could possibly mean. The only thing she could think of was a com-

mand to a horse. She suppressed her own desire to laugh.

"Turn to the north," Alison said, and they did. She said, "May the air be temperate. May the winds speed us on our tasks."

Bernie decided she liked the way she'd sounded before and added another "Ho." Ann squeezed her hand in warning, but even as she did Ellen added her own "Ho."

"It's all right," Bernie whispered to Ann. "Keep it light."

"Isn't that irreverent?" Ann whispered back. Bernie nodded.

Clarissa seeing the two girls whisper, thought, I see. This is girl's camp. They're having a ball. She had a momentary wave of loneliness, the way she felt as a child whenever she'd been left out of a game.

"Turn to the east," Alison instructed. They turned to face the bright moon. "May the energy of the rising sun support us and give us strength to grow. May the light of the moon inspire and guide us through our fears and the darkness of night."

Suddenly Rachel spoke. "May we realize our desires. May we be of help to others." This was her dream come true. This was what she had been waiting for, and in some strange way she felt closer to the church than she had in years.

"Ho," Bernie said again, and Rachel was momentarily annoyed.

"Turn south," Alison said, raising her hands in that direction. "I call upon the Goddess of Earth for direction. May she be with us tonight as we gather our strength, as we find our sustenance from the Earth to be her champions."

There was silence and then Bernie added her final "Ho," reminding everyone of Santa Claus. There was a smothered giggle, and Alison turned to smile at Bernie.

"Laughter is welcome in The Craft. We try not to take ourselves too seriously."

She turned back and continued, "The circle is now open. This is the time for song, poetry, statements of concern. We have admitted the powers that be, and now we do our work. What will you have?"

"You tell us," Grace said to Alison. "We've never done this before."

"That's all right," Alison replied. "Each person does what she needs to do." She paused and then seeing that the women were still waiting for her, she said, "All right. Let's sing. The words are simple–a kind of chant which describes our connection to the earth." She began, "We all come from the Mother and to her we shall return . . . ." and then they were joining her, singing the ancient chant, circling, bowing, weaving together.

When the song had slowly faded away, Ann said, "I have a poem I'd like to share," and she pulled a scrap of paper from her pocket. "I wrote this when I was part of a really successful project where a kind of magic was at work. For a while, everyone really cared about each other, and they made good things happen. It feels right to read it here:

Electric, we shall sing
Essential change.
Renewed, we, too
Are messengers.
Our Delphic delirium
Commands these stones
To speak
Their granite grievances.
Sea-wind and spring
Should answer them,
Shall fire unmoving
Stones to dance
With our delight.

"Beautiful, Ann," Grace said. "You are a poet. It sounds like it was written just for us–and for this beach, these stones. That has to be a kind of magic."

Ann smiled shyly in acknowledgement.

"Then let's put the magic to work. Let's focus on someone that needs our help," Bernie said enthusiastically.

"I say we should vanquish the people who would destroy this island as it presently is," Rachel said, waving her arm dramatically towards an invisible enemy, her bracelets jangling. "Throw the developers out."

"Onward," Solange said, delighting Bernie and Ann who had not seen Solange in such an expansive mood for months. She continued, apparently unaware that they were amused. "We've heard Ellen speak of these people, these developers who would take away the land and use it for purposes which can only destroy the environment, the quality of life here. We've all sensed from the beginning, haven't we, that there might be something for us to focus on here?"

Rachel said, "Yes, but how do we do it? It doesn't seem that prayer–or whatever it is we're doing here–is enough. If I say vanquish it sounds so medieval as if we were knights in shining armor. But I'm also a practical person. I know we can't just cast a spell–not in this day and age. And we are also against violence. How does witchcraft approach a problem like this?"

All eyes turned to Alison.

"There are many ways, and I wouldn't necessarily dismiss the idea of spells–you might just want to use a more modern word. Spells have their place in the scheme of things, but let's begin at the beginning. I will ask each of you to offer your own particular help when the time comes. Out of your offerings rest assured a plan of action will evolve."

"Let's do that then," Ann said. "I don't think we're real clear on exactly what it is we want to work on yet, but we are philosophically–or should I say spiritually, in agreement with Rachel."

"I certainly am." This was from Grace, even after promising herself she would stay out of things.

Clarissa was now thinking how harmless it all seemed. Where exactly was the evil, she wanted to know? Suddenly she was sorely tempted to join the circle, but she saw no way of doing it.

"After we close the circle," Alison said, "we'll begin our next phase. We must seal our intent with one more ritual. Will someone sing for us?"

Solange had never sung publicly, but she was hardly surprised to find Alison looking at her with anticipation. She closed her eyes and began to sing. The sounds came from her as if she had known they were there–sweet and strong. Her voice rang out with the words of a folk song that seemed appropriate to her, one she had loved for years. "Blackbird singing in the dark of night . . . ." Her voice was both eerie and comforting, soft and harsh. Rachel turned away to stifle her own inner song that insisted not only the melody was familiar, but also the voice.

When Solange ended her song, Alison took up the opening chant and the group joined in. This time even Clarissa sang and the circle opened for her so that she could join them. When their voices faded away there was only the lapping of the incoming tide.

Looking down they saw the water almost at their toes. "Hey, we're going to have to swim home," Ann said, laughing.

Alison broke in, "Time to leave. Let's return to the house where we can begin the work. I've brought my magic tools. I want you to see what they are." She raised her hands for the last time and everyone waited. "We thank you for being with us, oh Spirits. Follow us when we close this circle. Guide us in our work. Blessed be. May it be well with us."

"Ho," Bernie said, and this time it seemed like "amen."

As the circle broke up, each woman took her torch and doused it in the water. The bonfire, now totally surrounded by the fast-moving tide, would shortly die. Since the beach was flooded, they cut back over the rocks. Stumbling and grunting, they scrambled over steep unfamiliar terrain overshadowed by towering trees. Finally they were back in the familiar blueberry field behind the house with the moon to guide them.

Alison, who had arrived in the kitchen before the rest, seemed a different woman from the one who had worn a wreath in her hair just moments ago. The others self-consciously laid their own wreaths aside.

"Ah," Ann said, observing the newsprint and easel, "a facilitator in a negotiation meeting. An arbitrator at work."

"Right." Alison said. "Magic."

Ann said. "I need to talk to you. I'd love to get into this kind of work–do something like this . . . ."

"Great. I'd be glad to talk to you about it later," Alison replied. "But for now," she was all business, "would everybody take a seat around the kitchen table? There are pens and paper available if you want to take notes, but I will also record everything as we go along–up here," she gestured to her easel, "where everyone can see and comment."

Could I have asked for a more spectacular case study, or what, Grace thought happily. Who would believe that witches combine ritual with the rational, deck themselves with flowers, and then settle down to do problem-solving in the kitchen? She heard the click of her tape recorder and leaned over to replace a filled tape.

She was smiling when she looked up to see Alison eyeing her. "I was thinking . . . ," she said, apologetically as if she knew what was coming.

Alison grinned. "I know. It is a strange combination–this mix of magic and method, especially for the rational mind, the uninitiated, but eventually you'll begin to see that it's a natural, confluent process. Remember I said we use whatever talents our members have. I hope you'll see that shortly. Now . . . ," she looked at the others to include them, "I'd like everyone's attention. We are going to begin our strategy session. We have to work hard because time is short. The first thing needed is to define carefully and thoroughly what the problem is.

"Ellen, this is your area of expertise. We need you to review for us in more detail, if possible, the problem as you see it."

Ellen was surprised, but entered into the new mode readily. "At the risk of repeating myself, let me just summarize. Developers are the problem. There are presently three, but one is worse than the other two–name of Jack Russell. His company had bought up a lot of land here for resale. They circumvent the local ordinances whenever it pleases them. The others, a husband and wife who are arriving here with him tonight seem to be–oh, I don't know–uninformed, I guess would be the nicest way to put it. I rather suspect they haven't taken the time to find out what their associate is up to. He is a partner in Logan-Russell Corporation, a powerful company which has been buying up land all over Maine–actually all over New England. He has no intentions of living here, and the couple he's bringing with him are thinking that condos would be just the ticket, although they say they want to spend time here, but what that means is, maybe one week or two a summer, if that much. You know how this share-a-condo things work.

"We have no way to keep them out or to control their plans. They are rich and powerful. They have lawyers. We do have a town lawyer who is not on a salary, but rather has to be paid by the hour. Needless to say the town can't afford many hours. Logan-Russell have already created havoc with sewage and slash.

"The worst part though is that their money looks awfully good to some people on the island–workers who have been promised jobs. It's bribery and there is no guarantee they'll actually get the work."

She paused, then added, "The people here have been brow-beaten by the man. They could go along with whatever is presented tonight, partly because he's a fast talker and knows the intricacies of zoning law and partly because they feel pressured to act. Is that enough?" she asked looking depressed.

Alison finished writing furiously everything she could of Ellen's description on the newsprint clipped to her easel. As she filled up the first paper, she tore it off and handed it to Rachel who taped it on the wall opposite Ellen.

"All right. Any questions for Ellen before we move on?" There were none. The women heard the urgency in Alison's voice and understood the necessity to keep working.

"We've seen what the problems are, the negative forces that are at work. What would be the best way for the island to take care of itself–say, if there were no developers, if they could in effect, take their time and do it right? Everyone, now. Let's idealize, allow our imaginations to run free. We'll build a description here of what the ideal would look like–trying to include the needs of all the islanders, not just our own idea of personal paradise. Mind, I'm not claiming that we know what's best for the islanders. That would be as bad as Jack Russell, coming in here and buying up the land without regard for their interests.

"No, what we want here is to imagine what it would be like to live on this island. Pick someone–a lobsterman, a school girl, a store clerk, a carpenter, a house wife, a retired person–and think the way he or she would think about land, water, school, whatever. We've got Ellen, after all, to keep us on the track, and Rachel, too. This is her place. She's been coming here for years as a summer person. It's not as if we have no one to remind us if we're being outrageous. Still, the reminders, as such, should come later. For now, I want you to let yourself imagine the perfect. We'll get to the criticism and the practicality later. For the short time of this exercise the rule is: dream your most imaginative and daring dream and refrain from stepping on someone else's dream. Got it?"

The women began calling out suggestions one at a time. As they did so Alison wrote them down, then posted them on the wall where they could look at the list as it grew: Keep things the way they are. Call a moratorium for a year or two to give the island time to plan. Buy shore land to give access to the people who've lost their shore property. Hold down taxes. Build affordable low-income housing on the waterfront. Change local property tax laws so people on fixed incomes get a break. Reserve more areas of shoreline for public swimming, boating, walking and biking. Restrict numbers and kinds of new homes built. Set aside a wilderness preserve. Design a tougher sewage and waste disposal law. Save historical landmarks. Provide a variety of ways for people to earn a living which will not destroy the island.

They slowed down after the first flurry of suggestions. Alison prompted them, "All right. That's a good list. You're doing very well, but some of those suggestions need expansion. We need to look at opportunities for people to earn a living here on the island–ways which would be beneficial both to the islanders and the island itself."

When Father Donahey reached the RV, he was totally exhausted. The sweat dripped from his chin. He yanked the wig from his head, loosened the laces of his borrowed British Walkers, and plucked the annoying things off his feet. He said ten "Our Fathers." By then he was cooler. For good measure he said ten more. He held out a hand, and saw that he wasn't trembling anymore. Placing the rosary onto the table he stood up.

"I've had all I can take of this. I'll have a shower," he said aloud, stepping clumsily out of the skirt. He unbuttoned the blouse and shrugged it off. Leaving both pieces of clothing on the floor, he stepped over them.

I'll feel better, he thought, entering the tiny bathroom cubicle in his underwear, when I put my own clothes back on. Then I'll go back to that house and make it known what I think of their unholy activities. He crossed himself and began to search for a towel. There was no room for a towel rack in the small enclosure. A poor design, but what would you expect of an RV? He went out and opened the closet and rummaged through Alison's clothes. A book fell to the floor. He picked it up and saw the name "Starhawk" on the cover. The girl was into astronomy, he thought absently. Tossing the book aside hurriedly, he continued his search for a towel. Only clothes were stored there. He slammed the door to the closet and moved to the kitchen area. He pulled out several drawers and finally found two terry cloth dish towels. They'll have to do, he thought dejectedly.

In the bathroom, he searched for a clue to the workings of the shower. Alison had said something about switching on a hot water tank, but he expected she'd taken care of that already. He looked for the switch anyway, and couldn't find it. He pulled the shower curtain to one side. It slid easily in a track that went above the window, around and over the door. That was funny. There was a lot of curtain, but no shower stall? Disappointed, he decided to wash up at the tiny bathroom sink. Confused by the unusual number of faucets, he turned one and got only cold water. He turned another and icy water poured on his head. What in God's name? The blasted room was raining. He was in his underwear and soaked. He leapt out of the cubicle as the water poured after him onto the floor of the RV. He reached one arm into the bathroom trying to avoid getting any wetter. He fumbled with the faucets and hot water poured down, scalding his shoulder, arm and hand. The RV was a lethal trap! He tried one more time and managed somehow to turn both faucets off.

Letting out a sob he turned away from the flooded bathroom. As he did, his right foot hit a stream of water flowing from under the door. With a yelp Father Donahey skidded crazily across the floor catching the other foot in the discarded blouse and skirt as he went. With a terrible crash he landed on his hands, knees and then the side of his face.

Stunned, he tried to stand, but the pain was incredible. He collapsed howling. This was no ordinary pain. Something was terribly wrong in this place. It was booby trapped. The water and his fall had been no accident. A demon was most certainly present. From now on, he would have to watch every step. His pain subsided somewhat and he made another effort to stand. Determining that he had no broken bones, Father Donahey moved gingerly, grabbing the skirt and blouse off the floor. They were slightly damp but salvageable. Hanging them up over the bathroom door to dry, he wiped his face with one of the two towels.

It was then he realized his face was beginning to swell. He went to look in the mirror. Holy Mother! He touched the place and cried out. Where his eye had been was a slit surrounded by an amazingly huge swelling, a multi-colored melon.

He hobbled, moaning, to the kitchen, where he dislodged two half empty trays of ice cubes from the small freezer compartment of the refrigerator. He emptied what there was into the sink and wrapped the ice in the remaining dishtowel. He must pack the eye quickly before he dressed. Looking around for something to put on while he treated his injury, he remembered he'd seen Alison's bright purple kimono in the closet. He wrapped it around himself quickly feeling comforted by its warmth.

He decided to pray while he worked on the eye. "Dear God," he said aloud, "I'd kneel but I might never get up. I've got to do something to protect myself. Maybe it's too late. If I could drive this RV, I'd be out of here, but I need instruction." He saw the futility of that kind of request of God and said so. He did not want God to think he was an idiot, not when he needed Him the most, but where could he go on the island that was safe anyway? People would never understand. They would think he'd been in a fight. Well, he had. But what Protestant would believe that he'd been in a fight with the devil? And he certainly knew no Catholics on the island, nor did he know the location of a church where he might take sanctuary. Here, they probably thought all the Irish were scrappers and booze hounds. Thinking of that, he realized a drink was what he needed.

"Forgive me, Father," he intoned, and then more conversationally, "I forgot I was praying. I'm at the mercy, it seems, of Satan."

Suddenly he understood that he himself might be possessed. The thought at once terrified and thrilled him. This was the price of going on a jaunt without the Bishop's blessing. He had been taken unawares, before he could do anything about it. When he rose to dump the melting ice pack into the sink, his knees hurt him so badly that he cried out again. He did his best to find the materials he had packed for exorcism. Was there a selection, he wondered, for self-exorcism? That sounded blasphemous, but if it was true that he was possessed, only the Lord knew what would happen next. He prayed for forgiveness and placed himself in God's hands. May you win out over The Beast, he said desperately, as he shuffled through his bag and took a double shot of the whiskey he had brought with him.

He searched his texts. There must be something to stop this onslaught. Everything he touched turned against him. He would not have been surprised to find rats or snakes pouring out of his holy books. "Oh, Jesus," he yelled, half crazy. "This is terrible, terrible. I need help."

There was a knock on the door. He jumped and the pain returned tenfold. Nothing but more bad luck that someone should knock at that moment, unless–unless God was answering his prayer. Even then, he hardly wanted to see anyone in his present state, not Alison and certainly none of those women. If he didn't answer, whoever it was might go away. Another knock, more urgent this time and a man's voice, "Are you all right in there?" He must know someone was inside. Father Donahey pulled Allison's kimono around him defensively and responded, "Yes," in falsetto tones, "Yes,

I'm here." He snatched up the wig and crushed it down over his head. Looking wildly about him, he saw that the room was a mess. Too late to clean it up.

"It's Captain Harrigan," the voice said. "I heard a cry for help, thought someone might be hurt."

Mother of God, what were the police doing here on this small island? No policeman would ever believe his story, but he had to answer. Perhaps allowing someone else inside would chase away the evil spirit.

He opened the door a crack to see a man who was not in uniform but rather casually dressed in dungarees and a flannel shirt.

"My God, you have been hurt! I was right to knock. I was wondering what the RV was doing here to begin with, but I decided to walk on by. Then I heard you cry out." Father Donahey cursed himself for his loss of control.

"You got yourself a real . . ." the man began sympathetically.

Father Donahey cut him short, not wanting to hear the words from someone else. Instead he said them himself. Forgetting his falsetto, he croaked angrily, "That's right. I've got a shiner. I slipped on the wet floor as I was about to take a shower."

The man looked puzzled. The old gal had a strange voice, similar to a boy going through puberty. She also looked remarkably like a frog. Even with her swollen cheek, one little eye popped out at him. The shiner was an awful one.

"Have you got anything for the pain?" he asked kindly. He was thinking of how he treated his own ailments. A stiff shot or two almost always took care of anything. "I've got some hair of the dog, ah, whiskey, I mean," he corrected himself quickly. "Back at the bunkhouse. By the by, I'm Captain Harrigan, pilot of the J. R. Higgins, the ferry which serves the island. I live by the ferry terminal. I could get you a spot of something, if it would help . . . . Actually you look a little shocky to me. You could use a drink."

At last a blessing. An Irishman to the rescue. Hair of the dog sounded perfect to Father Donahey. Truly a miracle. But here was a predicament. The man thought he was an old lady.

It wouldn't be proper to let him in. Ah, but this was an emergency.

"Oh, Captain," Father Donahey resumed his lady's voice weakly, "I'd be much obliged to you. My name is Clovis, er . . . Donahey. It's good to see an Irish face.

"Only too glad to oblige," the captain told Mrs. Donahey, and he went away to get the bottle.

"What shall I wear?" Father Donahey spoke aloud to himself again. "Should I put on my own clothes and tell him the truth? No, he'll be thinking I've gone mad. It's not becoming for a priest to go around impersonating a woman. If only he hadn't seen the wig and listened to me talk in that silly voice." He went through Alison's closet again in a frantic effort to find something to wear. It was no good. He'd have to put on the woman's outfit again, damp or not. Perhaps the captain would leave the bottle and go home.

Captain Harrigan had no intentions of leaving the bottle. He hated drinking alone, although as the relief captain, a man from the mainland, and single, he spent many lonely hours in the crew's quarters, some of them with only a bottle for company. Once in a great while, however, an evening was enlivened by an island woman, who he might say, liked a little entertainment.

"By heavens," he said politely to the person he now called Mrs. Donahey, "You're a brave thing managin' all on your own, like this. Is there no one with you? I could go and get someone to help you, if you want." He poured a drink for the lady and just as an afterthought, one for himself. "I'll join you, if you don't mind," he said hesitating, as if it weren't the thing he always said.

"Not at all," Father Donahey said hoarsely. It was not the best of situations, his sitting there in his damp underwear which had soaked through Alison's robe, yet it would have been a companionable arrangement otherwise. If only his feet were not so icy cold and his eye not throbbing.

"Actually," Father Donahey said, "I have a housekeeper with me. She's down at that house on Lily point," he gestured with his thumb, "visiting her friends. I don't want to disturb her right now. She'd get too upset." Well, a little lie for the time being wouldn't hurt.

"Strange kind of housekeeper who couldn't tear herself away to be of help to her employer," the Captain said angrily. "You're too easy on her. That's not the way to run a tight ship." Then he laughed and realized the little lady's one good eye was glaring at him. She didn't like anyone telling her what to do, he could see. He took a long swig of the whiskey straight. He felt its warmth move down into his very being. "Good stuff this," he remarked as a way of changing the subject.

"Very fine and I thank you," croaked the lady.

They were both feeling more comfortable with each other so words seemed less important. Yet they were strangers, after all, and Father Donahey felt obliged to make conversation. "I appreciate your kind gesture. I suppose you're a Catholic, are you?"

The Captain nodded agreeably. "Not what you'd call regular, Mrs. Donahey. I go when the mood hits me."

Father Donahey was irritated. God had sent him a lazy Catholic. He took another swallow of the whiskey and realized that the throbbing in his eye had subsided. "You're not worried for your soul, Captain Harrigan?" he said stiffly.

"Not a bit, little lady," was the reply. "I've sinned too long and too much to repent. No priest could clear the decks for me now. I'm a sure thing for Davy Jones." He laughed uproariously.

Father Donahey was not amused. "I'd think again if I were you. The devil's ways are not a laughing matter. Hell's fires are far worse than you can imagine."

Captain Harrigan knew he'd struck a sour note with a religious woman and he thought it best to smooth her ruffled feathers. "Ah, a good person like you has nothing to fear, I'm sure," he said, "and perhaps I'll go to confession, myself, one of these days."

"None too soon," the old woman asserted, and Captain Harrigan noticed a slight slur to her speech. He poured a drop more in the bottom of his glass and sat warming in his thoughts of past sins.

"None too soon," the old woman repeated and tipped her glass up for the last of the whiskey.

Noticing her empty glass the Captain leaned over and generously filled it to the top.

"Why thank you, sir," she said, and, warming to his kindness she took it and drank it down in one long gulp. "None too soon," she said, cackling strangely.

"Now, little lady," Harrigan said with genuine concern. "You've had a traumatic fall here. It wouldn't be good for you to take too much whiskey too fast. You might fall again."

"Not on your life," came the answer in the deeper voice he had heard earlier. "This is exactly what I need. It's giving me back my strength which I will shortly need."

Father Donahey was feeling quite fine by now. He cast aside his ice pack. Being a bit beyond his limit of three drinks, he was rationalizing now that he needed a few more in order to get on with an exorcism. Then he was struck with a thought. What if this fallen Catholic sitting right there before him was Lucifer himself? What if he was just another of the many works of the devil? Hadn't he just admitted he was a candidate for Davy Jones? Davy Jones was another name for the devil, after all. Even a child knew that. How could he have missed it? He must get this man out of here as soon as possible.

Captain Harrigan had missed the last part of what the lady said. He was so impressed with her ability to take her whiskey straight that he followed suit and poured them both another double shot. That done, he watched as Mrs. Donahey swigged her drink again. They had settled into serious drinking. Still, you never knew who your drinking partners might turn out to be on a place as God-forsaken as this island. Why he'd had a wonderful night with two lonely fishermen's wives only last winter during a helluva storm. They'd modeled their catalog-bought negligees for him while their husbands were away at a hearing about lobsters at the State House in Augusta. Grand it was. It was plain that there was no prospect tonight for that kind of thing. He would only stay until the bottle was empty. Still, looks aside, the old gal could hold her liquor; she was quite a woman.

"Don't you think we've got it all up there, now?" Bernie said, her eyes beginning to tire from squinting at the newsprint in the kerosene light.

"Well, perhaps not all," Ann mused. "This process can go on for a long time, but . . . ."

"We've got quite a bit to go on," Rachel interjected hopefully.

"Yes," Ann agreed, "and I think we ought to focus on one or two items–things we can act on now."

"What's the immediate problem?" Solange asked and stopped herself short. "Of course. We have to prevent the DEVELOPERS (she realized she'd been thinking of whoever it was in capital letters)–this Jack Russell and company from getting to the meeting tonight. That would: (a) give us time to figure out a better strategy, or (b) help the board figure out theirs."

"Whoa," Ellen said. "I'm not sure I can go along with not meeting them at all . . . and who knows if the planning board is going to welcome help from a group of . . . ." she hesitated to say witches. It did seem strange to be calling these articulate, intelligent women by a name that had such strong negative connotations.

"So we won't say we are witches," Rachel said, filling in the blank for Ellen. "Does anyone ask what your religion is in this country? Especially when you are offering to provide a public service? What's our next step?" Rachel asked. "Alison?"

"Well, we could decide on c) none of the above. I'd like to say that you certainly don't have to act on any of the suggestions." Everyone laughed, and she continued. "There is still plenty of time for Ellen to go and pick up the developers."

"Just a minute." Ann said. "Don't you think it really is a great idea to delay these people from reaching the planning board meeting tonight. I mean, why not?"

"Begins to look like I'm the only one that's holding up this plan," Ellen said, but she chuckled when she said it.

"Oh, all right. Detain them, temporarily. Is that what you are proposing?"

"Step One," Ann said happily as everyone nodded their heads. "Who is going to do the deed and how?"

Ellen glanced at her watch. "Time is getting short. Whoever it is had better start soon."

"Let's make up our minds then," Bernie said urgently.

"Who's going out there?" Solange asked.

"I'd love to," Bernie said. "I'll go out there, pull a spark plug and pretend the car has broken down or something."

Ellen said, "I can tell you how to take a road that circles around. You could keep on doing that–pretend to get lost. At night in particular, there are no easy landmarks. Then I'll come out and 'find' you after the meeting."

"But how can you turn up at the meeting without them? They're expecting you to be the chauffeur," Rachel asked.

Grace was unable to contain herself anymore. "Look. Say Ellen was here for a party. Something happened that caused her to be delayed. Her car had a flat, whatever . . . . One of the people at the party volunteered to go pick up the developers for Ellen. Then when Ellen is ready, she goes straight on to the meeting."

"But then," Bernie said, "if I don't show up in a reasonable amount of time, won't they send you or someone else out to find me? They'll figure I got lost."

"They might. We'll just have to take a chance," Ellen said seriously.

"God, this is getting complicated," Solange said. "Can't we just tell the board the developers decided not to come after all?"

"No way," Ellen said. "They're in touch by ship-to-shore radio on their yacht. They could call and check."

"Not once they're in our car, they can't," Bernie said.

"So, Bernie loses them somehow, then she returns without them, saying she couldn't find them," Ann suggested.

"That won't work either. Remember? Someone on the planning board would drive out there. The car will have to break down and Bernie will have to start walking or stay with them . . . to make it look real. We'll have to do some heavy talking at the meeting in the meantime," Solange said.

"Maybe the developers will be so annoyed they won't feel like dealing with island people anymore," Clarissa said naively.

"I wouldn't count on it," Ellen said. "It's true that they can easily afford to go elsewhere; still they've seen the land, at least one has, and now tonight by moonlight–that would clinch it for most people. They'll know a good thing when they see it."

"Just a minute," Solange said. Her face lit up with an incredible smile. "You're talking about people with money... well, talk to one now. Me!"

Their planning came to a swift halt and all eyes fastened on Solange.

"What are you saying?" Bernie asked.

"Remember that game we played this morning on the way here–the one where we bought the university, then zapped the people we didn't like that work there?"

"So?"

"Well, we can zap a few here."

"Solange," Ann said patiently, "That's what we're trying to do. Get on with it."

"I'll buy the land from them," Solange said happily, "and return it to the island."

"Christ," Bernie said. Except for Ann, the rest of the group looked totally dumbfounded.

"Be serious, Solange," Ann said.

"I am. I'll make an offer they can't refuse."

"The developers?"

"Sure. You make it hard for them, by helping the planning committee to stick with their guidelines and when the developers get fed up, I'll buy them out."

Ellen said, thoughtfully. "I didn't realize who we were dealing with here."

"Who did?" Alison said. "That's the way magic works sometimes. But hold on. Saying is not necessarily doing. Solange, you don't want to buy land without looking into it carefully. You should have a good attorney and lots of time to think this through. Even if the developers were interested in reselling the land without developing it, you might get into a bidding contest. They could end up getting at least double what they paid. They already jacked the price up once. You'd be defeating our whole purpose. If you buy the land at an inflationary price, land values here will skyrocket. You'd be doing exactly what we're trying to prevent the others from doing."

"Remember," Rachel said feeling responsible suddenly for this woman who she had been increasingly identifying as her long-lost daughter. "You spoke earlier tonight about using your money wisely. You owe it to yourself to take some time to learn what the possibilities are."

Solange was suddenly aware of what a rush of power felt like. It was as if she had taken off in an airplane in a dream and suddenly realized that she didn't know how to land. "I thought I had the answer," she said in a tired voice.

"Perhaps you do," Alison said. "Wait and see."

"In the meantime," Rachel said, "Let's try to convince the planning board to hold to their rules. If we can do that and keep the developers away from the meeting tonight, we'll have accomplished a lot."

Clarissa said, "I think that's a great plan."

"Me too," Ann echoed, "but what part will each of us play? What should we do?"

Clarissa could not hold back any longer. "Rachel's good with people, and she does own property here after all. She can speak as an older person, as well as represent some of the retired people."

Rachel shot Clarissa an appreciative glance and said, "I could do just that–speak in their behalf, plead with the planning committee to hold off. As Clarissa says, I am a taxpayer, even if they do think of me as someone from away."

"Will there be many people there tonight?" Grace asked.

"It's hard to say." Ellen said. "This is Saturday night don't forget. They seldom go to meetings anyway, but if there's nothing else to do, you never can tell. They might show up in droves. I'm sure that canceling out and coming late, like this, is part of the developers strategy to get things done when people aren't paying close attention."

The women let their minds run on idle for a moment, and then Ann said, "Alison, you could use your skills as an arbitrator to help the planning board."

Alison said, "Not without invitation, but if asked, I'd be happy to. And you could assist me."

Ann swallowed hard. "Oh, I don't know how good I'd be. I don't have the experience . . . ."

"That's all right . . . . You'd be working with me. Lots of arbitrators learn through apprenticeship. That's part of their training. You've already had courses in group dynamics and communications, right?"

"Yes, but . . ."

"No buts. If we have an opportunity to help out, you'll be my partner for tonight. We'll take our newsprint with us and show them the ideas here."

Ann couldn't help offering one more but. She said, "But do you think maybe you should start with blank paper and write stuff down as we talk? Maybe people will think we're being too pushy if they find out we've been working on this behind their backs."

"What do you think?" Alison asked Ellen.

"It's hard to say," Ellen replied, "but you need to catch their attention and keep it. If you take too long to get the information up on the board it may not work. I'd use the newsprint we already have here. I personally think it shows a lot of work. That may impress people enough to make them stop and think."

"Ellen," Rachel said, "you could introduce Alison and Ann."

Grace said, "Yes, that would keep it in the family–having you start first. We shouldn't volunteer solutions that aren't asked for though, or before there seems to be a need for help. They might feel as if you're usurping their power, interfering in their business." She smiled apologetically recognizing herself as an interloper, even as welcome as they had made her feel. It was almost too good to be true, she thought, being here, making friends with these women. A streak of superstition worked inside her now, the same one that made her knock on wood mentally whenever things were going her way.

"I can take those newsprint sheets to the meeting myself, Ellen suggested. "I've been known to do stranger things on this island than carrying paper and magic markers to a meeting . . . so they'll take it in stride if I show up with such things," she chuckled. "After I introduce you, I'll turn the paper over to you. That should help."

"But in this context . . . ?" Ann asked doubtfully, "won't it look as if it we planned ahead?"

Alison nodded. "Sure, but is that a bad thing?"

"Who knows?" Bernie said, seemingly untroubled by the ambiguity.

Ellen said. "It might be tricky, but let me worry about it. I know how they operate, and generally speaking they're distrustful of people from away. Experience has taught them to be that way, and I'm inclined to agree with them. They have watched people come here and buy land and right away want to pull up the drawbridge and keep everyone else from buying land. Outsiders also become arbiters of what is in good taste. They sneer at people who have to live in trailers–that kind of thing. Islanders are not any more naive than the rest of the world. In a way they are the world in microcosm. They have learned from experience about hardship and isolation. Some of them, at least, will be receptive to accepting my word that you have expertise to offer. Some won't. One thing I'm sure of. People know that I care about the future of this island."

"Sounds like you're the woman for the introductions, then," Bernie said approvingly.

"Now. Any other jobs that need doing? Any people without a task?" Alison prompted, beginning to see the need to get at the job.

"I think," Grace said, "that it makes sense for me to tape the proceedings–just go on doing what I am doing. Then we can go back over the tape later to see who said what."

"Terrific," Ellen said. "No one ever takes notes at these meetings. Just do it unobtrusively if you can. Sit by yourself–away from Alison and Ann."

By now Clarissa was feeling left out. She spoke hesitatingly, "I don't know what to say. There doesn't seem to be much that I can do . . . but I'd like to go to the meeting as an observer, anyway."

"No way," Bernie said. "I need you with me."

"Oh, my," Clarissa said, flushing. She was both delighted and embarrassed to have been singled out. "Yes, I could go along–but will there be room in the car for everybody?"

"You'll only be picking up three people," Ellen said.

"It's time to leave, right now," Bernie said rising from the kitchen table and shoving her chair in. "We'll plan how this is going to work on the way out. See you people later."

"Wait. I'll walk to the car with you–give you better directions," Ellen said. "I wouldn't want you to get lost."

Rachel called after them as they went through the door. "We'll meet here after the meeting to discuss results and next steps."

The planning board meeting was usually held weekly at seven p.m. in the school house, but this special meeting, called because of the Logan-Russell Corporation, was to start at the unheard of hour of ten-thirty. Waiting for the meeting to begin were Winner Brent, the First Selectman, middle-aged and gaunt-looking because of his unusual height, and two other selectmen, Lenny Jones, just turned thirty, and Bob Miller, a short muscular man in his late fifties with white hair. They stood around their pickups finishing their beer.

"Jesus, it's a helluva way to spend Saturday night," Bob said taking a long drag on his cigar.

"What was you doing with it so far?" Lenny said grinning. "Watching the tube or arguing with your old lady? Nothing good on tonight anyway–just re-runs, and you could use a rest from Darlene." He considered himself fortunate whenever he thought of Bob's wife. She was trouble. Living with her, he thought, was like living with a prickly cactus.

"We'll get this over quick enough," Winner said, noticing that Bob as usual ignored the remark about his wife. Lenny was insensitive to Darlene, a woman who had spent the last ten years in a wheelchair because of a car accident. "These developers get carried away, ya know," he continued. "All we gotta do is thank 'em and tell 'em we'll take their requests under advisement."

Lenny blinked and rubbed his crew cut. When Winner started his official talk, it confused him. Was he saying that things had to be finished tonight or not? They'd met before with the Logan-Russell Corporation, and he guessed they was getting twisted by these people with all their God-damned money. Still, island contractors planned on getting started clearing lots and building foundations the first of the month. Russell was supposed to start hiring Monday. A good number of fellahs here expected to get on the payroll. Himself included. Lenny grabbed a bunch of his sweatshirt and rubbed at his mid-section. Better take a bath when he got home. Sue Ann didn't like his sweat smell, she said, and Saturday night was his best chance to get in. Hell, it was his only chance. It was the one time she tied it on. Now this damn meeting had screwed things up. If they'd only cancel, he could get home before she passed out.

"So what's the hitch?" he asked. "Where is ever'body?"

Winner said, "Dunno." He shifted uncomfortably. "They'll be along in a minute. Big Shot Russell and the others is gettin' a ride in with Little Miss Muffet."

They all laughed at that. Ellen was not like an island woman, Lenny thought. She was always doing a man's work. It puzzled him why she would want to.

"Might'a said Monday," Bob offered, "but the plannin' board has other ways of seein' it. They got theirselfs worked up over a little shit might get into the water. You'd think they'd never used an outhouse. You'd think they never seen the ones on the shore opens right over the water. Where'd they think they was droppin' it all this time?"

Lenny guffawed. "They been haulin' lobsters and diggin' clams from the same water for years and nobody got sick. 'Cept for Martin, no one on that plannin' board ever hauled a thing 'cept maybe someone's ashes." Lenny cackled wildly at his own joke, and Winner, who was sensitive to jokes about sex, turned away.

"Can't talk no sense into the rest of them, no way," Len finished.

"That's not true," Winner said. "Martin's a good chair, and just 'cause the rest of them don't agree with you don't make them stupid."

Lenny shook his head. Winner made no sense at times. "So what do we do?" he said, getting restless and wondering if another beer might make things easier. "They're still fartin' around with their plans. We should set a fire under their bums. We done it before. Who makes the decisions, anyway?" It was puzzling him that Winner was shuffling his feet on this one. "We shoulda been done and over a month ago," he complained. The need for another beer overpowered him; he opened the door of his pick-up and reached in on the floor for another can. Snapping the top off, he flipped it away and took a swig. An unpleasant thought hit him. Maybe Winner was gettin' paid a little something on the side for this delay. No, somehow that didn't fit with Winner's ways.

Bob, too, was puzzled by Winner's seeming reluctance to step in. Usually he and Winner worked things out between them, then the two of them told Lenny what was what. If there was a real problem, Lenny always went with whatever they wanted. He wasn't all that sure of himself; still he could be convinced to come down on the right side, and stand solid with them whenever somebody questioned what was happenin'. That counted for a lot.

"Damn," Winner said, and his voice sounded forlorn. "We gotta begin enforcing them reg'lations sometime or they won't be worth the powder to blow 'em to hell."

Bob belched. "We been letting people get away with murder up to now. Them plans was always for the summer crowd. We never had 'em before, wouldn't a missed 'em if they had disappeared."

"Fact is . . . ," Winner said, leaning back on his pick-up hood solemnly, "fact is we got screwed a lot cause we had no zonin'. Nobody knows nothin' about boundary lines either. I'll be damned if I know where my own place ends on the east side. Deed says twenty degrees east of the apple tree north of the stone wall. Well, there ain't no apple tree. Ain't even a stump. And the stone wall's long sunk. Can't hardly see most of it. Deed was recorded back in 1840."

"Shit, you ain't gonna sell anyway, Winner," Lenny said. He was getting sleepy, but talk of boundary lines roused him. He was still trying to sell the house his mother had left him and every time he had a good customer, sooner or later they'd come to figuring the property lines. It was one of those things that couldn't be done. A number of smartass surveyors and lawyers had given it up for a bad cause. He was still waiting on the sucker who'd take a quit-claim deed and forget the matter. He was sure one would come along.

"No, I'm just sayin'," Winner continued, "we gotta start payin' attention to things like zonin' and property lines. We been movin' some fast. We're gonna wake up one foggy mornin' and the whole island will belong to the summer crowd."

"You sayin' you don't want ta do business with Logan-Russell?" Bob said growing concerned.

"Naw, it's not what I'm sayin'," Winner said. He flicked his cigarette ashes onto the playground between them. "We gotta stop lettin' people from away make decisions for us. Be good to take a breather here."

"Jesus, Winner," Bob said finding himself at odds for the first time ever with his friend. "What about all the guys waitin' for work? Plenty folks right about now need somethin' for the next five months or so, so's they'll be able to get through winter. Just because a body is old don't mean he don't need somethin' better than social security. Ain't enough, I tell ya."

"True," Winner said, sympathetically, "but like I said. They's two sides to this. Old man Swinson and Auntie Laurie, and a lotta other folks can't stay in their houses too much longer if taxes go up. And the old ones is not the only people in trouble. My son, Sam, and his wife and kids, they're havin' a hard time gettin' started. Fishin's been bad and they got back taxes already–plus interest. I don't wanna see them leave the island. This land deal has a double edge to it." He looked upset.

Bob saw the problem now. "Yeah," he answered more sympathetically. "But maybe Sam could get work with the Big Shot."

"Jesus, Bob," Winner said, losing patience. "Think beyond a paycheck will ya? Sam loves fishin'."

"There's Little Miss Muffet," Lenny said and he felt fuzzy as he swigged down the last of the warm beer. "She's got a car load'a people. Don't look like no Big Shot to me. All wimmin."

Winner did not recognize the people with Ellen. "Where's Russell?" he called over to her as she slid out of her van.

"I sent a friend to pick him up. I was at a party and my tire was flat when I came out. Thought it would be quicker. Didn't want to hold up the meeting." She approached his pick-up, the other women behind her. "Guess I was wrong to worry," she said with an engaging grin.

"Hey, Winner, this is Rachel." She tapped Rachel gently on the shoulder. "She owns the place at Lily Point."

Winner nodded. "Think I've seen you around."

"And this is Ann, Solange, Grace and Alison," she indicated, patting each on the arm.

"Pleased to meet ya," Winner said. Solange shook his hand, and so did Alison.

"These are the other two town selectmen," Ellen continued, "Lenny and Bob." She repeated the women's names one more time.

"Where is everybody?" she asked.

"Guess they don't like givin' up their Saturday night no more'n us, " Lenny grumbled. "They don't hurry and get here, I'm leavin'. Don't know about the rest." He glanced at his watch. "Five minutes," he said, then turned and went to sit in his pick-up.

"I guess I'll go in," Ellen said to Winner, who shrugged and smiled.

"Be in when I finish this," he said, gesturing with his cigarette.

The schoolhouse was a small square building of one story. Two classrooms opened up on each side of a short central corridor that ended in a small office. Ellen saw that the meeting was to be held in the second classroom on the left where a few people had already taken seats on the far side of the room. "This is the fifth and sixth graders' room," she told them as she waved a hand in greeting to the group across the room.

Rachel was delighted with the place. She and Solange wandered around looking at the student work displayed artfully on the walls. "This reminds me of my own grammar school. I didn't think they shared classrooms anymore," Rachel said wonderingly. They made their way to where Ellen was standing with Ann and Alison. Grace had moved off and taken a seat by herself.

"Most of the Maine islands still have small schoolhouses like this," Ellen said. "There are too few children to put in a room all by themselves, and besides they learn from each other–the older kids serve as tutors sometimes. When they finish eighth grade they have to leave the island for their high school years. Some commute daily, others board off island."

"Sad that they have to leave their homes so young. Their families must hate that," Ann said.

"This is a great room," Solange said, feeling nostalgic. "The children must feel welcome and loved. I liked grade school so much better than high school."

"Why was that?" Rachel asked realizing how little she knew about this woman. She had missed her own daughter's school years. It was all so confusing, being reminded of your own child who might be sitting somewhere talking like this to a stranger–and she, Rachel, would never know her, never see her.

"In grade school," Solange was saying, "the teachers were warm and loving–quite different from my foster mother who was not an affectionate person."

"Are you bitter?" Rachel asked wistfully, "about growing up in a foster home . . . ."

"Well, it wasn't always pleasant, and sometimes I wondered what it might have been like had they been my real parents, or even if they had liked me. Yes, I was bitter at times, but not anymore," Solange said smiling. "I've been away from there for years. I've made my own life, and it's turning out to be an exciting one, I think."

"Solange . . . ," Rachel began abruptly, then hesitated when the door opened and another group of people walked in. One was a woman who struck Rachel as being Dutch in looks. She was short and round with blond hair braided tightly around her head. She had on a brightly embroidered blouse with short puffed sleeves and a full skirt that reached to her ankles. She carried a large straw bag. One of the men looked like a billy goat, with a kind of pointed face and a straggly gray beard. He looked vaguely familiar to Rachel, as if she had seen him at church suppers or at the post office on the island. She recalled that he always looked like he could use a good scrubbing and cleaning. Seedy was the word. Another man slouched as he shuffled into the room. His brown hair hung in an unruly tangle over his forehead and he had on dark, mirror-style glasses and a tired corduroy jacket that was too small for his well-muscled body.

The three moved down the aisle and settled awkwardly into desks at the front near Ellen. The woman immediately took her knitting out of the straw bag and began to knit. She called out to the room in general, "Sorry to be late, but I was canning tonight, believe it or not–making sauce out of winter apples." She freed one hand from her knitting and reached over to Ellen and tugged her by the sleeve. "Introduce me to your friends."

"Hi, Leeann. Hi George," Ellen said to her and to the man with the glasses, Leeann's husband. "How are you, Jonathan," she inquired of the man with the beard. She introduced the group from Lily Point.

Another man ambled through the door and went to stand at the windows. "Nice evenin'," he remarked shyly from his distance, continuing to stare out into the night sky as he spoke.

"That it is, Martin," Jonathan replied. "The harbor's lit up with moonlight. Wonderful night to take out a canoe and paddle around the harbor."

"Haven't been in a canoe since I was a tyke," Martin answered.

"Just as well, Martin," George said to him. "Till you learn to swim."

Martin turned and smiled. "I don't know, George. Not much use at my age. Can't survive in that temperature for more'n five minutes anyhow."

"You fishermen amaze me," George said. "If you ask me it's as crazy as it would be for an electrician to disregard the possibility of getting electrocuted."

"No one asked you," Leeann said shortly.

"Now, now," a cheerful voice from the back of the room called. "No fightin' 'lowed at this meetin', specially married folk. Let's get this show on the road. I got better things to do with my time." A short, stubby, curly-headed man came bounding down the aisle and plunked himself in the seat next to Jonathan.

"You mean watch the boob tube and drink beer? Unbecoming for a member of this august group," George said.

"He means you're marked for life, Jimmy," Leeann said, turning to smile at him. "Too bad, you could be home watching *The Dating Game.*"

Jimmy laughed good naturedly, "Hey I learned all I need to know watching you two caterwaulin' away. It's safer being a bachelor."

"Well, since the committee is here," Martin looked at the group seated by Ellen, "I think we could begin." He moved away from the window, slowly, letting his hand slide across the windowsill. He sat down in the teacher's chair.

"Thank you, Martin," Leeann said.

The three selectmen made their way into the room followed by a group of islanders. Winner, Bob and Lenny moved down front and sat on the other side of the aisle from the planning committee members. The other islanders sat at the back of the room, leaning against the wall, as if they were still children in school, Rachel thought, reluctant to get too close to the teacher. What did that say about their education? She looked around, and to her surprise, she saw there were at least fifty people now in the classroom. Anyone else who came in would have to stand anyway.

Martin acknowledged the selectmen with a perfunctory nod.

"What the hell, Martin," Bob began. "Maybe you can shed some light here. I thought this whole thing was settled. What're you doin'? Spinnin' your wheels one more time?"

"There are some serious objections to the latest set of plans presented by the Logan-Russell Corporation," Jonathan pronounced as Martin sat silent.

"Some say," Lenny said, leaning back in his chair and tilting on its back legs. "Some say not."

"Where are they anyway–Logan and Russell?"

"Been delayed. Should be here shortly," offered Winner.

"I say we should postpone any discussion until our regular meeting next month. If these people can't get here on time why should we take any action?" Leeann said crossly. "I've had a long day."

"Where are they anyway?" George echoed as if he were just waking up to the fact of their absence.

"They're stuck out there at their yacht. Ellen didn't pick 'em up," Bob said giving her an accusing look.

Ellen said calmly, "They'll be here shortly."

"Serves 'em right," Jimmy, said cheerfully. "Can't come by the ferry like the rest of us . . . let 'em set there an cool their heels till we send for 'em."

People at the back of the room laughed and clapped their hands. More people slipped in and stood quietly along the side nearest the door.

Martin began diffidently, "If we can, I'd like to see us take some . . . action here tonight. Maybe we could wait another ten minutes to give the Logan-Russell representatives time to get here."

"You mean Big Shot?" Winner asked wryly. He was twiddling his thumbs.

"Big Shot and his Beebees," George said and laughed harshly.

"I'm for postponing action until Logan-Russell, or their representatives arrive," Leeann said again. "We can hardly proceed before the persons whose plans we are examining answer our questions. And I for one have questions."

Lenny grunted. Long-winded woman, he thought, looking at Leeann and wondering why she didn't get her hair cut like other women.

A few more islanders trickled into the room. There was a general murmur of disgruntlement as the room filled up.

"Do you want to open the meeting for discussion from the floor?" Jimmy asked Martin.

Bob was immediately suspicious. "We've been over all this before," he complained. "People've had plenty time for talk."

"I've no objections," Martin said mildly, and Bob settled back in his seat as if for a long wait in a doctor's office.

"At least, we wouldn't waste our time just sittin' here," George remarked.

"It is a waste," an unidentified man said. "I'm for grantin' permission to Logan-Russell to get on with their plans without any further delay." A few people at the back applauded his statement.

"Me, too," Lenny said, happy with the applause.

"In case you were wonderin'," Martin said gently, "this is not a selectmen's meetin'. We're still in a plannin' session."

Winner stared hard at Martin and then he said, "That's right. Do what you have to do. People want to talk. Let 'em. We'll make the final decisions in a while." He sat back, looked out over the room, and twiddled his fingers some more.

Alison studied Winner's face and wondered what side he would come down on. Did he have his mind made up already? She hoped not.

"I'd like to say a word," a woman with frayed greying hair struggled to stand up from her desk at the back. "I'm just a summer person," she hesitated apologetically, "but I do think you have a beautiful island. It would be a shame to spoil its beauty by putting in condos."

Several people who sat near her applauded. She warmed to their support and continued, "I own land and I pay taxes, and it seems to me that there must be something we can do to control unnecessary growth, to hold down the taxes." More applause.

Shit, Bob thought to himself. Who's she to say? She could pay taxes till the cows come home. She has a million socked away somewhere, but always tries to bargain before she hires anybody to do some little job. The woman sat down meekly, and a man began to speak without rising from his seat. People in the front could not see who it was.

"Let's get at the real issue here," the voice said. "Summer people are all alike. Each of them wants to be the last person to buy property here. Nobody wants newcomers. Now we got newcomers who are going to make a real difference to the economy. Provide jobs for a change. You're worried about the beauty of the island. We worry about keeping our homes." There was a heavy round of cheers and foot-stamping. He continued, "Hell, I like the island for its beauty. I was born and brought up here. I know it's special, but I'm gonna be packin' up soon if I can't get steady work. I won't be enjoyin' the beauty nor nothin' if I have to leave." The cheering broke out again.

"Thank you, Joe." Martin said, solemnly . . . "Anyone else care to speak?"

A woman who sat alone at the front spoke up. "I hear tell the developer's gonna dump swill into the water over to Lily Cove and also into the harbor. Is that right?"

A voice from the back yelled out, "Worse 'n that. It's raw sewage."

"How'd ya like that with your clam chowder?" Someone belched loudly, and the crowd roared. Ellen looked at Alison and the others and shook her head ever so lightly. It was not time for suggestions yet.

"Jesus Christ," Lenny exploded, "you're all a bunch of sissies. We been eatin' clams from the harbor all our lives. Raw sewage gets swallowed up in there regular, always has. Tide sweeps it outta there. No one died from it yet."

A woman stood at the back. "I'd like to identify myself for the record, although you probably all know me by now. I'm Suzette Pellotte, the public health nurse. I'm on island once a week–more sometimes, and I've taken care of a lot of you. It's a fact that there is going to be more sewage than you ever had before dumped into that water, but it's going to be treated. There'll be a big plant for the sewage built on the land the developer is buying. To be honest, I don't think it's going to be a problem."

"How can we be sure?" Jonathan asked her.

"Well, there have been studies done, and it's easy enough to test the effluent."

"But, it's possible isn't it that they might not build the right kind of plant, that something could go wrong?" Jonathan insisted, testily.

"Well of course," the nurse conceded, a tone of impatience in her voice. "You just have to make sure you know what kind of plant they are going to install. Consult with the state environmental protection agency."

"No way," Bob yelled at the nurse. "We don't want no interferin' from Augusta. We've had them down here before."

"That's your choice," the nurse said quietly and sat down.

"What I want to know," came a voice from the back, which Rachel realized had become packed with people in the last few minutes, "is why we're meeting here without them developers anyway, if they didn't have the decency to show. I call that poor manners."

There was loud applause and someone said, "What the hell. We don't have to wait. Why don't we close shop and go home. It's typical of some city bastard to come here and take up our hard earned weekend with their problems."

Rachel could feel the hostility building in the room. She felt it was her time to speak.

She stood and said, "I'm Rachel Beattie, and although I live in Portland, I own the old McKnight house on Lily Point and I've spent many a wonderful summer here. I've just retired and I worry about taxes going up because I'll be living on a fixed income. I also worry about sewage being piped into Lily Cove. I think we ought to take time to study what kinds of sewage treatment plants there are before deciding which one, if any, should be used on the island. I know there are usually materials about such things in the library. You don't need to consult with Augusta." Much of the material in the library was supplied by the DEP, Rachel knew, but information offered there would seem far less threatening somehow because it was on paper.

She had struck a positive note, and she saw some heads nodding. She watched Ellen rise to add her own remarks.

"Yes, I've read some things that were helpful. Sarah, are they available at the library now?"

"Yes," a woman standing at the back replied. "Anyone may borrow them."

A voice said, "I'll be in on Monday, Sarah," and there was a roar of laughter, as people recognized it was her husband who spoke.

Another voice called out, "Sure, and Sarah can help you read the stuff while you're there."

The tone of the gathering had turned convivial. People were making the best of their spoiled Saturday night, Rachel thought, or maybe this was a better Saturday night than usual.

A tall man with strikingly pale gray eyes shuffled to his feet. He ran his fingers through the few strands of silver hair he had left, and confronted the subject everyone had been avoiding. "Sorry to inject another serious note here, but we haven't talked much about this company–Logan-Russell–who they are and what they've been doing elsewhere. I have some information I'd like to share with you. As taxpayers I think you have a right to know." He gazed calmly about him.

The selectmen, Rachel noticed, seemed uncomfortable with his presence. "I'm Larry Prentice, and I'm a retired biologist, living here year round. I happen to have a few friends who work at the State House in Augusta. They pretty much know what's going on in Maine since they work on economic development." He hesitated and then plunged on. "The truth is, this company has had problems elsewhere in Maine. Perhaps you'd like to hear what they've been doing and then you can decide for yourself how you feel about them.

"I know some of you are expecting to get hired on by Logan-Russell, even as early as next week, but don't be too sure you'll get a job. Even if you are hired on, that doesn't mean permanent employment and Logan Russell usually brings its own crew. They say what they need to say just to get a foot onto the land, then they may hire a few locals–or they may not. Whoever gets hired locally, I hear, does the scut work, gets paid minimum wages for short-term jobs. No benefits. No opportunity for advancement. No future work.

"There are three other things I'd like to bring to your attention, examples of Logan-Russell's conduct in business. First: a woman up in East Holden bought some land from Jack Russell to build her retirement home on. After she signed the papers she took a trip to Europe for three months, something she'd wanted to do all her life. When she returned she went to the site to begin planning her home. She found that Logan-Russell had built a road right through the middle of her property. She is involved in a suit against them.

"Second: one of the men who worked for the DEP was involved in testing sites for Logan-Russell. He approved various proposals by the company, some of which local authorities say overlooked town zoning ordinances. That man is now on the payroll of Logan-Russell, and the proposals he approved are being challenged in court.

"Third: closer to home, a family bought some land from Logan-Russell over in Bernard. They're from Texas and they couldn't get to the land until the following summer. When they came back they found their five acres had been stripped of trees. All there was was slash."

Lenny looked up from where he had been drowsily scribbling on the desk in front of him. "Serves 'em right. They should 'a stayed in Texas."

Sometimes Winner wished Lenny was not a selectman. "That's not the point," he told him sternly. "The man in question is Bill Sawyer, the surveyor–the same man we've been dealing with over here."

There was a low whistle and everyone began talking at once.

"Quiet. Quiet, please. We need quiet here," Martin said thumping on the teacher's desk self-consciously with his fist.

"What are we supposed to do?" Bob said over the fading voices. "Throw out these people just cause they hired someone from the DEP. That don't prove nothin'."

"But what about the people who bought the land? Look what happened to them." It was the woman who had spoken earlier about controlling growth and holding down taxes.

"Caveat emptor–let the buyer beware," Jonathan said smugly.

"Oh, come on, Jonathan, you can't really mean that," Ellen said. She was furious.

"Certainly, I do," Jonathan said and stroked his beard. "That's a business matter for the individual land owner to decide for himself. We can't interfere."

"I say we go home, take some time," Leeann said one more time, "and do some reading."

"Chris' sakes, Leeann," George said. "All you ever do is stick your nose in some damn book. Reading isn't the answer to all problems."

"No, but I might get rid of one problem by consulting a book on do-it-yourself divorce," Leeann shot back at him, and the schoolhouse rocked with laughter.

George rallied immediately. "You'd sure miss my home cooking then, wouldn't you?" Leeann reached over and shook him.

When the laughter subsided, Martin spoke. "I think this is information we might use. Are you sure of the facts, Larry?"

"Yes. I'd be glad to give you names and addresses."

"Thank you. I'd like that."

There was a lull in the room and Ellen decided that the time was right for her to do her bit. She stood gracefully, looking out at her friends and neighbors, "We've been talking tonight about what happens when we lose control of our land and even lose control of our future. Everybody looks at it differently, but we all have needs and we all have feelings about the matter. We're in a state of confusion about how to take things in hand—to get control. So far we seem to think there are only two choices open to us: to accept or to reject Logan-Russell's set of plans. Actually, there are some important decisions we should make about the island before we even think about Logan-Russell since they may be only the tip of the iceberg. Other developers may follow their lead shortly. And there are still things we can do about Logan-Russell. We've gotten stuck in a rut, and that rut was created, not by Logan-Russell, but by us."

There was a murmur of agreement in the room.

She continued, "We can change all that. All we have to do is take the time to do it right, to think about strategies of our own. We do not have to be outsmarted, but we are up against professional developers who know how to get around land use ordinances, and that is intimidating. For that reason I think Leeann's advice is sound. We should give ourselves a gift of time . . . .

"There are many possibilities," she said. Her eyes searching the room, trying to gage the reaction to her words. Bernie could arrive any second with Jack Russell and his clients. It was time, she thought, for Solange to make her unusual proposal. "I'd like you to meet a woman who has an option to offer you . . . ."

Solange dove into the task headfirst. "I know you have committed yourself to dealing with this company and I am a newcomer," she said breathlessly, "and I understand anyone's reluctance to accept suggestions from a stranger, but I am definitely interested in purchasing property here on this beautiful island–with a view to starting a business of some kind–one perhaps related to fishing." As soon as she said the words business and fishing the room became silent. Surprisingly she grew calmer. "My father, whom I never knew, died recently and left me a fortune. Up to this point I've always earned my own living and I'm now finishing a degree at the university. I never dreamt of having money. I don't believe it's the most important thing in the world. I've been pretty content without it, but I do want to put the money to good use so that others will benefit." She looked out at the faces. If nothing else she had their undivided attention. "When I heard what is happening here, my first impulse was to buy the land from the developer and give it back to the island."

"Why not?" came a cry from the back of the room.

"Sure!" someone said good naturedly and there were whistles and some stamping of feet.

"Because," she said, and gave them her best smile, "I don't live here and I have no right to just barge in thinking I can solve all your problems with money. Also, as I was told earlier tonight, if I did enter the market at this juncture, tried to convince Logan-Russell to sell, the price of the land would undoubtedly rise astronomically and along with it your taxes as well as mine.

"The other reason why I hesitate to get involved in purchasing land immediately is that I am new to this whole business of being a philanthropist. It's a bit heavy and I'm not sure I'm going to like it. I do know I need some guidance from people who know the financial ropes. In the meantime I want you to know that I am definitely interested in helping the island to find solutions to land development problems. So you see, you do have some choices." She had run out of things to say for the moment and so she turned to Ellen who stood and faced the gathering.

"Earlier this evening, I did some brain-storming," Ellen said, acknowledging Rachel and her guests. "We made up a list of possibilities for projects which might benefit the island. We were surprised at how many we came up with. If you have never done that kind of list making before, you might want to try it." She held up the role of newsprint she had brought with her.

"Why not show us your list?" came the genial voice of Jimmy.

She turned apologetically to Martin, and said, "Would that be out of order at this time?"

"Well . . ." Martin began, and George interrupted him, "We seem to be stuck here anyway. Why don't you go ahead."

There was a round of applause and Ellen said, "I'd like you to meet Alison and Ann. They're experienced in helping people work things out–arbitration, that kind of thing. Alison does it for a living in the court in Portland, and Ann is a student from the university." Alison and Ann rose, made a little bow to the delight of the audience, and began to post the newsprint list on the blackboard walls. Grace unobtrusively moved her recorder closer to where they stood. "I think we're fortunate that they happened to be here this weekend." Ellen added and sat down.

Bob was beginning to feel uncomfortable with the sudden onslaught of outsiders, but for the life of him he couldn't find a reason to interrupt. Lenny had already decided that it wouldn't amount to much anyway. He slumped down in his chair and closed his eyes.

Winner, however, continued to twiddle his thumbs contentedly. He was amused with the turn of events. Wouldn't Jack Russell be surprised to walk in right about now? Wouldn't it be nice if he had to sit here and wait for someone else for a change? Maybe he should send somebody out to check up on what was keeping him. Lenny? He glanced at Lenny who had dozed off. Winner gave him a sharp jab in the ribs. Lenny started and looked groggily out over the room. "What'd ya do that for?" he mumbled.

"Forget it," Winner said, disgustedly and turned his attention back to the board.

Lenny nodded off.

"Today, we listened to Ellen talk about the problems of taxes and underemployment on the island, but we had no idea about some of the other things." Alison said, and Ann added, "We hadn't heard about the woman whose land has an illegal road on it, or some of the septic system problems."

"We hadn't heard it either, lady," someone shouted.

"Based on what we did learn from Ellen," Alison continued, "we came up with a list of possible projects and we'd like your comments on what we have here."

"And you can give us additional ideas if you like," Ann added.

Alison cautioned the listeners. "This is only a wish list, but dreams never come true if you don't begin somewhere." She gave people a few moments to study the lists.

A woman who had moved up front ventured, "There's some things on your list that we've thought about doing before, but we never could get funded."

"Ayuh," Martin agreed. "We lost a grant from the fisheries because we didn't get our papers in on time."

"There was the cannery deal. That was all set to go, then the owners backed out at the last minute," Jimmy said.

"We did work on historical sites, this year," Jonathan added. "We have a committee trying to preserve records and mark land where important buildings once stood. We've got our eye on a possible site for a larger museum."

"What we're trying to do is to ensure that the island history is preserved," continued Sarah, the librarian. "The library is sponsoring that project. Send your donations today," she added with a giggle.

A woman at the back spoke up. "We had a jewelry group started using stones from the beaches. We was sendin' our bracelets and necklaces to Boston and New York, but we couldn't keep up with the orders. Some of the women didn't want to work at it any more. It is sort of borin'," she confessed and looked around her for confirmation. "Still, 'twas a good idea. Some of us wouldn't mind doin' it again if we could get extra help."

There was a loud crash, and the door to the classroom opened. Two people entered the room. One was a man, the other an old woman with a black eye visible all the way to the front of the room.

Alison gasped aloud, but quickly contained herself even as she recognized Father Donahey. What happened to him, she thought wildly. And what's he doing here? Who is that man with him? They're both drunk beyond reason.

Bernie and Clarissa followed Ellen's directions, driving west toward the harbor. At a crossroads they turned off, drove down a steep hill and across an isthmus. On their right they could look back in the moonlight at Lily Cove. On their left Changeable Cove glistened, a path of moonlight stretched across its center toward the open ocean.

The least populated part of the island, most of this land had recently been purchased by Logan-Russell Inc., which was promising buyers a romanticized replica of early Martha's Vineyard or Nantucket. Both women had seen the ads Ellen carried with her, ads that touted the unspoiled wilderness, the most untrammeled, uncommercialized beauty; the most private, yet accessible world. Until recently, it was only those out for an afternoon's spin or lovers out for an evening's spoon, as Rachel put it, who drove across this wooded hilly terrain. Distant peninsulas and coves which had been accessible only to the intrepid hiker now had rough bulldozed roads for everyone.

"What a romantic setting, but I think Rachel may be wrong about lovers coming here to make out," Bernie said. "Did you hear Ellen talking about the kids on the island? They tend to park near the stores."

"To see and be seen," Clarissa mused. "On an island the ends of the roads are too near the edge of the world–where everything falls off into the darkness. I might be frightened if I were a kid going parking. I'd feel safer near the store where there are people around."

"Even their parents, dropping by for a bottle of milk?" Bernie chuckled. "I don't know. It seems strange to me," she continued, "but of course there is no entertainment for kids here, no movies, no video games, no McDonalds. It may seem boring to go off into the dark all the time. The other thing is, parents all know where the ends of the roads are. They probably parked there when they were kids."

"But they didn't have cars then, did they?" Clarissa said. "You know, when I was young, we went to the school dances, and to church suppers. We sang in the choir. That's how we met and socialized. We didn't have all these commercial entertainments, and we weren't allowed out of the house all that often," Clarissa was complacent. "I think we grew up the better for it."

"How are you feeling about our gathering, by the way?" Bernie said. "You seem more comfortable."

"Much better. I don't think what we're doing is related to real religion. And certainly not satanism, not after what everyone did." She was hoping for Bernie's agreement.

Bernie drove silently, watching the road.

Clarissa did not interpret her silence as disagreement. "I can't take it all that seriously," she continued. "It's fun to be here. I like trying to help other people. We both needed something like that, I guess."

Bernie knew the "we" included Rachel.

"So you don't necessarily call it 'charity' or 'Christian' when someone tries to help strangers?" Bernie ventured. It might not hurt to point out some comparisons. "Well, it certainly seems Christian–of course–and it is charity. I mean I can't see that it's all that different. Can you?"

"Depends on what you call Christian. I'm Jewish myself."

Clarissa stifled an, "Oh," and glanced covertly at Bernie.

"So," Bernie continued. "I think of doing good–being charitable–as part of my heritage too, but I also view witchcraft as self-empowering for women. There are very few women rabbis. In shul I could never make a decision of the kind we have been making tonight. I couldn't call a meeting–gather everyone together to take action. That's been a male prerogative in Judaism."

"There are no women priests at all in the Roman Catholic church," Clarissa added cautiously, wondering what that really meant. She had never questioned it before. These days you heard about nuns who challenged the church and said they were called to be priests, and she admired them, even though she thought of them as a little crazy. Would she be considered crazy now by Father Donahey, she wondered? She felt a flash of discomfort.

"It's confusing, isn't it, Clare?" Bernie said, not insensitive to what Clarissa might feel. "When you try to figure out why each religion is so certain of its status as the one true way, and better than all the rest–with a copyright on all the good stuff, you get to thinking that maybe they've got blinders on."

Clarissa didn't know what to say to that. She only knew that her church was the best. Still she liked Bernie, and Bernie was the first Jew she'd ever really talked with about anything serious. One thing she knew. Some Jews were serious about diet. She gave them points for that.

"Are you kosher?" she said taking Bernie by surprise.

"That went out with my grandparents," Bernie said, laughing heartily.

Clarissa was disappointed. She would have liked to talk to a Jew about diet.

Bernie was watching the road more carefully now. "We're almost there I think. We should plan what we want to do if this thing is to go smoothly," Bernie said, her voice sounding more serious. "I don't suppose there's that much to rehearse; still, they're bound to make conversation with us, and we might get asked questions which could foul us up, make them suspicious."

"Like what?"

"Well, Clarissa . . . Do you mind if I shorten that to Clare?"

"No, not at all," Clarissa said. "I take it you don't like old-fashioned names like yours and mine."

Bernie cleared her throat. "Right. No one calls me Bernice except my mother when she's mad at me. Anyway, it should be easy enough at least, at the beginning, when we meet these people. We'll say that we came to pick them up since Ellen had car trouble. Then we'll drive till the road splits, take the left fork. About five miles later the road comes out into an open field. We'll see that field just before we enter the woods on this road about three miles down, I think. That's important because it's where the two roads are connected by another smaller road. We have to find that smaller road, it's a right turn again, and then another back onto this road. Then all we have to do is circle until we admit we're lost. Then we'll play it by ear."

Clarissa began to feel excited about making it work. "What then?" she said. "What if they get annoyed?"

"We may have to soothe them a bit, make them think that everything is all right, even if they believe we're basically incompetent."

"I wonder how the others are doing back at the meeting? They must have begun by now," Clarissa said. "I hope everything goes well."

Bernie fervently hoped so. She began looking for signs of the ocean through the trees. The road led through several open areas and then back into deep woods. "Ellen said we'd see water to our left for quite a ways before we reached the cove where the boat is anchored. They've been hacking down trees here. They want customers to see the view from the shore better. Probably no one would buy it if it was just untouched forest."

Shortly they saw a glimmer of moonlight through the trees

and then its reflection on the water. The point had to be close by.

"Now," Bernie said, "a mile or two from here ought to do it; we should see lights from their boat. They were also supposed to light a fire on shore."

Clarissa shifted nervously in her seat. She wondered what kind of question they might ask. Nothing personal, she hoped. "Should we tell them the truth about everything else?" she asked Bernie. "I mean our names and where we live. What if they find out that this has been a trick? Could they sue us?"

"How could they prove Ellen didn't have a flat? That would be kind of difficult. She'd have more than enough time to make her tire flat."

"I don't know," Clarissa said anxiously. "I just don't know about telling lies. Even in this situation."

Futile, Bernie thought to herself, to philosophize with Clarissa about morals. "Do what you think best, Clare," she said, "and anyway, I'll probably do most of the talking. I always do." She chuckled self-indulgently. "You don't have to say anything unless someone asks you a question. Just say you came along for the ride."

Relief flooded Clarissa. "I'm sorry, but I have mixed emotions about this." She laughed. "My Catholic's conscience is always nagging me."

"Hey," Bernie said, "Nothing to be sorry about. I understand."

"Wait," Clarissa said. "I see lights up ahead. There's a fire along the shore. Can you spot it? Over there to the right."

Bernie saw a spot of flickering yellow, and they drove with growing excitement till they reached the edge of the woods where the road stopped. Bernie was suddenly alarmed. "I didn't see the road we're supposed to take back. I missed the damn thing. I was so busy looking for water on my left."

"Should we backtrack and find it now? Clarissa was alarmed.

"We can't. They must have seen us. They'll be on there way to meet us. I'll just have to wing it. On the way back, be on the lookout for the road. You can tell me when you see it. We'll be fine," she assured Clarissa.

They could see people standing on the shore with smaller lights bobbing beside the fire. Flashlights. Then the fire abruptly disappeared leaving only the flashlights to identify the spot.

Bernie turned off the motor, grabbed her own flashlight and started walking toward the shore. "Stay there," she called back to Clarissa, "I'll be right back. This is rough ground–lots of slash." She made her way around stumps and through broken limbs of trees. Raspberry brambles grabbed at her clothes. Conversation floating toward her, she decided to wait where she was. "Hello," she called out, "I've come to get you. Sorry about the delay."

She heard a male voice give a grunt and then a muffled remark and a low laugh from a woman. The man said loudly, "What kept you? We could have motored around to the harbor by now if we'd known there would be this much delay."

"Sorry. Flat tire," Bernie called, putting authority into her voice. She would not accept a scolding from the enemy.

Three people, two men and one woman, made their way gingerly to her side. She shot out her hand to catch the woman who almost fell as she leapt a tangle of fallen branches. "Watch your step. My name's Bernie. The car is over this way." She turned and led the way.

"Thank you for coming," the woman said. Bernie heard the smile in her voice. "My name is Lyla."

Bernie nodded, moving on. Although she was curious to know which of the men was Jack Russell, she did not wait for introductions.

She opened the back door and the three climbed in. Clarissa turned and greeted them cheerfully, "Hi, I'm along for the ride. My name's Clarissa."

"Humph," said the grunter.

"How do you do," said Lyla, and she graciously introduced the others to Clarissa and Bernie. The grunter, it turned out, was Jack Russell.

Figures, Bernie thought wryly. The other two were a married couple, Jess and Lyla Hewitt. "How was the sailing today?" she asked to lighten things a bit.

"Grand," Jess said. "We had a terrible day yesterday, lost a lot of time hung up on that rock, but once we got the engine started everything turned around. We finally got the sails up this afternoon. Took us longer than we thought to get here. This is a beautiful part of the world, and we're anxious to begin building here."

"Then you've bought land?" Bernie said deciding to play innocent.

"I own the land you're driving through," Russell said shortly. "Two hundred and fifty acres. By the way, where is Ellen? She was supposed to meet us. She was supposed to be here half an hour ago."

"Wow," Bernie said, trying for a tone of apologetic innocence. "I had no idea I was that late. When Ellen had her flat, there was a delay, and when she saw it would be a while before her van was ready, she sent me out just so you wouldn't be late to the meeting."

"How nasty about the flat," Lyla said sympathetically.

"Well, I'd no idea it took that long to get across the island," Jess said somewhat uncomfortably. "I thought you said . . . ."

"Nothing to worry about, Jess," Russell said smoothly. "People use boats to get around. That's part of the fun of being here." He was trying to sound jovial, like he was the outdoors type who really loved sailing. Bernie bet the only time he put the sails up on his boat was when he had guests on board. Real sailors called his kind of luxury yacht a 'smoke stack with status sticks.'

"Well, yes," Jess said. "Still there are times when the sea is rough. A person might like to go into town. I just had no idea it was that far. How far would you say it is?" he asked Bernie.

"Oh, it's not really a town," Bernie said, and then elaborated on her lie, "and what roads there are are real rough, bad on the car's suspension."

"Nonsense," Jack Russell snapped. "You must be a tourist. The island has a town, small though it is. The island itself is only twenty by eleven miles if you figure the peninsulas and all."

Bernie caught his eye in the rear view mirror and his expression told her he would at that moment gladly throw her out of the car window. "These roads are winding and there are a lot of hills. We're not talking as the crow flies," she persisted. She was getting into this. The man was easy to annoy, and he was a jerk. On the other hand, Jess and Lyla seemed nice enough.

"Will you be living out here for the summer or longer?" Clarissa asked turning around to look at Lyla when she spoke.

"Oh, I do hope we'll spend a lot of time here. We're thinking of building not only for ourselves, but also for others. We'll have a small place, yes, but we travel so much. We have a ranch in Wyoming and a home in St. Croix, besides the little flat in London. It's so hard." She sighed. "We just get settled and then we're off again." She sounded genuinely perplexed as if she didn't quite know why she kept moving from place to place.

Jess said, "We've never spent time in Maine. It's going to be fun, Lyla. We can stay into the fall if you like, go to Wyoming a little late. We could even skip Wyoming this year–go straight to St. Croix for Christmas." He was comforting her, Bernie saw. All this property business was obviously not really Lyla's main interest.

Bernie watched the side of the road without turning her head. Maybe they wouldn't notice how slowly she was going. The roughness of the road was on her side, after all. The car harshly jounced up and down without too much need for her to deliberately aim at bumps and holes. But there was still time to kill. She hadn't the least idea what she could do next.

Clarissa saw the other road before she did. "Mind the turn," she said to Bernie. It's just ahead."

"No," Russell said shortly. "That's only a side road I had built for other lots. Keep straight ahead. It's quicker." He was absolutely decisive. There was no sense in challenging him.

"Oh," Clarissa said daringly, "but I thought it was much shorter to take that road. Didn't someone say something about a tree being down at the other end of the one we're on?"

"What are you saying?" Russell demanded suspiciously.

Going on to the circle is out, Bernie thought. He knows the route well. Unless I warn her, Clarissa is going to get us in trouble.

"It's all right, Clarissa," she said pointedly. "I'll take this route. The tree's not a problem. Remember, we didn't see it on the way out here." She began to comb her mind for some scheme which would buy them some time. If only she knew of a little swamp area that she could somehow drive into and get mired down. A stupid thought. Ann could not afford to have her car wrecked, no matter how devoted she might be to the idea of helping the island.

Clarissa's desperate voice intruded on her concentration. "I'm going to be sick. Could you please stop, Bernie?"

Amazed, Bernie pulled over to the side and stopped. As she did Clarissa burst from the door and rushed into the brush. She was swallowed up by the darkness.

Bernie said, "Gee, I wonder what it is. Maybe something we ate tonight." She was a little worried for Clarissa. She rummaged around in the front seat and found a small package of tissues. "I'll take these to her in case she needs them."

Lyla made soft sounds of sympathy; Russell grunted impatiently, "Try to hurry her along."

"Jack," Lyla said warningly.

Jess said, "Will we be too late for the meeting?"

"We are already late, Jess," Russell responded instantly. "But they'll wait. Believe me." Bernie could hear the fury in his voice and was relieved that she had grabbed the keys and tucked them in her denim jacket. He would probably have left Clarissa alone in the bushes if it were his car.

She made her way into the trees calling to Clarissa, hoping that she was not seriously ill.

"Over here," came a whisper. As Bernie made out Clarissa's face in the darkness, she suddenly understood that Clarissa was faking it–stalling for time. "Tell them I have diarrhea, bad cramps. They'll have to wait. Let's keep moving further away."

"Boy," Bernie's whisper was full of awe. "That was sure convincing. I really thought you were sick."

"No, nothing's wrong. I just figured we had to do something fast. It was the first thing that came to my mind. Funny, I feel perfectly fine." She smothered a giggle. "So far. I can always go to confession, if it hits me later."

Bernie squatted by Clarissa who had found a stump to sit on. They could barely make out each other's face two feet away. "Stay with me till they holler," Clarissa whispered. "We need all the time we can get. Might as well try their patience rather than placate them."

"You're incredible," Bernie whispered back, amazed at Clarissa's sudden transformation. A minute passed and then they heard the car door open and Lyla call out, "How is she? Is Clarissa all right? Do you need help?" Bernie could hear her trying to make her way through the brush at the side of the road.

Winner looked up as a ruckus at the school room door interrupted the proceedings. His first thought was that here was more entertainment, his second was concern for the safety of all.

His own physical strength impressed Winner. It impressed everyone. He was the tallest man on the island, and under the right circumstances, he could and did intimidate anyone who had not totally lost a sense of reality. He was island law, a strange combination of brute strength and home-cooked justice.

Winner mopped up after Saturday night drinking sprees, stopped adolescent drivers from careening around after decent folks had called it a night, and counseled in various island quarrels. He could, on occasion, look the other way, but there were two things he would not tolerate: physical violence and the interruption of a good night's sleep.

Now he saw what looked like a tussle between an old woman and the Captain, whose periodic drunken binges were familiar to everyone on the island. Winner stood to his full height and moved his impressive, lanky body in John-Wayne-slow motion toward the back of the room, an act which people anticipated with appreciation. The strong-arm tactics which followed would offer not only immediate gratification, but their description would be embellished tomorrow and take on myth-like proportions in years to come.

The crowd parted like the Red Sea to provide Winner a path. He reached the side of the old woman, whose wig was askew over one ear and who struggled to regain her footing. Frank Harrigan was by her side, his arm slung over her shoulder. He couldn't have stood otherwise. Winner asked himself for the fiftieth time how this off-island pilot managed to retain his license when his periods of sobriety were so few and far between. But the immediate questions were how such an unlikely twosome had found each other, and who his equally plastered partner was.

"Leave me alone, I tell you," the lady croaked. "I can manage nicely on my own." She struggled valiantly to free herself from Frank's arm and then stood gasping to get her breath.

"What seems to be the problem here?" Winner asked in his deepest, most authoritative voice to the out-of-breath woman.

"This man," she said to Winner, "is drunk, and furthermore, he wouldn't believe me when I said there were witches on this island."

So he'd been right, for God's sake, Winner thought disgustedly. They're both stinko. Frank must be hard up to take on this old varmint as a drinking partner.

"She had an accident, Winner," the Captain protested, gesturing towards the shiner. "I offered her a drink," his words were slurred. "I don't think she knows what she's saying."

"Where'd the black eye come from then?" Winner said patiently.

"Whatever he says, don't believe him, Winner," someone in the room shouted and there were gales of laughter. People were craning their heads to get a better look at the scene.

Alison, standing at the far end of the room, wished ardently that she could vanish. She was presently shielded from Father Donahey by the crowd, but there was the whole matter of her connection to Clovis which Rachel would undoubtedly think of shortly. How could this have happened? Never had she imagined that Father Donahey would go on a bender with some local man. A part of her wanted to watch the scene. The other cautioned her to hide.

Winner said, "You didn't answer me, Frank."

The Captain responded. "She took a fall. I offered her a little whiskey to soften the pain." There were cat calls and jeers, and he was sensitive to the tone of the crowd. He turned angrily and said without thinking, "You're gonna need to get off the island one of these days when there are too many cars, and I will have to make a decision as to who goes and who stays."

"That sounds like a threat to me," Winner said ominously. "You still haven't explained what's going on."

"No, no, surely not." The Captain backed off, clearly alarmed. He saw he still owed an explanation of what was happening. "Well, I joined the lady for a drink, that's all," he said lamely, and there was more laughter which he did his best to ignore. "She got drunk," he offered.

"I did not. You did," came the hoarse reply from the puffy little woman. "I was simply trying to recover, so I could go about my business."

"And what was that?" Winner asked, feeling that, in this case, her business became his concern.

"I wanted to investigate matters on Lily Point."

All ears in the room tuned in and suddenly the women from Lily Point understood who this was. Rachel felt stricken.

"Excuse me," she said, moving through the crowd till she reached Winner's side. She stared at the little woman before her, who looked oddly familiar.

"Clovis," she said, "is that you?" and the little woman started. "This is Clovis and she is my guest," Rachel said, reaching out to put a hand on the old woman's arm. "I'm sure there's been a mistake. She was resting in her RV tonight. Did this man break in and attack you?" The thought alarmed Rachel. They should never have left the poor thing on her own. It was obvious that something terrible had happened to her while the rest of the women were all enjoying themselves. She looked around for Alison but could not see her in the crowd.

"That's not the case, Madam," the Captain replied assuming his authority as an officer of the sea, and thrusting his chest as if standing at attention. He was definitely alarmed. This was a nightmare. Would he lose his pilot 's license? Better do some fast talking. "I simply went to the lady's assistance. I was out taking my evening walk and I heard her cry out. I felt I should investigate."

Winner pursued the facts. "And how did you both land here?"

"She told me some wild story about witches, said that they were down on the point. I went with her. There was not one person there. The house was dark. She said they might be down on the water. I went and looked. All I could find was the remains of a camp fire where somebody'd had a cook out."

"Mine," Rachel said promptly, looking Winner right in the eye.

"The lady," the Captain continued, grinning now, "insisted then that we look for them on the island–the 'them' she referred to was supposedly witches."

Winner had a glint of amusement in his eye for the Captain, who, encouraged, continued on. "Well, I decided to humor her. We drove around the island in my car, but the only lights, the only sign of activity was here. She insisted we come in to warn the people. I tried to stop her."

"Warn us of what?" Winner said fascinated now. Liquor could do strange and wonderful things. He knew a good show when he saw one, and so, he felt certain, did the others in the room. There wasn't a soul here who was sorry they'd come to the meeting even if it was Saturday night.

The Captain had had enough. "Ask her," he said. "It's her trip. Not mine." He wiped his brow with the back of his hand, and staggered to an empty chair and sat down to watch.

"Did this man hurt you?" Winner asked the woman.

The sight of all the people, the bright lights and the absolute attention being paid him were having an effect on Father

Donahey. He was rapidly sobering up and was concerned about the possibility of being identified. This was no Halloween ball. He decided not to make a big thing of the fact that the Captain had grabbed his rear end when they were getting out of the car. If they called the state police, he would have to identify himself.

"Well, not really," he said as shyly as he could sound. "I just wanted to come in here, and he tried to stop me in a way that lacked good taste."

There were a few more snickers in the audience, then silence.

"Now," Winner said, getting back to the subject at hand, "what were you gonna warn us about?"

Here Father Donahey looked at Rachel and a puzzled look came over his face. Through his alcoholic haze he remembered who she was. He was silenced by the fact that she was in a totally alien context; she was a former parishioner. Still she'd come forward straight away to rescue him. He had to give her credit for that. Instantly he recalled listening under the window as she said some outrageous things. What were they, anyway? He tried to remember details–words, sentences–incantations. Nothing came to mind. There was, however, a strong chance that he would look the fool shortly if he didn't gauge his accusations carefully. "Well," he said slowly, trying to think in his panic. "I was concerned because I came here for a weekend of rest. My cook/housekeeper drove me. After we got here she said she wanted to go to some kind of summer solstice celebration here on the point at this woman's house." He stared fixedly at Rachel trying to will her to understand the danger of her situation. "She said something about witches."

Rachel tried to comprehend what was going on. Wasn't Clovis the one who had answered the ad? Why would she be frightened then? More importantly, where had Rachel seen her before? Whoever it was, she was obviously drunk and disoriented, was lying, or didn't remember that she, herself, had answered the ad. She must have become frightened at the last moment. How best to explain without seeming ominous? She turned around her, looking for support, hoping Alison would appear. Instead she found Ann and Grace standing close by. She gave them a nervous look. Grace squeezed her arm and said, "You're doing fine."

She turned back to Winner. "This is the summer solstice," she said calmly and loud enough for everyone in the room to hear. "That means it's the longest day of the year–the most sunlight. People often celebrate, as we did with the fire on the end of the point and a pot luck supper."

"That's right," Grace said. "I can corroborate her story. We are her guests," she gestured to Ann. "We've had a pleasant evening together. You're aware of how we spent part of our time, from the conversation in this room."

Ellen spoke, "That's right, Winner. There's nothing spooky about it. I was there for dinner too." She turned to the woman who was obviously Clovis and said, not unkindly, "You should get some rest. You've had a long day." There were murmurs of approval and finally sympathy from the surrounding people. The story had a familiar ending. Everybody knew somebody who had gone a little crazy from drink. Winters were long, and people felt cooped up after a while. Nobody here knew what this old woman's life was like. In the morning she'd probably have a hard time remembering what she'd said here tonight.

Winner nodded, "Ayuh. Time to let someone take you along home." He looked back at Suzette Pellotte, the public health nurse, and beckoned to her. She rose and came forward. "I'd be glad to take you home. I stay just up by Lily Point." She smiled at Father Donahey and said, "You'll feel better in the morning."

Once more laughter erupted in the room, but the sound was good natured. Winner leaned over and whispered in Suzette's ear, "Stay with her till you're sure she's asleep."

Father Donahey felt annoyed and defeated. Warning these people seemed out of the question now. They'd never take a drunk person's word against all these witches. They were probably spellbound. That was the way the devil worked. He could cause a person to be discredited so easily. By this time Father Donahey was totally exhausted. Tomorrow, however, he would confront Rachel. Get her alone and confront her with her evil work. The thought comforted him. He gave

Captain Harrigan a dirty look and departed with the nurse. There was a round of applause as she escorted him through the door.

Phew, thought Alison. That was close. What would have happened if everyone here suddenly focused on witchcraft? She looked around and saw the scowl on Jonathan's face. He might be going to do just that.

She made a move toward where he was sitting and gave him a kind smile. "Sounds crazy, doesn't it? Must be difficult to get your work done with interruptions from everywhere. Logan-Russell aren't terribly considerate business people are they, asking you to meet on Saturday night. I can't imagine where they are." She glanced at her watch.

"This whole evening has been disgraceful," he said sharply, eyeing Alison. "I wouldn't be surprised if you were in collusion with Jack Russell."

"Don't you ever take people at their word?" she said smiling sweetly. "I never heard of Russell until today when Ellen spoke of the island development. Actually, I became interested in island problems essentially because it seemed to be a situation where mediation might be helpful. I work part-time as an arbitrator in a district court."

"I've found in this life," Jonathan answered as if she had not spoken and adjusting his wire rim glasses, "everyone serves himself. There's no such thing as pure altruism."

"That might be true," Alison said mildly, "but I can say I enjoy working with people, helping them to work out their problems, and still enjoy getting paid for it."

"There you are," Jonathan replied.

"There I am," Alison repeated good naturedly. "I'm not afraid to admit it." She grinned mischievously, "What do you get out of being on the planning board, then?"

"A chance to see life on the island," he answered and laughed. "I'm a student of life," he continued. "I like to keep an eye on island affairs. A lot of people here don't appreciate the history of this island, don't know their own heritage. I do."

Ann, who had just joined Alison, raised an eyebrow. He ignored her and continued "I want to live my life as I have been living it, in peace and quiet. I won't survive if the place turns into a commercialized summer retreat for the wealthy. I intend to preserve the atmosphere as well as the history of this place."

"I see," Alison said quietly. "No altruism there."

"Precisely," he answered smugly, "and you are an interloper, and I don't need your approval."

"What was that about?" Ann asked Alison when they had moved back to their seats.

"Got me," Alison said, "but he perceives us as the enemy."

"Okay, okay," Winner said having returned to settle himself heavily in his chair. "What do you think, Martin?"

Martin knocked on the side of the desk, and the room quieted down. He coughed lightly. "Hmmm . . . where were we?" he asked politely.

Alison stepped forward. "We were simply outlining possibilities for island development which might be more to the liking of the islanders themselves."

"Looked pretty idealistic," Jonathan said, waving his arm aloft to signify light-headed.

"Pipe dreams," Bob seconded the thought, finally able to express his annoyance with the idea of strangers mixing into the business of the taxpayers. "What property do you own here?" he asked Alison.

"None," she replied. "I have no irons in the fire, nothing to gain or lose." She realized that this sounded impossible to the pragmatic ears of her listeners and added quickly, "But I wouldn't mind working for you if you needed a consultant. This is a sample of my working style." It was a risk she had to take.

"That figures," Bob answered. "You come on island and pretend to be an expert, and you don't even know what's going on."

"Now wait a minute, Bob. That's not exactly true," George said. "They know all right. They want a piece of the pie. They're just trying to outfox Logan-Russell."

"And what's wrong with that?" Leeann countered.

"Where the hell are they, anyway," Lenny asked waking briefly to the last remark. He scratched his belly and looked around the room. To his great surprise he saw his wife sitting in the crowd. He winked, hoping that would remind her of their little fun later in the evening. She gave him one of her ugly smirks and his heart sank. That was the end of that.

Leeann ignored Lenny and continued on, "Jack Russell's from away, too, and some of you people have been very interested in what he has to say."

Winner liked Leeann's bluntness. He understood why she found it hard to get along with George. No matter what you said, he always took the other side and thought he was clever. Leeann had been patient to put up with him as long as she had, particularly raising their five kids just about single-handedly. George was notably absent whenever there were decisions to be made about the girls. Leeann was a warm loving mother, but a practical woman–liked to get things done. And George . . . George was slower than molasses in January, always tinkering, never finishing a project. His favorite words were, "Well, now wait a minute."

Winner said to the room in general, "What do you people want to do here anyway?"

The impatience in his voice was enough to stir Martin, who ruffled the few strands left on the top of his balding head and sighed. He looked gray and tired. "Seems to me to be some ideas here worth lookin' at," he said, then he rallied, casting an appreciative grin at Alison. Attempting to get a laugh from the crowd, he drawled, "We aren't exactly married to Logan-Russell, now are we? If we was, I'd say this is a pretty poor excuse for a honeymoon."

The crowd crowed in pleasure. Logan-Russell was counted down and out. "Throw the buggers out of bed," someone shouted. As the roar of the crowd died down Ellen injected a serious note, "Just a moment. They did buy land here, and their proposal is before your committee. Even though they're not here to speak for themselves, the committee doesn't have to love them to carry out its work–that is, to determine whether their proposal fits island guidelines."

"Which it doesn't," Leeann said sharply.

Ellen shrugged her shoulders, and shot Leeann a questioning look to encourage her to continue, but before Leeann could open her mouth an older woman with white hair and little half-glasses that perched on the end of her nose, shouted angrily, "Every time somebody wants to build something on the water, every time somebody wants gravel, or wants to dump their trash, they go ahead, put up their buildings, dig their holes, spill their garbage–wherever they want, no matter what you people say. You should be ashamed to call yourselves a planning board. We aren't talking about marriage here. We're talkin' about assault and battery."

She paused and then in a lower voice she used a word she was obviously uncomfortable saying in public, "It's rape–of the land and the water, that's what it is." She sat down, her face flushed and turned for support to an elderly white-haired man who sat next to her. He put his arm around her shoulder and then joined her protest, "I agree. It's a disgrace. And you, Winner . . . . You've got yourself the wrong name. I say we ought to stand up and defend ourselves. We're all losers here."

A few voices chimed in in agreement, but for the most part people in the room seemed to feel that Winner was not at fault. Martin looked dismayed. He was about to speak when Bob unleashed his own frustrations at the older couple.

"Easy for you to say," he said looking around the room angrily because he could not look the two people in the eyes. "You don't need work. Your old man, Harriet, he retired early on what he made with all his fancy sonar equipment. And you, Arvin, you're as bad as your sister, there. You made plenty big bucks over the years fishin'. They's some of us here who can't afford to retire."

The white-haired woman stood again, and shook her fist at Bob. "You don't know what living on a fixed income is, not for all your years, or you wouldn't be so quick to criticize those who've worked so long . . ." she choked up, unable to finish.

Bob snorted, but he leaned back in his chair, turning his back to the pair. Ann and Alison watched nervously for what might come of this angry exchange. Finally, when it seemed that silence would prevail, Alison spoke. "Is there any reason to believe that Logan-Russell's plans are carved in stone? What if you disapprove? Can't you present them with alternatives? Maybe you can convince them to sell to someone else who will do what's right."

Bob swung around and eyed her contemptuously, then he stood up and walked to the back of the room as if to put distance between himself and her opinions. He wanted to tell her off, but something held him back.

"Don't you worry, dearie," a woman spoke up. "They'll do what they want anyway. Bob, he'll be right there with Jack Russell. As long as he's paid, he don't care if the island turns to a pile of chicken shit."

"Hold on," Bob said, walking in the woman's direction. Winner stood quickly to intervene. Putting an amiable hand on Bob's shoulder he said something that only Bob could hear. Bob shook his head and turned away, muttering. Winner went back and sat down.

A man who looked like he was dressed from an L. L. Bean catalog began to speak in a quiet reserved voice. "There are a number of lawyers on this island, both retired and summer people, who might be willing to stand by the town if it were necessary to litigate. I certainly would be willing to donate time to the cause."

The room was galvanized as people grappled with the idea of unexpected reinforcements. They had not wanted to ask for or expected help from summer people. Now when the opportunity presented itself there was a mixture of responses which created a general buzz in the room.

Lenny woke momentarily, the change in climate penetrating his fuzzy head. "Whazzat?" he asked, but nobody answered.

A tiny woman dressed in faded dungaree shirt and pants made her way from the back where she'd been standing near the door. "I'll donate some of my time. My partner will too, I'm sure. We've both had many happy summer days on Lily, and I'd very much like to see the island have some new means of providing income for those of you who need work." She paused, "But in the process of starting fresh, which is what I hope you will see the benefit of doing, please, let's work together to prevent spoiling the character of this place. We tend to take it for granted."

She had a soothing manner about her and when she smiled at the board members she gestured towards Alison and Ann. "These women have started the ball rolling. They've already presented some healthy options." She pointed a finger at the newsprint along the blackboard wall. "There are ideas here worth pursuing, and there could be more. We can all contribute. We should have been coming to planning board meetings all along. At least I should have." She glanced across the room at the gray-haired lawyer. He acknowledged her look graciously.

"I would say Ms. Longstaff is right. We could benefit from calling a halt right here. I think a moratorium might be in order–give you time to go back to the drawing board, do a little investigating," he suggested.

"Which was what I said at the last meeting," Leeann said tiredly.

"Now, wait a minute," George said, and Leeann snapped, "No, George. We have been waiting long enough."

Martin, thought about the next move. He patted the back of his head nervously again and then he said, "You're sayin', we can legally delay Jack Russell, that we have a right to postpone a decision?"

"They forfeited their right to a hearing by being too late, tonight. We can damn well ask them to wait for us," Jimmy crowed happily.

Winner was now impatient. "Of course. We all knew that already. We can turn 'em down if we want to. What's new here is that if they challenge us and start work without our O.K., we can take 'em to court. We got some teeth here finally." As he said the words, he suddenly felt a kinship with summer people he'd never felt before. Maybe these city lawyers were worth something after all.

Leeann said, "Well, this is what I've been hoping for," and there was a general sound of approval. "I move we adjourn for the evening and meet next week at the earliest possible convenience of the members of the planning board. I also say we don't meet with Logan-Russell until we've decided what we are going to do. No more casual conversation with these people."

Martin, looking extremely uncomfortable because he saw that he should reply using parliamentary language to bring the meeting to a close. He never did like the words, but he had to get done somehow. "All in favor?" he asked, but George said gruffly, "No, wait a minute Martin, you need a second and then . . . ," he added, "Oh, all right–never mind. I second it," and everyone on the planning board raised a hand and the meeting adjourned in a great flurry of conversation.

Clarissa lay in a heap under a towering white spruce and moaned loudly. Bernie whispered in her ear, "She's coming." They both could hear Lyla picking her way closer over the roots, and then they saw a flashlight flickering. Bernie watched Lyla as her feet sank in the duff and her ankles wobbled. Layers of pine needles and other decaying matter had made the ground spongy and all but impossible for high heels to negotiate.

"How are you?" Lyla called anxiously, "Are you terribly ill?" and then cried out "Oh, oh damn," as she turned an ankle.

Clarissa moaned again and Bernie called back, "Must be something she ate tonight. We had mussels. Maybe it's the red tide."

"Oh, I'm so sorry. Should we get help?"

Clarissa answered, "I'll be all right in a minute, I hope. It comes and goes." She sat up just as Lyla clambered over a bush and hovered over her.

"Poor thing," she said sympathetically. "Can you walk?"

Clarissa tried to sound weak, "I don't know. The motion of the car over all those bumps might do it again." She groaned again and rubbed her stomach.

Bernie put a hand on Clarissa's forehead and said, "She's cold and clammy–almost shocky. We'd better cover her." She stood and took her dungaree jacket off and put it around Clarissa's shoulders. Lyla struggled out of her cashmere sweater and handed it to Bernie who tucked it over Clarissa's head. Clarissa began to have a genuine hot flash. She thanked God for the timing, and sat back against the tree. It took all she could to keep from discarding the two extra pieces of apparel. From her place under the tree she could see a tempting sliver of shoreline in the distance through the brush. She wanted to strip and dash into the ocean. Instead, she panted and fanned herself. "I feel feverish," she gasped, convincingly, and it was the first true thing she'd said in ten minutes. In the beam of the flashlight the sweat stood out on her forehead.

"Looks like food poisoning, to me," Lyla said. "I think we should get her to a doctor at once."

"Unfortunately," Bernie said, "there is no doctor."

"What?" Lyla was stunned. "No doctor? I can't imagine living in a place where there's no doctor. Jack didn't tell us about that."

Bernie grinned in the darkness. She said, "They have an ambulance for emergencies. The ferry will take a special trip to the mainland–takes around forty minutes, costs over one hundred dollars." Bernie waited for the reaction.

"My lord. What shall we do?" Lyla was clearly alarmed, and Bernie felt guilty for lying.

"I'll be all right." Clarissa, too, felt somewhat culpable, but she'd made up her mind which side she was on and was going to see it through to the end. "I don't need to go to the mainland. I have some camomile tea at Rachel's house and if that doesn't do it I'll have some comfrey. Besides, I'd still have to go another seventy-five or more miles to the hospital once on the mainland."

Bernie remembered passing a small hospital not five miles from the ferry terminal on the other side. She winked at Clarissa who moaned a little for good measure.

Jack and Jess were now standing beside them, a large five volt flashlight aimed directly into Clarissa's face. "How are you doing?" Jack asked with barely concealed impatience.

"Better, I think," Clarissa answered and then bent over.

Bernie smoothed her hand across Clarissa's forehead. "Clammy again," she said.

"Well, we'd better carry her out," Jess said with genuine sympathy. "Can you stand up? We'll make a bridge of our arms, and you can sit back. We'll get you out of here in no time."

"Jess," Lyla said in a cool dramatic voice Bernie and Clarissa had not heard before, "Jack never told us. There's no doctor on this island. I find that incredible."

Jack Russell lost his temper then. "I'm sure there's a doctor. It's just that there isn't one who lives here year round." He snarled at Bernie. "Where did you get your information? They have a clinic. A doctor comes twice a month."

Lyla was not impressed. "I can't believe you failed to tell us," she said angrily. "What else did you leave out?"

"Now Lyla," Jack said.

"Don't Lyla me," she retorted. "I'm beginning to think we should be very careful about signing any agreement with you about this land or any other."

Jack sighed but said nothing, and Jess looked troubled. The two men, carrying Clarissa, made their way back through the underbrush, Jess on one side and Jack on the other. In a tone of concern Clarissa asked, "Is it terribly late?"

"I'm afraid it is. We're an hour and a half late, but you couldn't help it, poor thing," Lyla said kindly. "The most important thing is for you to get some help, some relief from your pain. Imagine, no doctor," she added in a tone of total disbelief.

"Lots of people live in places where there's no doctor," Jack Russell said shortly. "Better for 'em, actually. They're less likely to get sick." He was so obviously annoyed with the evening's events that Bernie couldn't help grinning into the darkness. "They rough it, and they're healthier for it," he continued in a badgering tone.

"And what about cases like this?" Lyla asked indignantly, not waiting for an answer. "Are you feeling any better, Clarissa?" she said holding her flashlight to the side of Clarissa's face and peering anxiously into her eyes.

Clarissa ducked her head, ostensibly to avoid a branch, but mostly to avoid the penetrating regard of Lyla's regard. Lying, she was learning, extracted its price. She decided to stand and walk the rest of the way. Struggling to get out of her helpers' arms, she said, "Look, I'm feeling better and I'll try to walk now." She handed Lyla her cashmere sweater, and then as she removing Bernie's jacket, her hand touched a bulge at the bottom of one of the pockets. She knew what it was. She slipped her hand into the pocket and her fingers curled around the keys to Ann's car.

"We did it!" Ann said gleefully to Solange and grabbed her by the arms. "We did it!" she repeated and they performed a kind of jig over to Alison who joined them as they circled the front lawn of the house at Lily Point.

"And when they meet again," Solange said breathlessly as they stopped their dance, "they will have an easier time because we have been here. We made it happen."

Ellen stood smiling quietly beside the front porch where Rachel and Grace sat.

"I have to thank you for letting me be part of this, even as an observer," Grace said emotionally. "It was simply a wonderful night; I've learned so much."

"It's true," Rachel said proudly. "You did a fantastic job, Ellen, and you, Alison and Ann, all of you. She turned to include Grace, "And you, our historian, you got it all recorded on tape?"

Grace was fervently thankful to report that she had. "I can't tell you how happy I am that I was there for all of this. I'm going to have one helluva transcript."

"How will you use your material?" Alison asked her.

Grace explained, "There's so little written about witchcraft as a positive force. The vast majority of stuff I've read concentrates on the oppression of innocent people accused of witchcraft hundreds of years ago. More recent material is written by sensationalists, tabloid stuff which focuses on satanic cults whose members weren't or aren't necessarily witches but have come to be called that." She smiled shyly at Alison. "I'm sure I don't have to tell you. I mean, it's obvious that we have all been enculturated to react to the wicked witch from *The Wizard of Oz.* How many children do you think would identify The Good Witch out of context–say in some other clothes? She was just a pretty woman, and fairly young compared to her counterpart. Witches are supposed to have pointed chins and long noses with great warts on them. Their bodies are bent and scrawny and their straggly gray hair keeps falling out from under their pointed black hats."

Ellen mused. "Think what religions could do if they all could manage to forget their differences and focus on their shared visions of love and peace."

"It's a shame," Rachel said, momentarily caught up in the vision of great protest marches and lobbying efforts in Washington with officials representing all the churches. "I never felt Catholicism used its power wisely–all that money tied up in the Vatican. It's like they were in a permanent beauty pageant, dressing up in fancy robes, with all that valuable art hanging over their heads–all that pomp and circumstance. If they had really wanted to end poverty they could have marshalled the bishops and cardinals, recruited all the priests and nuns, sold all the treasure and waged all out war. All Catholicism does is threaten and promise. Hell if you're bad, heaven if you're good, but nothing in between. It's like 'jam yesterday, jam tomorrow, but never jam today.' Remember that dialogue between Alice and the White Queen?"

"Mmmm," Grace said, "and Lewis Carroll knew, I'm sure, how apt that remark was." Suddenly, for no apparent reason, Grace rose from the step where she was seated and did her own little dance, hugging herself happily and humming. The moon shone on her audience of women. Their faces were serene.

When Grace came to a standstill, Alison confessed, "I feel as if I've been living two lives the last few weeks and I've just got to share with you what's been happening to me. I want to tell you about Clovis."

Rachel said, "Yes, you must. I've been wanting to know more about her–but, wait–please come in the house and have a cup of coffee while we talk. We'll be warmer there. The dew is sneaking up on us." She ran her hand over the porch step and exhibited her wet palm in the moonlight.

"What time is it anyway?" Solange was worrying about Bernie and Clarissa. "Shouldn't they be back by now? I'd really like to wait for them before we start rehashing the evening."

"Perhaps I should go after them," Ellen said anxiously.

"Oh, I'd give them more time," Ann said. "What could possibly happen? I mean, this man Russell may be a greedy land developer, but he isn't physically violent, certainly?"

Ellen was sure that he was not.

"Give them another half-hour, then we can take a drive out that way," Rachel suggested, and they all agreed. Even as they walked towards the kitchen door, they could hear Ann's car returning.

"What news?" Rachel shouted at them. "How did it go?"

"You'll never believe this woman," Bernie said, tugging at Clarissa to hurry her across the lawn. "She did it. She saved the day. Our heroine–Clare," she called out, holding Clarissa's hand high in the air in a victor's salute.

They bustled around in the kitchen, finding cups and tea bags, measuring their instant coffee, raiding the refrigerator hungrily, talking simultaneously trying to tell it all at once. Eventually they reconvened in the living room.

Bernie began at once to tell the story of the drive. Clarissa shyly received Bernie's praise as if from an older, authoritative person.

With growing amazement, Rachel listened as Bernie described 'Clare's' faked illness, and how she managed by a stroke of luck to steal the car keys and keep them while everyone searched vainly in the duff.

"After half an hour of fruitless searching, Jack Russell lost it," Bernie said. "He swore and shouted and finally struck out on his own to walk to the meeting. The rest of us continued to look for the key for another half hour. Then when we'd had about all we could take and were about ready to walk back, Clare told everyone she needed to search just one more time. She was feeling responsible, she told us, so she took the only bright flashlight of the lot and searched the whole area again." Bernie hooted, "What an actress she is!" Clarissa overwhelmed by her elevation to stardom, waved a hand helplessly as if to stop Bernie.

Bernie just grinned at her. "I watched her out there grubbing around in the pine needles. I was sure the key had gotten lost somehow–slipped out when I was putting the jacket around her shoulders. I had no idea what she was up to. Then suddenly she pops up with it and says dramatically, 'Here they are!' "

"So was anyone there when you got to the schoolhouse?"

"Not a soul. The lights were out. The door was locked," Clarissa crowed. "Jack was furious. He had blisters on his heels–was limping when Bernie and I picked him up. I was almost sorry for the man."

"Huh," Bernie said, "Had he waited for us . . ." she spoke pseudo-righteously, a twinkle in her eye, "had he waited, well, he was just lucky he didn't wait. Clare might have buried him in pine needles."

They all laughed in delight and Rachel drank in the picture of her friends in their new found glory, promising herself never to forget this night.

Ellen said, "Jack Russell deserves whatever he gets."

"So what did they do when they arrived too late?" Ann asked.

"Jack exploded. The only thing he said that made any sense was that it figured."

"And so it does . . . figure," Rachel said.

"What about the other two–Lyla and Jess?" Grace asked.

"They are honest people, essentially well meaning and they took it well, at least with us . . ." Clarissa answered.

"But they were upset with Jack Russell?"

"That was the best part," Bernie said. "I wish you could have been there to hear Lyla. She dismissed Russell, said, 'I'm finished. I will not do business with you. Your attitude is unforgivably rude.' She said that," Bernie repeated, "and Jess sided with her."

"What do you think that means?" Grace asked. "Will they be finished as business partners or is it just for this one piece of land? Will it change what's going on on the island as far as development?"

"Who knows?" Ellen replied. "We'll just have to wait and see. But it sure looks promising."

"Anyway," Bernie continued, "we gave them a ride back to the boat. You should have heard the silence."

"Well, Lyla spoke to us and so did Jess," Clarissa added, "but it was mighty quiet just the same. You could cut it with a knife. I wouldn't be surprised if they took off in the yacht and left Jack high and dry on the island."

"I say we did good work tonight," Rachel beamed. "Hip, hip, hooray." She rose from her chair and went to Clarissa and gave her a hug. "You never cease to surprise me, you know."

"My, heavens," Clarissa said, and hugged Rachel back; then, disentangling herself, she smiled at Rachel and said, "I guess I surprised myself."

"So, tell us the other side," Bernie said. "How did the evening go for you?"

"I believe it went pretty much as we hoped it would," Alison began. "Some people were angry, some were frustrated and others just plain disappointed. But they did some work. People reviewed some of the things they've done and are doing. Others offered suggestions. Two lawyers offered their services pro bono. The islanders looked at what we presented and I think they'll try to make a fresh start, don't you, Ellen?"

"Definitely," Ellen agreed. "I was particularly encouraged to see the lawyers volunteer. That will be a great help when we have to take somebody to court."

Bernie was clearly impressed. "So it went like clockwork then?"

"Not exactly," Ann said. "One of our members turned up late. By the way, Alison, you disappeared while that was going on? How come?"

"I made myself scarce, that's what. When you're finished describing the events, I will explain about all that."

"Anyway, Clovis showed up, and she was drunk and with a man," Ann said.

"She was what? She did what?" Bernie and Clarissa were stunned by the information.

"When we stopped by to see her earlier, on our way back from the store, she looked fine. She didn't look like that kind of person . . ." Bernie faltered.

"She certainly didn't, but we can all testify to what we saw there tonight."

"What about the man?" Clarissa was wide-eyed. "Who was he?"

"The relief Captain of the ferry. It seemed they went on a drinking spree together," Ann said.

Rachel was puzzled. "I have to admit I am a bit flabbergasted by Clovis's conduct. I don't know what the islanders will think of me. I should have been the one to bring her home. I feel bad about that."

"Well, don't. The job could just as easily have been mine, and you notice I'm feeling no shame," Alison replied bluntly. "Now is as good a time as any, I think, to give you the inside story." She glanced around at the other faces in the room and the only one she worried about was Clarissa. Her Catholicism might make her sensitive to criticism of a priest. "I'm sure you've all wondered to some degree why Clovis was such a recluse throughout this whole adventure. She was the one who was so interested in the coven to begin with."

"Yes," Ann said seriously. "I had some thoughts about that."

"I did too," Solange concurred.

Alison took a deep breath and plunged into her explanation. "Clovis was looking for the Devil and a cult of satanism. She expected to find one here. Actually Clovis is not a . . . a she, not a woman at all. He's a priest who wanted to do an exorcism."

"You're kidding!" Ann said.

"No, I'm absolutely serious. I'm his housekeeper. That much is true. He didn't know about my neopaganist views, or he never would have hired me. And I probably wouldn't have worked for him, but I needed the money for graduate school. I just don't make enough as an arbitrator to put anything in a savings account.

"When he first answered the Widdershins ad I was amused with his secret letter writing. I thought he was having a little fling. I found out about the letter when he asked me if he could use my address, and he pretended it was church business. I think he really believed that what he was up to was legitimate. The replies from Rachel came to my apartment, not to the parish house. I mean it's a small community in some ways—even the mail carrier is a member of the parish. Then, of course, when he decided to come to the coven," Alison continued, "he couldn't figure how to get to the island and remain hidden. He needed to use my van, and he couldn't drive it, so he ended up by telling me the truth." Alison shrugged her shoulders. "Later he began to suspect that I was a witch." She chuckled and added, "My red hair—I guess was the connection—made me a child of the devil. An easy step with his rich imagination from there to seeing this whole event as a work of Satan."

"Incredible," Grace said imagining how difficult it would be to do justice to this event in the language of academe.

"Where is he now?" Bernie asked.

"Sleeping it off at the RV," Alison said chuckling. "I don't hold it against him, you know," she smiled. "Actually he's quite harmless."

"What's his name?" Grace asked.

"That's for him to tell you," Alison replied cautiously, thinking of Clarissa and Rachel. "He's miserable enough as it is right now. If he wants to reveal himself, he will. He may march down here tomorrow morning in an attempt to save your souls."

Clarissa was disgusted. "I can't imagine a priest behaving in such an undignified manner. It's one thing to be worried about people involved in cult-like activities, but another entirely to come around and bother a group of women who are trying to do something of value for a community."

Rachel, smiled inwardly. How quickly Clarissa had forgotten her own objections earlier this evening. Another revelation struck Rachel. The face at the schoolhouse had looked so familiar, and now–now she had the context. She knew who it was. Clarissa would be in for a shocking revelation. An insane desire to laugh sweep over her. She could not hold it back. She began with a little chuckle and the chuckle grew till the tears were falling and she was rocking back and forth. Like a wave, her laughter swept over them, catching each woman in its wake until they all went under. Then as one began to get control of herself, another would be inundated. Inevitably, someone paused long enough to ask Rachel what was so hysterical, and she waved her hand, wiped her eyes, and choked out the word "priest," covered her mouth and began to laugh again. At that point, the idea of a priest dressed like a woman was sufficient reason to make anyone laugh.

Exhausted and trembling, Rachel tottered off to the kitchen for a refill of her tea. "We really should go to bed," Clarissa said, trying to be sensible.

"Yes, but what about tomorrow? What if he shows up here?" Ann asked.

Yes, indeed, thought Rachel, listening from the kitchen. "We'll cross that bridge when we come to it," she called to them and the answer satisfied everyone.

Alison said, "You have nothing to fear. He's dying to do an exorcism. You might want to consider letting him try." There was a grin on her face that was irresistible. Everyone began to laugh again.

"Oh, no. Please," Grace said, holding her stomach.

Bernie said, "He really does look a lot like The Church Lady on Saturday Night Live."

"No, he looks like Toad dressed up as the washerwoman in *The Wind in the Willows,*" Ann said, "Remember him?"

"Oh, god," Alison said, totally delighted. "I wondered if anyone else would see that resemblance."

Clarissa was instantly sober. "I wouldn't give him the satis faction of talking about him anymore, whoever he is. He's a disgrace to the Church, disguising himself in women's clothes."

"Let's call it a night," Solange said.

"In the morning," Alison added, "you'll know better what to do. I'll get the whole story about what happened with the captain and let you know. Good night." She slipped out the screen door and started up the road.

There was a general gathering of shoes and sweaters by Ann, Solange and Bernie preparatory to departure for their tent. Grace had claimed the living room couch and was already curled up in her sleeping bag. Ellen made the rounds, giving each a hug. "Thank you all so much for your help," she said affectionately. "It was a great boost for me and for the islanders."

"You're so welcome, dear," Rachel said and kissed her on the cheek.

"What about your cat, Grace?" Ann asked, remembering that Increase had disappeared.

"Oh, that's right." Rachel was instantly concerned. "Shouldn't we go and look for him now? You stay here, Grace. I know you're tired."

"You are not to go looking for him now," Grace said. "I've put out a dish of food," she motioned to the outside windowsill beside her where a small screen was propped in the window. "He'll be back and I'll let him in. He always managed to find his way home–back in his wandering minstrel days. I just hope he doesn't sing for you tonight after we finally get to sleep."

"If he does, we'll recognize his song. We've heard it before, remember?" Solange said giving Grace a bear hug. "Not to worry. I've got to go to sleep, right now," she said and those were the last words of the evening.

Rachel focused on the wallpaper that covered the ceiling. Tiny carnations danced stem to stem with bachelor buttons and blue forget-me-nots. The paper was at least

fifty years old. Younger than me, Rachel thought, yet already distinguished in its own right. Practically an antique. She chuckled.

Clarissa, lying awake in the next room, heard her. "What's so funny?" she asked.

"I don't know. I've got that light-headedness that comes when you can't sleep even though you desperately need to. The wallpaper was amusing me."

"Go back to sleep for a half hour. I'll wake you with fried eggs and bacon."

"Hmmmm," Rachel said, "That sounds great, Clare, but I know what you think of bacon and eggs–all cholesterol."

There was a silence on the other side of the wall. "Not you too," Clarissa said.

Rachel was disappointed. "I was only kidding about the cholesterol, Clarissa. Just make me a cup of tea."

"Not that," Clarissa sounded sulky. "You called me Clare. I let a stranger get away with it, but not you."

Rachel hadn't heard herself do it, but she recovered quickly. "All the more reason, Clarissa. Why shouldn't I call you Clare? You allow a young woman to call you that–you should allow me to do so–without giving it a thought." She giggled and Clarissa was overcome with tenderness for her. She smiled happily, and pulled herself out of bed. "I'll get up and make breakfast. Go back to sleep."

"Actually, I've decided I don't want to go back to sleep. Come in here for a minute. I've something to tell you."

Clarissa came dutifully, wrapping herself in her old flannel bathrobe and settling at the end of the bed.

"I want to talk about a couple of things." Rachel looked stern, almost forbidding.

"Heavens, you should have something to eat first. You shouldn't talk about serious things on an empty stomach."

"It's this," Rachel began, ignoring what she characterized as Clarissa's nutritional peckishness. "The priest," she hesitated and stared at Clarissa willing her to know so she wouldn't have to say the words.

"The priest . . ." Clarissa repeated dully after her. "What about the priest?"

"Oh, Clarissa," Rachel was exasperated. "Don't you realize who he is?"

Clarissa grasped for understanding and failed. She was impatient. "No, Rachel. I'm afraid I don't. Is it important?"

"It should be to you," Rachel asserted.

And Clarissa understood. "Father Donahey," she said softly.

Rachel nodded solemnly. "We're going to have to face him, Clarissa."

Clarissa did not argue the point. Instead she listened to Rachel, watching her with a glassy look. Finally Rachel asked, "Are you afraid of his being here–that he might condemn you, Clarissa? If so, I'd be glad to tell him that you have not been a part of the rituals."

Clarissa shook her head. "I can't think straight. It's so crazy–this whole thing is."

"Well?"

Clarissa thought for a moment. "I guess I'm a bit angry. I think what he has done is insane, but he did it because he believed he was acting in behalf of the church. That's what bothers me. The fact that he could get that idea . . . oh, I can't think clearly just now."

"But you had fun last night–you liked being a part of the group didn't you?"

"Yes, but I didn't feel as if it had anything to do with religion."

"But you knew it did for me."

"I guess so, but even when you left the church I believed you'd eventually return. In some ways it all seems so foolish–the stuff we did this weekend–I mean the part in the moonlight. Now really, how could the Catholic Church consider that sinful?"

Rachel shook her head. "They think a lot of stuff is sinful that I never looked at as bad. But you understand, don't you, that if they didn't think our ritual was evil, it might be because they don't think it's significant. Isn't that what you're doing?"

"Dismissing it, you mean?" Clarissa asked. She thought for a moment. "Well, maybe. I don't think it deserves to be called a serious ritual–that part in the moonlight. It's kid stuff really. Not nearly as impressive as what the church offers." She looked out at the point of land where they had been last night. "Best of everything I've loved about the church is the ritual."

"Me too," Rachel empathized. "I miss it sometimes.

Still . . . ," she pondered for a moment, "most ritual practiced today has its origins in ancient religion. Things were simpler then without all the pomp and ceremony. They probably worshipped in the wilderness. Certainly Jesus did not have the Vatican and all the impressive wealth and power to back him up. He did his magic with parables, with words and acts of love and gentleness."

"Come back," Clarissa said mournfully.

Rachel was startled. She had moved beyond Catholicism to her own personal and mystical view of early Christianity. She smiled sadly when she understood what Clarissa meant. "Too late," she murmured, reaching out to hold Clarissa's hand. "I'd like to think I could take part in designing new rituals. No woman will ever do that in the Catholic Church. And as far as last night–a real coven would probably have been much more impressive in its ceremony. Alison, after all, had to do it all on her own."

"But they'll never have the Mass, and all the stained glass, all the statues, the stations of the cross, all that."

"No, but whatever there is, I can be more actively a participant in it–a real part, not just a member of the congregation."

"Oh, Rachel. You know that's unfair. We participate. We have roles to play. What about Communion?"

"Clarissa, if I told you what I think of transubstantiation, you'd be furious."

"You already did, don't you remember? You think it's symbolic cannibalism."

Rachel nodded solemnly. "That kind of God-eating was going on long before Christianity. It started with the real thing centuries before Jesus." She paused and released Clarissa's hand.

"Never mind me. I understand why you love the church. When I was a kid I used to dress up and play altar boy. A friend and I had our own ritual. We carried it out, unbeknownst to my parents, on the front steps of the Episcopal Church down the street from my house. I loved it, because it was mysterious and brought me closer to the magic.

"Yet, on another level I understood that I was blasphemous. I loved the daring, the act of defiance against both the Episcopal and the Catholic churches."

"But you were a Catholic," Clarissa protested.

"But I was also a child, Clarissa, a girl child. Don't you understand? I could never be an altar boy, never a priest, only in make-believe."

"Funny, I never wanted to be an altar boy or priest."

"Most women have been brought up to see themselves only in female roles. I'm one of the exceptions, but there should be room for the exceptions to serve as well. They shouldn't be excluded."

They sat quietly staring out at the cove and then Clarissa said, "So you think the church got its rituals from paganism?"

"You must know the answer to that, Clarissa," Rachel said softly.

"So in a way, the church started out like you did–playing on someone else's altar, just as you all were in the moonlight –looking for ways to express reverence for the mysteries of life, or ways to show their love for God."

"Yes, but they left us out."

"Not really. Mary is the mother of God, after all."

"She once was The Goddess, Earth Mother, then she got dethroned, tossed down so to speak. She's not God, Clarissa, and although in some places Mary receives honor as the Mother of God, in the Protestant religions she all but disappeared.

"I think Christianity incorporated her as a way to convert the pagans who still worshiped her. They had to find a place for her or the people wouldn't try the new religion. Mary was once called Brigit, the Triple Goddess–virgin, mother, and crone."

"That's your version, and I respect your right to your own opinion." Clarissa was firm.

"No, Clarissa. That's not my version. It's written in many mythology books. I'll lend you my copy of *The White Goddess* by Robert Graves anytime."

"But Christianity isn't a myth," Clarissa insisted. Rachel saw that the discussion was at a stand still. She turned back to the crisis at hand. "What are you going to do about Father Donahey?"

"Does he know I'm here–that I've been part of this?"

"I don't see how he could."

"Oh," Clarissa said in exasperation, "I think he's been an ass about this whole thing. I don't care what he thinks anymore. I'll see him eventually. Meanwhile I'll get us some breakfast."

"Wait a minute, Clarissa. I know you really don't want to make bacon and eggs, and anyway, I've something else I want to tell you, something I haven't talked about with anyone. I promise it's not about the church."

Clarissa looked down at Rachel's hands absently smoothing the bedspread. They were so familiar with their prominent dark veins and liver spots. She felt especially close to Rachel and understood that this was an unusual moment in their friendship. Rachel seldom confided in her.

"When I was a mere child, I had a baby," Rachel said quietly, her voice almost a whisper.

Clarissa could think of nothing to say to this startling revelation, and Rachel continued, "I think that child, that daughter might be here. Solange might be my daughter."

"Solange? How could that be?"

Rachel told her the story of her brief love affair with the music teacher.

"But Solange has an English last name. And you say his name was Artolla."

"She had her foster parent's name, but you can see she looks Spanish?"

Clarissa acknowledged that she certainly did.

"And did you hear that beautiful voice when she sang? Music has to be in her genes."

Clarissa was beginning to see the possibilities. "She's lived in Portland five blocks from you all these years, and you never even knew where she was?"

"No."

"What are you going to do?"

"I don't know yet. I've grown fond of her. I'm not sure I can tell her. She might be disappointed–or angry."

"This is so difficult." Clarissa said. "I had no idea. Rachel, why have you never spoken about your having a baby?"

"I wanted to put it behind me. I never expected this to happen. Never in my wildest fantasies. I'd given her up for lost. I'd been determined not to think about it for years before I met you, and most of the time I succeeded. Then when Solange told her story last night, it hit me. I think she might–just might be my child–my own child grown up."

"I think she is," Clarissa announced decisively as if the knowledge had been there in her head all along.

Rachel looked out the east window and gasped. Across the lawn she saw Father Donahey making his way toward the house, his clerical collar in place.

"What is it?" Clarissa said.

"Father Donahey," Rachel said, knowing this was going to be a confrontation. She wanted to be the first to talk with him. From the days when she had listened to him pontificate, she knew he would convey a kind of angry righteousness that could intimidate Clarissa. Perhaps she could say something to dissuade him . . . send him off before Clarissa had to get involved. It seemed important to shelter her from his vindictiveness.

She crawled out of bed carefully, but even then her right knee wrenched painfully. She was always stiff in the morning, but after last night's expedition to the beach and back over the rocks, she was particularly lame. She picked up her clothes hurriedly and began to put them on. "Listen, let me be the one to make breakfast. You stay here for a bit. I'd really like to spend some time alone with him. Then you can have your turn later, all right?" she asked winningly.

Clarissa was not at all reluctant to do as she suggested.

"Stay here, or get back into bed. I'll have someone bring you an herbal tea when I make some for him. Some fruit and yogurt too. I'll tell you what's happened when I come back."

She fumbled with the last button of her skirt, damning the osteoarthritis in her fingers, pulled her blouse over her head and tossed her shawl across her shoulders. She limped down the stairs favoring the right knee.

As she walked through the living room she discovered Grace curled up in her sleeping bag on the couch, still asleep. Quietly she pulled the living room door closed behind her as she stepped down into the kitchen.

At the stove, she dipped water from the big pot into the tea kettle and lit the burner. None too soon. When she looked up Father Donahey was already on the top step peering in through the door window. That'll teach me to put curtains up, Rachel thought as she saw him frowning at her. Oh, well, might as well get this over with.

"Come on in," she told the priest reluctantly, and noticed the peculiar look on his face–a kind of smile for the doomed, she imagined, and was surprised by her own ability to see the humor in her thought. Twenty years ago she would have been down on her knees begging him for forgiveness.

As she issued her invitation, Solange appeared at the door, yawning. Would there be an opportunity to talk to her alone, Rachel wondered silently. Everyone would be awake shortly. She ushered them both in, deciding it would be wiser to serve the priest his tea outside where she could talk to him privately.

"Help yourself to breakfast, Solange," she said smiling. "There's hot water in the kettle and there'll be more in the big pot shortly. I'll serve Father Donahey a cup of tea on the lawn."

Father Donahey turned to acknowledge the woman behind him, a look of dismay passing over his face. "Not you, too. You were a member of the parish all your childhood days–until–when was it?" He didn't bother to finish his thought, but turned and brushed by her in a nasty way.

Unruffled, though obviously as shocked as he was, Solange replied, "Right."

Rachel briskly filled three cups, pulled some fruit and yogurt from the crowded refrigerator. She grabbed a spoon and napkin. "Here, Solange. Would you just take these to my guest upstairs, and help yourself," she added. She gave a knowing look and said no more. Rachel took the other two cups of tea. Holding the door open with her foot, she ushered the priest outside to the gentle rise of land in back of the house where the view of the cove was commanding.

She handed him his cup. "You know her, Father Donahey?"

"Yes, of course. A nice person from a good Catholic home. A shame . . ." he paused and looked hard at her. "And you know her, too, of course."

"What do you mean?" Rachel felt a chill. What if he knew this was her child. Should she ask? She felt breathless, and her heart lurched. She took a deep breath and plunged on, deciding not to wait for his answer. "What can I do for you Father Donahey? I've a busy day ahead."

"You must know, Rachel, that your soul is in mortal danger, as is Solange's."

"I know no such thing," she replied tartly.

"Of course," he said sarcastically. "You've lost your faith."

"Actually, I think I'm beginning to regain it," Rachel said.

"Oh?" He raised an eyebrow and waited.

She wanted to keep him that way–hold him in suspense until he could stand it no longer, but he replied, "You still have time to redeem yourself. This is evil business you've gotten involved in."

She thought fleetingly of giving a recital of her list of grievances with the church, but she knew he would have only the one set of answers to give. The outcome would be satisfying to neither of them.

"Look, I'm not one of your lost sheep. I've found my own way, as an adult. Each day I realize with growing satisfaction that what I'm doing is right for me. I've had to find my own salvation."

He looked at her pityingly. She'd seen that look on his face in the past, but this time it had no powers. "We have a disagreement, Father, about what is evil, that's all. Why don't we just let it go at that."

"Because my understanding of evil is not based on personal opinion, as is yours. It's based on the authority of the Church."

"I don't really want to debate with you," Rachel said. "Why don't you sit here and enjoy your tea and the view. I've got to get breakfast for my guests." She turned to walk away from him to find Clarissa crossing the lawn toward her, a cup of tea in hand.

Father Donahey turned at the same time and she heard him let out his breath, "No."

"Hello, Father," Clarissa said quietly. So calm, Rachel thought. She's been transformed.

"My child," Father Donahey said, and Rachel squirmed inside. Clarissa tucked herself neatly into one of the lawn chairs and with a graceful gesture invited Father Donahey to occupy the chaise near her. He lifted his tea bag from his cup, glanced at Rachel. She took it from him neatly and threw it in the bushes.

He said, "I'd like to be alone with Clarissa."

Rachel turned to go, but Clarissa stopped her.

"There's nothing confidential here as far as I'm concerned. This is Rachel's home. You can say anything you want in front of her. She's been my best, actually my only friend, for years."

Rachel felt tears start in her eyes. She would not leave Clarissa alone now under any circumstances. She let herself down gingerly into the nearest deck chair.

"Clarissa," Father Donahey began pompously, "your soul is in peril."

"Perhaps," Clarissa faltered, "but who knows?"

"The Church knows. Trust me," he said. "Your soul is hovering over an abyss. This woman and the others like her have gone over the edge already. They're trying to take you with them."

"Why would they do that, Father?" Clarissa asked, seemingly innocent.

"They are possessed by the Devil," he said triumphantly.

"Such nonsense," Clarissa said, suddenly angry. "That's archaic foolishness, Father Donahey. There is no devil connected with this group. Furthermore, if the church wants to hold people like me, it is going to have to stop trying to intimidate us. I can get my spiritual support elsewhere. I don't need to hear all that superstitious gobbledegook. The next thing you'll be doing is holding an exorcism."

Father Donahey's face turned red.

"This," Clarissa said pointing at Rachel, "is not Rosemary,

and I am not her baby." She smiled lightly. "And I know you're feeling like you've lost one of your parishioners, but that may not necessarily be true. I will be back. There are too many things about the Church I love."

"Unless you renounce this unholy alliance and ask for forgiveness, that might not be possible," Father Donahey said threateningly, but he saw the look on her face and knew she was unmoved. He changed tack. "This is most depressing," he said. "I am deeply saddened by your callous behavior. You are only hurting yourself I'm afraid."

"No, Father. You're the one that's hurting." She looked at Rachel and gave her a sly, quick wink. She continued. "I'll tell you what–if you let me come back to Mass on my own terms, I'll see to it that no one, not the Bishop, or anyone in our parish ever finds out about Clovis and the Captain."

She watched his eyes which seemed to bulge beyond their usual extent. "And another thing. You've just said you felt depressed. I suggest you try tryptophan. It's a mood elevator–helps when you're feeling down. Yogurt or turkey are good sources."

"But that's blackmail." Father Donahey said, jumping to his feet. He swayed back and forth and his face was purple. Rachel considered the possibility that he might have a stroke. She reached for him, but he warded her off.

Clarissa continued unmoved. "Not at all. I'm just offering you a nutritional tip." She sounded almost flip. Rachel was stunned.

The priest made the sign of the cross and began an incantation. It was all that was left to do at this point. He'd never expected his great adventure to come to such a horrible end.

Clarissa watched a second longer as he flapped his rosary in the wind, then waved him off, "No, Father, don't do that. It's embarrassing. Besides I have to go in and get my breakfast. See you in church." She gave Rachel a hand to pull her gently from the deck chair. Together they walked away. Father Donahey sat down heavily, his teacup tilting precariously on the arm of the chaise.

Gathered around the kitchen table, Ann, Bernie and Solange were spooning in mouthfuls of yogurt mixed with granola. They had been bemoaning the fact that they had missed Clarissa's latest declaration of independence.

"I thought I'd seen it all last night," Bernie said, her arm draped over Clarissa's chair. "You're moving too fast for me, Clare."

"When you get to be my age, you make the best of your time . . . ," Clarissa eyed them soberly, "that was not a pleasant confrontation and I'm still feeling it."

"Understandably," Solange said. "I took the easy way out and avoided him."

"And the other thing is," Clarissa continued, "I find at my time of life . . . I want to change without changing."

"Sounds impossible," Ann said.

"No, she's saying she wants to have her wheat germ, and eat it too," Rachel quipped from the stove where she was scraping the last bit of bacon and eggs from the pan.

Clarissa continued dauntlessly. "In a way. I want to stop time but keep on gaining the wisdom that comes with aging," she laughed softly. "No. What I really meant, I guess, is to keep what there is of value from my past experience in the Church, and also join you people when you meet . . . if you meet again?"

"That's great, Clare. I knew you'd find a way to be with us." Bernie was jubilant.

"But when are we meeting?" Ann asked.

"I hate to have this weekend be over," Solange added sorrowfully. "It's been so wonderful–all of us working together. The least we could do is get together once a year."

"I want you all to return next summer, that's for sure." Rachel said. "Let's make the Solstice an annual event."

"I feel as if we're just beginning to know one another. I don't know about anybody else, but I'd like us to meet more often–perhaps once a month," Ann suggested.

"We have more to do than decide on when we meet again." Alison stepped through the kitchen door and slid into a chair as if she had been at the table all along. "We've got some unfinished business to take care of before we go back to the mainland."

"How do you read people's minds anyway?" Bernie demanded.

Alison chuckled, "It's a skill. Such things come in time to those who are open to them."

"I hope so," Rachel said. "because I'm willing to be open."

"Meanwhile," Alison said, "there are at least two bits of work to do and some good things yet to happen. I tracked Father Donahey down here this morning. He was determined to expose the evil doings, as he called them, and I couldn't talk him out of it, so I followed at a discreet distance. I stood in the shower stall just in case you needed me, but you handled him beautifully. That was not an easy job you had to do–either of you."

"We have had some practice over the years after all," Rachel said wryly, "especially Clarissa who is still among the faithful."

"Thanks, but I'm not sure being faithful helped all that much," Clarissa said briefly. She had been thinking of Rachel and her need to speak to Solange. "I think we should all go outside instead of wasting what's left of our day inside. You people have an afternoon boat to catch and I only have until tomorrow morning."

Rachel saw her opportunity. "Yes, please go and enjoy the morning. Solange, would you mind staying for just a minute? I'd like to talk with you."

"We'll be down fighting over who gets the hammock. Come join us when you've finished," Ann called back.

Rachel settled herself across the table from Solange. She wondered if, after these next few moments of revelation, she would ever feel comfortable with this woman again. "I might as well tell you that I was staggered by your initial introduction last night, the part about your life as a child." She continued hesitantly, "You talked about being in a foster home. They never offered to adopt you?"

"No. I used to think my father or mother had stipulated

that. I guess I wanted to believe one of or both of them intended to come back and get me. Obviously that was a childish fantasy. No," she repeated. "From birth, I stayed with one family who got paid more than what the state would pay under ordinary circumstances. My foster parents liked having the money."

"Did they mistreat you?" Rachel was swept with remorse that her own child might have been subjected to abuse, that she herself could not have prevented it.

"No, not physically. It was more a case of being invisible. They knew I was there, but in a way it didn't mean anything to them. Nobody was cruel, nobody was loving. They did what they thought was expected. I went to church, was fed, clothed. I got presents at Christmas and on my birthday, but they were presents that were given matter-of-factly, like you'd put a dime in a parking meter.

"I never asked for anything," she continued, matter-of-factly. "I always felt like I was on hold, waiting for my father or mother to come back."

"They never did," Rachel said sadly.

She shook her head. "My father sent me small amounts of money once in awhile. In a way that fueled my hopes."

"And your mother?"

"I know nothing about her."

"Do you know your real date of birth?

"My foster-mother made a big thing over the fact that she had to make up a date. It's the one I have always used: February 2, 1934 and it's on the birth certificate."

Well, the year was right, anyway. The correct date was January 15, 1934. Rachel's hands turned to ice. "That could be it," she breathed, her heart beating rapidly. She sat back in her chair to wait. She wasn't quite sure for what.

Solange looked on questioningly. Rachel's words made no sense, and yet there was something . . . .

"When I was eighteen," Rachel began falteringly, "my parents were very strict. Not like your foster parents though. They were loving. They did care, but they weren't exactly enlightened. I had no social life to speak of, except in the classroom. I was expected to do well in school and I did. I was to learn the arts and literature, and I was to be a lady. I went to Bates College, but I had to live at home. Dormitory facilities as we know them today were non-existent." She laughed, "Heavens! My parents would never have allowed me to live in the kind of dorm today with both boys and girls."

Solange was tense. She wanted to hear each word, but she needed Rachel to get to the point quickly.

Rachel, aware only of her own struggle, went on, "I took piano lessons while I was at Bates with a visiting pianist–an artist in residence, only they wouldn't have called him that back then. He was just a piano teacher. His name was Roberto Artolla."

Solange took a deep breath as she looked at Rachel for the first time, a look of understanding growing in her expression. She studied Rachel's face to discover some gesture, some sign that would reveal a connection between them.

"I fell in love with him," Rachel said simply.

"So," Solange blurted. It was the only word she could find.

"I think . . . I'm pretty sure, I'm your mother." Rachel rushed onward, knowing the next thing she had to say was crucial. "I was not allowed to keep my baby. My parents . . . ," her voice cracked and she was unable to finish. When she had gained a measure of control she continued, "In those days it was a disgrace. There was never a question of marriage, even though I loved him terribly. He was not acceptable because he was not American. So you see . . . ," she broke down again, then recovered, "you might be my lost daughter."

Solange had tears in her eyes. "Oh, Rachel, how incredible this is." Her mind raced for clues, evidence that Rachel might be her real mother. Rachel watched her anxiously. "I don't know what to say, the idea is so overwhelming. I do know one thing. Having a mother at long last is like a dream come true. It doesn't even matter whether it turns out to be fact. I will accept you as my mother, my friend. It's all right. Really it is. Don't cry." She tipped over her chair as she attempted to reach Rachel and hold her. They began to laugh and weep simultaneously.

"I have wanted to know about my mother all this time, wondered who she was, where she was, and now . . . ," she stopped suddenly. "You realize I do not know my father's name. There's no way I can legally acquire that knowledge. His estate was transferred with the condition–that I never be told."

"Oh," Rachel gasped, feeling as if her link to Solange had weakened somehow. "Then we can never know for sure."

"Not necessarily. You might be able to find out. You could use the name of Roberto Artolla as a beginning. We could search his records. In the meantime," Solange said, "You've wanted a daughter. You've got one. I hereby declare myself as willing to serve in that capacity. Even if nothing comes of our search, we don't have to be blood relations to be family. Why not?"

Rachel's felt the familiar fluttering in her chest and she felt breathless. She sat quietly for a moment listening to her heart until it was regular again. She looked at Solange and felt deeply moved by this would-be daughter. She said, "Why not?"

They took their story between them tenderly, as if it were a precious live thing, out of the kitchen, over the lawn and the blueberry field to the shore where it was joyfully received by their friends.

"How will Alison deal with Father Donahey?" Rachel wondered aloud. "He must be completely unhinged by now." It was later in the morning when they had all returned to the house. "She'll be the one to bear the brunt of his reaction."

"Ah, but he needs her," Solange said wisely.

"I'd love to be a fly on the wall," Bernie said.

"If she doesn't show up in a little while, we could take a walk up there," Ann said. "She might need rescuing."

"She'll be fine," Bernie said, dismissing Ann's nervousness. "It's the priest I'd worry about."

Suddenly Clarissa remembered Grace, still sleeping in the next room. "Think how much she has missed in just a few short hours? We really should wake her," she said to the others.

As if she'd been heard, the door to the living room opened and Grace stood smiling, her arms around a bundle of purring cat.

"Well, look who's back! The return of the prodigal son," Ann said.

"Wow. I slept so late," Grace said wonderingly.

"It's the sea air and all the excitement," Rachel said.

Grace released Increase who was struggling to get down and then she went to the stove to make herself some tea.

"Careful," Clarissa warned, "you don't want him to escape again." She reached over to hook the screen door.

"I have to tell you," Grace said happily. "He came to the windowsill, ate the food in his dish, then asked to be let in."

"You're kidding," Ann said.

"Nope. I've caught him that way before. I knew it would work. So what's been happening? Have I missed something?"

"Have you missed something?" Bernie fairly shouted. "You'd better believe it."

"You only missed the reunion of a mother and daughter!" Ann said, gesturing to Rachel and Solange.

"Well, we have decided that's what it is," Rachel said and told the story. Solange sat happily by her side, more than pleased to interject her parts of the tale.

"What a thing to wake up to!" Grace said. She came to Rachel and Solange and held them, and once again everyone laughed and wept together.

Bernie resumed as if there had been no interruption, "And then there is the news about Clovis, who is really Father Donahey. We learned that while you were sleeping, too!"

"Just a minute." Grace said dumbfounded. "Who's Father Donahey? I can't keep up here."

Rachel chuckled happily. "This was a rare morning, Grace, and you slept right through it. So much for your primary research." Everyone roared.

"Father Donahey," Grace said wonderingly. "Should I know that name? Oh, of course I do. He's the priest at . . ." she hesitated, then memory flooded back. "Doesn't he have the parish over on Munjoy Hill in Portland? I did a story once on the church. Is it St. Bernadette's?"

"That's the one. That's him," Clarissa said.

Solange looked at Rachel and said, "And there are two of us who flew his coop, mother and daughter renegades, each in her own time."

"And never once saw each other at mass before that," Rachel added.

"Well, I hope to get you both back," Clarissa said, confidently, as if it would be easier with two than it would with one.

"I can't believe your persistence," Rachel said, but not snappishly as she might have in the past. "Most people wouldn't attempt to mix witchcraft with Catholicism as casually as you. I certainly couldn't."

"And most people wouldn't intimidate their priest, either," Alison said, as she tugged at the locked screen door, Ellen waiting behind her.

"Hold on," Rachel crowed, unlatching the door, "wait till you hear what happened while you were gone." As she spoke she had the uncanny feeling that Alison already knew. Instinctively, she turned to Ellen and told the story one more time.

"You should take out another ad in the paper to let the whole world know. Maybe somebody will know something that you don't know." Ellen warmed to the obvious joy of Rachel and Solange.

"Believe me, the Portland paper will be interested. You won't have to place an ad," Grace said. "That's the kind of human interest story editors die for."

"At any rate," Ellen added, "congratulations, or is that the right thing to say when one has been part of a near-miracle? I want you to know I'm very happy for you both." She turned to Clarissa. "I hear you had a little confrontation with Clovis, alias Father Donahey, this morning."

"Yes, indeed, and I've been a bit worried how Alison was

going to manage after that little conflict. Has he talked to you about what happened here this morning?"

"Has he stopped talking, you mean! His version is that you are blackmailing him."

Clarissa looked a bit taken back.

Rachel saw her reaction. "Come on, you knew he'd see it that way. You counted on it."

"Oh, dear," Clarissa moaned. "Maybe I shouldn't have said what I did."

"Oh, pooh. He's fine," Alison said, dismissing Clarissa's concern with a wave of her hand. "Listen, he has me to contend with. I'm his mixed blessing, remember? He needs a ride home. Isn't that a riot? I have him over a barrel.

"Anyway, he doesn't really believe you would do anything to hurt him. You're a lost soul, a victim. I, on the other hand, am the perpetrator, the devil incarnate. He can't fire me because he knows that I, unlike you, have nothing to lose if I go and speak to the Bishop. I could reveal how I traveled with a strange old lady to Lily Island. He's terrified that the Bishop will think he's possessed. Secretly, I think he harbors the notion that he can still perform an exorcism–on himself."

She shrugged her shoulders. "He's a complicated person, really. Part of him knows that what he did here was incredibly stupid, putting his position in the Church in jeopardy. Part of him loves the voodoo, the hocus-pocus, devil stuff. Then there is also the homebody part of him who is tickled pink that I will be staying on as his housekeeper. He loves my cooking. That's a venial sin, I think." She seemed pleased with the thought.

"What's he doing now?" Rachel asked.

"What he needed to do."

"He's praying," Grace said.

Alison shook her head.

"He's eating?"

"No. He's finished breakfast. I made him his favorite tomato and cheese omelet."

"That would do it," Solange said.

"Almost." Alison said. There was a twinkle in her eye.

"So what else did it take?"

"Pet Semetary, one of Stephen King's books. I had it hidden in the RV. I knew I might need it as my ace in the hole. He's like a dog with a chew stick."

"Now I know you are a witch." Bernie said, laughing.

The sound of voices moved toward them down the driveway and Alison called out the door to Martin and Winner who strode purposefully toward the house. They stood looking like Bible salesman, in their best Sunday suits. Winner was the first to speak. "Ladies. Hope we're not interruptin' your Sunday. We just wanted to catch you before you leave. Rachel," he nodded politely in recognition that this was her house, then he turned to Martin whose hand rushed to his head.

"I guess . . ." Martin stalled, his fingers still running through his few strands of hair. "Ah . . . , we'd like to talk some more about . . . if you could come back again, if you would? Ellen, here, said that the two of you," he acknowledged Ann and Alison, "have some experience in settlin' disputes. Now, we'll be goin' back to the drawin' board here shortly, as you heard last night. We got some proposals from Logan-Russell long overdue for action. They been sort of . . . stagnatin', but maybe if we could sit down together and take a look, put some order–priority, we could make some sense–er, ah . . . get on with it . . . ." He cleared his throat and looked over their heads at some distant point. They could tell that he wished he were somewhere else. "Miss, er . . . ah, Solange, is it?" He pronounced the "g" hard. "We are also interested in talking with you about your, ah, possible investment in the island."

Winner nodded. "That we are."

"I'd be pleased to meet with you," Solange answered.

Ellen turned to the women. "Martin and Winner have worked incredibly long hours to the benefit of this island. They're a top notch team, real diplomats, and they could use the expertise you have to offer. They've had some real tough sledding and, I gather, there'll be more before this issue of land use is resolved."

"Well, I don't know how much good diplomacy does when you're dealin' with rascals. Can't see as we've got very far . . . ," Martin said, "but t'wouldn't hurt us to listen to a few outsiders–get your opinion on all this."

"Right," Winner intervened briskly. "So if you're interested, we'd like to set up a time?" He looked at all three women. "We'd like to have you come back in two or three weeks at the latest, so's we can get this thing cleaned up."

"The island would expect to pay for your services," Martin added quickly to Ann and Alison.

"Why that's great!" Alison said. "I'm sure we can arrange something." She glanced at Ann and Solange. "We'll let you know the first of the week–send you our fee schedule and other particulars. Actually, we could give Ellen a call, and she can let you know."

"That would be dandy," Martin said, visibly relieved. He reached over and poked Ellen ever so lightly on the shoulder and said, "Good day, ladies."

Rachel was ecstatic, "Did you see that? That was another miracle–people working together! I have to say what an incredible feeling of joy it gives me to see our coming together provide some benefit to the community." She was glowing with the feeling of success.

The women's approaching departure closed in on them, and their sense of elation turned inward. Rachel and Clarissa puttered around the kitchen finishing small domestic tasks while the others focused on leave-taking. There was that pleasant kind of quiet that arises after people complete a difficult undertaking. Finally Grace dipped one more time into their recent success. "You must be proud, Alison, to have brought us along so well in this process."

"I'm feeling content," Alison said, "with a very fine beginning. In fact, I'm thinking of writing about it. Maybe we could share our perceptions of events, exchange manuscripts at some point." She regarded Grace quietly, and then continued. "I know you understand that what happened here didn't evolve out of a need for domination or control."

Grace nodded. "Precisely the opposite."

"I came along on Father Donahey's journey with the sense that fortune takes you where you are needed–The Goddess Fortuna, that is." She laughed and added, "I knew I wouldn't find Satan. Father Donahey is the closest I've ever come to a devil."

She continued, "What I found here encouraged me. It was great working with women so keen, so open and ready to learn about creating a spiritual realm." She perched on the stair between the kitchen and the living room watching Grace pack her gear. "In my opinion, the most important events were brought about through the combined imagination and intelligence of everyone, not just what anyone did individually. That's what gives me the most pleasure in The Craft–that kind of counterclockwise collaboration–a kind of web of support that opposes the forces of domination."

Grace followed Alison's words intently. "I did see that kind of effort. It was exhilarating, but can it be put to work in larger groups?"

"Has it ever been tried?" Alison returned. "Have we ever taught the skills of negotiating a no-lose resolution, for instance, to children in the public schools? We've been so used to having a hierarchy in which the orders come from on high." She glanced around the room to include the others, then realized it was not the best time for a philosophical discussion. "Another time," she conceded.

"Synergy," Clarissa echoed thoughtfully to herself, as if she had finally got the meaning. Everyone in the room heard her.

"Plus strength in numbers," Alison said going over to hug Clarissa.

Rachel, elbows on either side of her coffee cup, sat at the kitchen table slowly returning from her reverie. The vision of eight women on the beach that first summer slipped into a review of solstice processions in succeeding years.

Clarissa, beside her in their sunny apartment, studied the view of Portland harbor outside their kitchen window. They began to chat idly, planning the following summer's trip to the island.

"This will be our sixth solstice, Clarissa," Rachel said. "We've added so many new people along the way, and lost a few. Still, I hope the original eight can all be there this spring." She dunked her donut, to Clarissa's dismay, into her coffee and continued with a growing sense of anticipation, "I wonder what this year's projects will be?"

"Well, we won't know that till we get there and do our work. Since Alison and Ann finished law school, it's harder to set a date for our meetings. We're beginning to compromise between the court calendar and the actual solstice." Clarissa laughed. "Anyway, Grace definitely will make it. Since she moved back to Maine and started teaching at the university she's been to every one."

"Bernie and Richard and the boys will be there," Rachel said. "Funny about her, isn't it? Changing her mind about law school? She and Richard make a great team as social workers though. It's also nice to have their sons as members of the coven. Bernie and Richard's project working with troubled families is working wonders. Combining the Outward Bound format for the whole family and interweaving counseling sessions for the abuser as well as the abused into the most rugged surroundings and the worst kinds of weather has turned a lot of bad situations around."

"And kept them turned around," Clarissa added emphatically.

"Another example of weaving rather than ripping," Rachel nodded, thinking of the slogan they had come up with at one solstice celebration. "Safety nets rather than bottomless pits of anguish and despair."

"Who said that?"

"We said it–the second summer when we talked about what it means to move in a different path from the traditional one. Actually it was Alison who said it first, but we added the last part. Don't tell me you've forgotten?"

"Of course not." Clarissa was affronted, but just as quickly pacified by the memory of their successes. "Solange is the one who delights me the most–she did what she said she would–learn to use her money wisely. Widdershins, Inc., as a think tank, is the most important spin-off of our original group's

effort. I love it when she refers to the think tank as boot camp for witches."

"And I love our being board members," Rachel said, deciding not to remind Clarissa that her thought patterns were sometimes disjointed and hard to follow. "Keeps us in touch with all the doings, and I get up in the morning which is an accomplishment in itself these days. If nothing else I hoped being a witch would do that." She chuckled and stretched, knowing that when she stood she would feel the ever-present arthritis. This would be the first year she would not try to walk down to the ritual on the beach. She would not tell the others until the last moment.

"The latest project, Rach," Clarissa said, as she began to wash the breakfast dishes, "is the one I'm concerned about. People are not convinced it will work."

"Well, there's always some resistance to any change. Remember when Ann and Alison made their first presentation at the schoolhouse that night? I had no idea that they would be invited back, and when they were, they managed to work so well with the planning committee that the Lily Island residents turned things around for themselves. Calling a moratorium on development gave them the time to draw up a good long range plan for their future."

"It was wonderful to see Logan-Russell plead for mercy from the various land owners, and when they finally agreed to sell back the land to the town it was a great victory," Clarissa agreed. "That loan to Lily Island was Solange's first investment, and it was a good one, too. The final blow was Jess and Lyla Hewitt's refusal to buy the remaining acreage. Jack Russell saw the writing on the wall then, and he wanted out."

Rachel dipped her donut again, then popped it in her mouth. "But Widdershins, Inc. didn't get off the ground until Ann and Alison helped the Lily Island selectmen lobby for the Maine Municipal Association bill. Now there's a law that says any poor small town who needs to go to court to fight infractions of local environmental codes can get a lawyer through Maine Municipal Association's funding. All they have to do is provide evidence through the DEP that there is a problem concerning the environment."

"Isn't there a deductible amount the town has to pay first for legal fees?"

"The town," Rachel said patiently, "has to provide the first thousand dollars in legal fees. That can be pro bono from a lawyer who is a resident, as long as the time donated equals a thousand. That's cheap when you think that lawyers can earn one hundred and fifty dollars an hour—sometimes more."

"It was so exciting to go to the hearing and listen to Ann and Alison speak out for that bill right along with Winner and Martin. Real synergy at work," Clarissa said, remembering her first legislative hearing.

"Yes. Do you remember the opposition? There were several mayors and town managers who argued that larger cities and towns should not have to help pay for the smaller towns' legal bills. Then the DEP made their pitch about the environment being everyone's responsibility, that one place's problems could spread to another."

"It was very convincing. Acid rain and the greenhouse effect are powerful evidence." Clarissa returned to the first solstice, "Amazing, how we worried at the first of it, that the whole organization of Widdershins, Inc. would just turn out to be another philanthropic group dispersing largess."

"One big lottery of Solange's money. We sure were tempted at first, especially Solange. I think she thought she'd be better off if she just gave it all away, and quickly. But Alison and Ann helped her think it through. And we did end up giving some money to projects, but not until applicants were willing to work on a collaborative approach of management. Some people got sick of hearing us say that and went elsewhere for their funding."

"Oh, I know that, Rach," Clarissa said, somewhat impatient with Rachel for repeating things she already knew. It was the price of an old friendship plus their living together, that they inevitably ended up being redundant in describing events.

"The one I worry about, Rach," Clarissa said, changing to the present, as she reached across the table to take Rachel's cup and refill it, "is the education project. We've got that summer conference with teachers and school administrators from twenty-two districts." She whisked the table with a napkin. "Are you done with the donuts?"

Rachel nodded. "You are right. It will be incredible if we can persuade teachers to teach conflict resolution. They almost always say they don't have enough time as it is for what they do teach."

Abruptly Rachel changed the subject. "So what's on the schedule for today?" She raised her voice over the water running in the sink where Clarissa had begun to rinse the dishes. She stood and added her cup to the other dishes in the soapy water. "Oh, of course," she reminded herself. "This afternoon we're going to the hearing on Ellen's project. She's going to handle the new housing development for elders in Portland. She'll do a great job–the Lily Island experience gave her a good name."

She gazed out the window and watched a small tugboat make its way past the Bath Iron Works. "Do you ever wonder what happened to Father Donahey?" she said, slipping back into her daydream of the first solstice one more time.

"Not really. Alison stays in touch–brings him goodies. She told me once that he complains about the cooking at that home for retired priests."

Rachel frowned as she was reminded of something. "Speaking of priests, I still can't believe you're serious about divinity school."

"I can't imagine why not. We've hashed it all out. First, I am not too old, and you, of all people should be willing to acknowledge that–you who have managed to defy the laws of aging. You should be willing to allow me to emulate you–to try to have my life now even though I am older. And second, I chose the Episcopal Church because it accepts women as priests. It accepted me into its theology school. I didn't give up my faith."

"Yes," Rachel said, trying her best to sound solicitous, "and I think you were remarkable to stick to your beliefs despite people like me who came at you from all sides. Still, I could have sworn you would never leave the Church."

"Did I really leave, Rach, or did the Church leave me? Oh, I think Father Donahey was the beginning of the end, not exactly the last straw, but close. I felt ex-communicated even though I wasn't."

"That I understand, but it seems like such a radical change in your life," Rachel said.

"Not really. The Catholics and the Episcopalians agree more than they disagree. They just don't emphasize it publicly as much as they could. I won't be gone forever. And hopefully, when I come back, I'll find a church nearby that will take me.

"And you, Rachel," Clarissa continued, "the most radical change in your life has been Solange. I never thought you'd adjust, and I always hesitated to bring the subject up because you never talked after the first revelation. It became something private between you and Solange."

"I'm glad you didn't. I wasn't really ready to talk about it. It took some doing, but I'm just as content now that she did not turn out to be my natural daughter. The whole thing opened up an area I thought I had finished with and it was very painful for me. I wondered if my parents had paid for the upbringing of my child, just as Solange's father did for her. They never left me a cent, so I had to wonder where their money went. Their will left me their love and the rest of the estate went to various charities and trusts of a sort that I didn't really understand and still don't."

She took a deep breath. "And we never found out who Solange's father was, as you know, but we did find out that Solange's mother has been dead for twenty years. Her father evidently felt incapable of caring for her even though he might easily have hired a nanny or governess and spent some time with her when he could. He never re-married.

"For me, the whole thing brought up a lot of psychological baggage, guilt for abandoning my baby." She paused and looked away to compose herself. "I don't know whether I could have handled actually having to face my daughter. Who knows how angry she would have been with me? Or whether she would ever forgive me? I might not even have liked her. Unlike Solange, whom I adore." She paused and looked around the kitchen. "Why did you put the donuts away? I want another one."

Clarissa was incredulous, but she grabbed the box from the cupboard and thrust them at Rachel, who took one and without a change in expression continued, "I mean, I've had to deal with my feelings second-hand through Solange, anyway. She is **somebody's** abandoned daughter. But because of the good person she is, I've managed to work my way through this thing feeling as if I could finally pay my debt to my long-lost daughter spiritually–by way of Solange–a kind of counter-clockwise restitution. Does that sound crazy?" She munched on the donut hungrily, devouring it in two gulps.

"Not at all, Rach. I'm glad you don't mind talking about it with me now."

Rachel went on in a quiet, determined voice, "I'm just grateful that Solange and I fell into being good friends–two adult women with a great deal of common ground to share."

"And love . . ." Clarissa added.

"Yes, love," Rachel agreed. "It feels more like what they

describe as grandmotherly love. I love working on ideas with her, being a part of Widdershins, Inc. I'm proud of her successes and our joint ones, but when she goes off about her business, when she goes home to her own place, I get along fine."

"You're one fortunate woman. So am I."

"I had no idea when I wrote that ad that so much would come of it," Rachel acknowledged. "And, here we are still reaping the benefits."

"Ah, Rachel," Clarissa said her eyes just a little bit misty as she began drying the tea cups, "long may we all continue to reap the benefits."

A Word About the Author

Libraries, reading and writing go hand in hand for Judith Wilcox Monroe who spent twenty-five years directing a model media center and library in a Maine school system.

She grew up in the town of Chatham in Columbia County, New York; she attended college in Boston, studied music at the New England Conservatory and was graduated in 1954 from Simmons College School of Library Science. In 1975 she received an M.A. in psychology from Goddard College which led to her first published book, *Peoplework,* co-authored with Robert B. Le Lieuvre (American Library Association, 1979).

She departed from library work in 1983 to pursue a career in writing. Her published works, in addition to this first novel, include poetry, essays, short stories and numerous articles.

She spends the summer months on a Maine island where she has become increasingly aware of and alarmed by the rush to develop some of the most beautiful rural areas in the state.